THE CRITICS ON COMMANDER SHAW:

THE
MAN
FROM
MOSCOW

Philip McCutchan

A BERKLEY MEDALLION BOOK
published by
BERKLEY PUBLISHING CORPORATION

ONE

For some days past all the military traffic had been going the one way—north, up the Kola Peninsula. Troops and military stores on the move were, however, nothing very new and no one thought much about it. On the whole the civilian population was, as ever, too preoccupied with its terrible climate to think much about anything else; this state of mind was almost endemic to the inhabitants of the grim, bleak towns and ports of the Peninsula. Certainly they connected the military movements, in a vague sort of way, with what had been going on in and around the Barents Sea and in particular on the islands of Novaya Zemlya; and to that extent they were interested, even excited, and they felt inside themselves that the Soviets were after the big prizes again. But there was nothing whatever to indicate that the wind of change, deserting Africa for the moment, was about to blow pretty strongly behind the scenes in Moscow.

At the moment it was scarcely a wind, of course. It was a mere breeze, a very gentle zephyr, light airs wafting phantom-like along the remote corridors of the Kremlin . . . but it was going to become a gale, and when it did, it would blow out of the Kremlin and into the streets of Moscow and beyond, far beyond the borders of the Soviet Union.

Shaw's tall figure, the starched shirt-front and white waistcoat a patch of gleaming lightness in the early autumn dusk, strode out from Kensington Palace Gardens past the top-hatted custodian at the gates and into the High Street. He crossed over the road by Barkers, behind a number 9 bus. When the bus had gone on he saw the gunman crossing a little farther up in the Knightsbridge direction and when Shaw turned into Palace Gate the man was not far behind him, presumably sticking tight until he was in the Daimler.

The Daimler was parked a couple of hundred yards up the road on the left and it was facing south. There were few people about, although it was not late. A young man and a girl in evening-dress came towards him, seemingly on the look-out for a taxi, and a group of teds, coats well below

5

their rumps, drifted along past the car, assing about and talking in high voices. On the other side of the road an old man, unkempt and tramp-like, made his way along, stopping now and then to pick up a dog-end from the gutter. Some way ahead a policeman crossed stolidly over from Queen's Gate, glanced without interest towards the vehicle and moved away along Gloucester Road, bored as hell.

The scene couldn't have been more ordinary.

Shaw approached the Daimler and put his head in at the front nearside window. He said, "Excuse me . . . can you tell me the way to Chelsea Square, please?"

The driver, a fat man in chauffeur's livery, looked at Shaw closely and then glanced over his shoulder at the two men sitting in the back. He said something in a language Shaw didn't recognize, but he had the feeling that he'd been identified quite apart from the password nonsense and that his identity was being confirmed to the Daimler's passengers; and he wondered coldly how many other people around London knew him on sight like this man did.

Just then one of the passengers, a pleasant-looking man in his middle forties with a soldierly touch about him, leaned forward and said in a heavily accented voice:

"That, my dear sir, is the way we shall go ourselves as it happens. If you care to accept, we shall be pleased to take you near there. So?"

Shaw's rangy shoulders moved slightly and he said, "Well —thanks. That's very good of you." The lower-deck lights of a passing bus flickered down into the car, glinted for a moment on metal, and Shaw noted whitened knuckles gripping a gun-butt. "I'd be delighted."

"I am so glad to be of help."

The man's companion pushed the door open and got out onto the pavement. Shaw could not have guessed at his nationality but he, too, had a military air. He also had a frank, open face—and he looked genuine. Shaw bent and got in and the man climbed back beside him. The first man gave a brief order and the chauffeur started up, heading along Palace Gate into Gloucester Road. Shaw, glancing sideways, said, "Well—here I am. And now can I know where I'm going?"

"It is wiser not. Please, no questions." The man's voice was polite and, like his appearance, pleasant enough. Leaning across Shaw he said quietly, "Now, Carl."

Carl grunted and fumbled in his pocket. He said, "I am sorry, but this is necessary. Please do not make it difficult for us, Commander Shaw. You must not know, afterwards, where you have been." He produced a length of some thick black material and slipped a broad swathe of it over Shaw's eyes. As it was pulled taut into a knot behind his head, Shaw felt the pressure of an automatic in his side.

The man on his right said, "Down on the floor, please. There is plenty of room . . . you will be uncomfortable, however, and I am sorry, but we must not risk a blindfolded man being seen. You will understand."

Shaw breathed hard, angrily, through his nose. He said, "I've only myself to blame for coming along at all, I know that—but aren't you rather overdoing the play-acting, chum?"

"We think not. You will see. Please do as I ask."

"Very well." Shaw slid down onto the carpet. "But it's got to be worth it. And if there's any funny business. . . ."

"There will not be." The man spoke with quiet assurance and sincerity. "You can trust us absolutely, and soon you will thank us, Commander Shaw. If you think that we are not trusting you in return, a little reflection will tell you that if we did not we would scarcely be doing—what we are doing. You will understand very soon."

Very soon, indeed!

It was high time somebody came clean, in Shaw's opinion. So far, the whole evening had been decidedly unusual, and it had started even before he'd arrived at the Embassy back in Kensington Palace Gardens—during the afternoon in fact, when an anonymous caller had come on the outside line to his flat and jammed the receiver down as soon as he had passed his message and without giving Shaw time to say a word of acceptance or rejection. However, Shaw's curiosity had been aroused, to say the least of it, and he had got Latymer to wangle him one of the Admiralty's quota of invitations to the Embassy function that his caller had suggested he attend; and then that evening he'd dressed in full tails and gone along.

It had been ordinary enough at the start.

A mid-European orchestra, its members wearing national costume, had been playing away on a dais at the far end of a long room; heavy chandeliers, the crystal glittering in a kaleidoscope of reflected colour, hung from the ornate moulded ceiling, their lights touching the diamonds of the women and the jewelled orders of the diplomats and the decorations of the high-ranking Service officers. Indeed the whole atmosphere had been one of sweetness and light—

7

which was welcome enough, but also strange enough, in the London Embassy of an Iron Curtain country in the nineteen-sixties.

And Shaw had felt instinctively that it was phoney.

This wasn't just because of that mysterious caller—the phoniness was absolutely basic and the sweetness was a mere oasis—or more accurately, in his view, the bitter-sweetness of a mirage—in the desert of suspicion and open hostility that characterized the cold war. It just didn't add up; all these gay fraternizers, peculiar enough bedfellows at any time, would be at one another's throats again the moment the Five Powers' Conference was over.

Shaw reached out a long arm, stretching round the back of a bulky Ambassador who was chatting to an Under-Secretary from the Commonwealth Relations Office. His fingers contacted a heavy silver box of cigarettes—black ones, with gold tips. Russian, and very expensive. Balancing his glass precariously in one hand, he revved his lighter and blew a long trail of smoke ceilingwards over the Ambassadorial head. Shaw's eyes were watchful—and hard. He was keyed-up and alert, yet a detached part of his mind was bored to death. He'd never been much of a man for parties or receptions, diplomatic or otherwise; in fact he loathed formal entertaining, it didn't mean a damn thing to him.

He sidestepped as the Ambassador's heavy backside came dangerously near his glass, and then he looked around the expensive mob that hemmed him in. So far he hadn't spoken to anyone; there were few familiar faces anyway, except for one or two acquaintances from the Admiralty and one of the First Secretaries from the American Embassy whom he knew in an intermittent kind of way. Now, Shaw was watching the faces and waiting for a sign, for the casual but unmistakable approach which would tell him he had made his contact. All these people . . . not one of them looked a likely bet. The men in full evening-dress, like himself, with those colourful orders and decorations won, he reflected cynically, largely on other men's efforts or the concealment of their own mistakes . . . the women, beautifully turned out and smelling like chemists' shops, with bare shoulders and revealing necklines, draped with diamonds and rubies and emeralds—all talking in loud, horsy voices and making sure that every one present knew who their husbands were. Drink was flowing pretty freely—and so, Esmonde Shaw observed, was talk. Earnest, rather feverish talk with a gay yet brittle air of sudden hope

8

behind it as though all problems of peace and war were about to be settled.

For there was much in the air and these men—diplomats, Privy Councillors, Members of Parliament, senior men from the ministries and, for good measure, what looked like half the aristocracy of England drawn from the backwoods and the fox-hunting coverts—were discussing it. The forthcoming Five Powers' Foreign Ministers' Conference here in London was news. London, once again if only temporarily, was back on the map and these people were here to prove it. And hopes were running very high indeed that this conference would prove a prelude to a summit conference. And a summit conference, that elusive panacea for all the world's ills, was always something to look forward to and, despite all the earlier disappointments, the mere fact of looking forward to it made everything seem right with the world and in its benevolent sunny rays all men became brothers—for a time. This time a summit conference appeared to be not only just around the corner but also to hold out every prospect of real success. The East had suddenly mellowed. Recent brinkmanship, perhaps, had paid off after all and the nations, seeing the pit, the chasm, yawning before them at last, seeing Armageddon plain, were going to get off the collision-course and were really going to talk. Jaw, jaw, as Sir Winston Churchill had said once, had been seen in the nick of time to be better than war, war.

Shaw drew on his cigarette and then sipped at his drink.

Emptying his glass half a minute later, he set it down on a Louis XIV table, stubbed out the cigarette in ash and glowing gold, and edged round the broad-beamed Ambassador. He moved away, passed a head-nodding group where the Chargé d'Affaires of the Chinese People's Republic was gravely lecturing some high officials of N.A.T.O., and went towards an elegant staircase rising to a half-landing where was set an enormous silver bowl filled with expensive out-of-season blooms. The staircase continued upward in graceful curves to left and right. Half the guests had overflowed up those stairs and Shaw felt it was time he investigated. He went up behind the uniformed back of a guardsman—Lord Harborough of the Coldstream Guards, Field Officer in Brigade Waiting, who had the Countess of Kildockery on his arm. Lady Kildockery had a look in her eye that said with engaging clarity that she would have liked to be in bed with Lord Harborough. Shaw went up the stairs and passed them, looked back casually at the soldier.

9

He said, "Good evening, Harborough."

"Ah—evening, Shaw, evening." The peer was red in the face and short of breath. He puffed, "Close—what?"

"Very." Shaw nodded and went on ahead, conscious of Lady Kildockery's gaze lingering on his back. He'd seen the sudden interest in her face when she glanced at him. That wasn't due to his work, of course, she wouldn't know him from Adam. But he'd noticed with some amusement that he often had that kind of effect on women. And it was at this precise moment that he realized that he was being followed up the staircase by someone other than Lord Harborough and his lady-friend. Some deeply ingrained instinct, a sixth sense of awareness which came from years of hard experience, told him that.

Casually he went on up the stairs.

Reaching the half-landing he glanced indifferently back as he followed the left-hand curve, a hard brown hand resting lightly on the polished banister. A tall, very thin, grey-haired man with the ribbon of some foreign order round his neck, was coming up, head bent. As he came level with Shaw, they glanced at each other and Shaw fancied he caught a flicker in the hooded eyes. Just a flicker and then the man looked downward again.

Shaw searched his mind, but he didn't recognize this man. And the voice on the phone had said that his contact would know him right away—a juxtaposition of facts that was disturbing in itself.

At the top of the stairs Shaw crossed a wide landing and went into a high-ceilinged room to his right. Here another orchestra was playing and the great room seemed even more crowded than the room downstairs had been. Shaw spoke formally to the Controller of the Navy, a full admiral, then nodded at a big bug from the War Office; as a mere matter of prudence he ignored, and was ignored by, a highly placed official of M.I.5, and then he moved over to where the crowd was thickest. You were never so private as in a crowd and you could talk in its midst with every assurance of not being overhead in the barrage of idiotic small-talk inseparable from official functions where wives were present.

A waiter brought a tray of drinks and Shaw took a glass of champagne.

That was when he saw the tall, grey-haired man again, chatting now with von Mittelburg, the Ambassador of the Federal German Republic. When von Mittelburg nodded dismissingly and turned his attention to a bulky dowager in black lace, the grey-haired man appeared to allow the crowd to elbow him towards Shaw.

Once again Shaw caught his eye and once again he saw the flicker of recognition. The man took out a silk handkerchief and, with a fastidious gesture, folded it and dabbed at his forehead. This was part of the recognition-code that had been described to Shaw on the phone. The man smiled, showing very white teeth beneath a clipped grey moustache.

He said, "So many people. It is hot."

"Very," Shaw agreed. "I see you haven't a drink." He waylaid a waiter, who held out a tray obsequiously to the grey-haired man.

"Thank you, that was kind of you." The man bowed slightly to Shaw and took a glass of champagne. He said, "Your very good health."

"And yours. . . ."

"Peace and prosperity to your great country." The man drank, then wiped his lips with his handkerchief. Shaw had detected a Hungarian accent, though the English itself was faultless. The orchestra went on thumping out some weird music and Shaw realized that the man's lips were moving. He bent his head closer. The Hungarian—if he was a Hungarian—said, "You were told to expect me, of course."

Shaw felt suddenly angry. This was amateurish. He hadn't even positively identified himself yet. Shaw didn't like amateurism in the game; it was always potentially dangerous. He asked, "How do you know who I am, anyway?"

"I cannot go into details now, but I assure you I know you, and I also assure you that your identity is safe with me —with us."

"Us?" Shaw's eyes narrowed. "What is all this?"

"Your pardon. Again, I cannot be too precise just now—"

"This is all a little vague for me. I wasn't told who you are or what you want to tell me. I might add that I don't like it at all."

"You will find out soon what I want with you, if you are prepared to trust me, Commander Shaw, and go where I ask you to go. You understand, I cannot talk here. My name I do not propose to reveal. I am sorry, but you will of course understand."

He stared into Shaw's eyes.

Shaw lit another cigarette from his own case, passed a hand over his long chin, and stared back. He said coolly, "No, I don't understand at all. You're asking one hell of a

11

lot of me—to go along to I don't know where, with I don't know whom!"

The man shrugged. "Naturally I see your point of view. But I cannot stress too strongly the importance of this matter. It is quite . . . vital. Yes, vital. You must trust me."

Shaw hesitated. He was a fair judge of people and this man undoubtedly gave him the impression of being on the level. He asked, "Can you be just a little more forthcoming?"

"A little, perhaps." The man seemed to consider, frowning and staring up at the ceiling. A moment later he said softly and with his lips almost motionless as though ventriloquizing, "There is someone who wishes to meet you."

"I see," Shaw said casually. "Can't he come here?"

"It must never be known that he has been in touch with you at all." The Hungarian's face came closer as he appeared to be brushing cigarette-ash off his white waistcoat and his voice was a mere whispering breath. "You will, I think, understand better when I tell you that this man is Rudintsev."

Rudintsev.

In the back of the Daimler Shaw's mind was still racing over the possibilities. As soon as he had heard the name of Rudintsev he had known he couldn't possibly let this thing go. Rudintsev was a senior official of the Russian Foreign Ministry and he had been in London for the past week, preparing the way and generally taking charge of the arrangements for the visit of his Minister for the Five Powers' Conference. What could Rudintsev, of all people, want with an agent of the Naval Intelligence Division?

Shaw had stared back at his nameless contact, questioningly, and had seen the set look in the man's face. Clearly he wasn't going to say anything more, seemed to feel he had already said more than was strictly wise. After that the man had obviously assumed that Shaw would be in on this whatever it was, and he'd simply given him his instructions for picking up the Daimler and said that, although he was being fully trusted, the matter was so vitally important that no chances could be taken and when he left the Embassy Shaw would be shadowed by a man with a silenced gun, all the way to Palace Gate. Ten minutes after Shaw had gone, the Hungarian said, he also would leave and would reach a certain house, whereabouts unspecified, ahead of him. Somehow Shaw had genuinely trusted the man but he still hadn't liked any of it, for there was still the amateurish touch and amateurs tended to slip up and leave every one else in the

12

cart. But the man had turned away then to chat amicably with some diplomat or other, and Shaw had shrugged and finished his drink, stubbed out his cigarette, and gone down the stairs, across the hall into the autumnal dark of Kensington Palace Gardens, and then his shadow had picked him up. Shaw had been aware of the man passing along behind the trees on the other side of the road—someone else, obviously, who knew him on sight.

The Daimler purred on fast and, so far as Shaw was concerned, in blank and total darkness. He hadn't the faintest idea where he was; all he knew was that they were going a long way and, in the later stages, swinging round one corner after another, possibly to throw off any pursuit. And they were travelling very fast. But at last the Daimler slowed, swung sharply left, and crunched over gravel. They appeared to be going up a fairly long drive and then the car glided to a stop. A moment later the door opened and he was helped to his feet and, still blindfolded, was taken up a flight of stone steps and into a hall. He was directed to his right and he felt his feet sink into the thick pile of a carpet. Then the material was pulled away from his eyes and, blinking in the sudden glare of electric light, he made out the distinguished, grey-haired man from the Embassy. This man nodded at the two escorts and Shaw heard them go out of the room. As his full vision came back, he saw that the room was a big one and elegantly furnished; and then he saw another man coming in.

He was heavily built and about his own age, maybe a little older, dark and clean-shaven and walking with a slight limp; wearing a dark suit with a white shirt and off-white tie, this man looked a typical ruling-class Russian. In a way, an echo of Krushchev—except for the face and eyes. These were kindly, humane; those brown eyes were trusting and friendly, though at the moment they were nervous as well, and held a curious look of hope and eagerness. This man would not have the ebullience, the thrust and the egotistical banter of a Nikita Krushchev, the cold deadliness of a Stalin or a Beria, the uncompromising nature of a Molotov. He was a Russian all right, but he was also a man of peace. Strong, Shaw thought—strong, but with the strength of a good man. Something in him appealed very much to Esmonde Shaw and when the grey-haired man took both their arms in a courtly gesture and introduced them, Shaw stretched out his hand and smiled into Teodor Rudintsev's eyes.

"They guard you well, Mr Rudintsev," he said quietly.

13

"And now—forgive me, but I can see you don't want to delay any more than I do—what is it you want to tell me?"

Rudintsev glanced quickly across at the grey-haired man and then met Shaw's inquiring scrutiny. He said, blinking a little with nerves, "I think that you are not going to believe what I shall say, and I cannot blame you for that. Also, you will think that I am a traitor to my own country, but this will be wrong. And I assure you most urgently that I shall be speaking the complete truth. Believe you must, my friend, for if you do not, it will be the end of your country and much of Europe as well."

The voice held conviction and Shaw felt a sudden cold chill in his spine. He said crisply, "Let's get on with it, then. I'll soon tell you whether I believe it or not."

Afterwards, when Teodor Rudintsev himself had left the house, Shaw was blindfolded again and led back to the Daimler with the two escorts and they headed quickly back into London. Within seventy-five minutes Shaw had left the car in the Hammersmith Road and it had driven off. He had memorized the number, but he knew that wouldn't help much; by the time he got to a phone those plates would be off and the genuine ones back on again. Not that it mattered very much. They could always pick Rudintsev up if they really wanted to, and to hell with diplomatic procedures.

He walked quickly into Gliddon Road and into his flat, an acute anxiety and impatience gripping his guts. For he believed that Rudintsev was absolutely on the square and was to be trusted. The man had clearly been terrified of his own side finding out his movements that night; anyone acting under orders to lay a smoke-screen could hardly feign that precise kind of fear. And more than that—his story, horrifying though it was, had integrity and consistency and urgent conviction.

Shaw delayed to mix himself a strong whisky-and-soda; he needed that badly. Then he took up the receiver of the closed line to the Admiralty. He hadn't many seconds to wait and when the Outfit's private exchange came on the wire he said briefly, "Shaw. Most urgent to Chief of Special Services, personal."

TWO

"First things first, Shaw. Before you give me the details, tell me this: why did the feller come to you rather than anyone else?" Latymer's heavy, pugnacious face seemed to snap at him over the top of pale-pink silk pyjamas and a dressing-gown with a violent Paisley pattern. "I can't see where the hell N.I.D. comes into contact with diplomats—except by way of collision! Well?"

Shaw said, "I don't know if it was flattery, but he said, and I quote, that I had 'a high reputation'—"

"Flattery without a doubt!"

Shaw grinned fleetingly. "Quite, sir. Anyway, he said I would understand, whereas certain of our ministers might be —er—hidebound. That's indisputable, in the circumstances —they just wouldn't believe it. I, Rudintsev said, could convince them. He added that his country had been impressed with the Redcap affair some while ago and—"

"All right, all right. Stop blowing your own trumpet, Shaw." Latymer rasped a hand across his chin. The softly shaded lights in the study of his luxurious Eaton Square flat muted the extensive skin grafts on his face, the face that had been so badly burned that distant night when the bomb had gone off, the night when Vice-Admiral Sir Henry Charteris, K.C.B., D.S.O. and two bars, D.S.C., had officially 'died'— for it had been expedient to let the would-be killers think they had been successful—and later, with the help of plastic surgery and the Official Secrets Act, had metamorphosed into 'Mr Latymer' and got his old job back. Now, the Old Man —as he was usually known in the Outfit—sipped at a glass of rare old brandy and stared broodingly at Shaw across the rim. He went on, "I may as well tell you right off, I don't like traitors. Never did, don't trust 'em either. If their own countries can't, why should I?"

Shaw shook his head. He said emphatically, "Rudintsev's no traitor, sir."

Latymer shifted irritably. "Tripe. A rose by any other name. . . . "

"No, sir, it's not that at all."

"Very well," Latymer said imperturbably. "I suppose you'd

better tell me the whole thing and then I'll be able to judge for myself, won't I? Let's have it, my boy."

"Right, sir." Shaw pulled at a cigarette and leaned towards Latymer, his eyes bright. "Rudintsev told me he was a Party Member and a convinced communist, also a patriot, but in spite of that he meant to put humanity first. He said humanity transcends frontiers and ideologies——"

"Cut it short, please." Latymer looked pointedly at the clock. "Remember you've dragged me out of bed."

"I'm sorry, sir. Well, here it is." Shaw took a deep breath and ran his fingers through his crisp brown hair, which had grown a little grey at the sides in recent years. "The Russians —not the lawful Government, Rudintsev was insistent about that, but a bunch of extremists who intend to seize power in the Kremlin—they're going to pull a Pearl Harbour on us. They're going to take over the Moscow Government in secret and then strike some blow, unspecified, at Britain while the Foreign Ministers' Conference is in session. And that's it, sir, in a nutshell."

Latymer only nodded, but his green-flecked eyes had gone suddenly steely. He said, "Go on. If that's the nutshell, let's have the tree."

"Yes, sir." Shaw dabbed at an ashtray. "Rudintsev said the Conference will go very well indeed and the East will appear to be making concessions—willing, gracious concessions—so that a summit conference can be arranged and every one will be happy. The newspapers, he said, will be optimistic and people everywhere will relax, feel the tension and the fear leaving them for the first time in twenty-five years and more. And when this feeling is at its height and all of us totally unsuspecting, not in the frame of mind for war at all, then they'll strike, and strike hard. So hard that Britain will be left pretty well impotent, militarily."

Latymer gave a harsh, grunting laugh, but his lips were pale now. "Cynical lot of bastards, aren't they?"

"The extremists are, sir, I agree . . . not the Government. I repeat that because Rudintsev wanted me to make that crystal clear." Shaw was looking into Latymer's eyes, his shoulders hunched as he sat forward. "The Kremlin as such is not concerned with this and in fact as a body they know nothing about it—and won't, of course, until it's too late and the extremist boys have taken over and arrested them. Rudintsev insisted that the Russian Government as constituted doesn't want war any more than we in the West

16

do and that they genuinely have no hostile intentions whatever against us—"

"Ha!"

"—though he also said that the Soviet has in fact got perfectly tenable excuses for her suspicions and fears of the West—that to some extent she's been driven into a corner and made to snarl like a bear. His exact words, sir. He said Russia is surrounded by hostile forces. American missiles point towards her, ready to be fired at a moment's notice. The Americans boast of this, and also of their spy flights over Soviet territory. He said they're indecently open about them, and the Soviet is forced to go further than perhaps normally they would go, to let the West know that they don't just sit tamely by. He said we can criticize them for that, but wouldn't we do the same in their shoes? We in Britain aren't free from blame either, according to Rudintsev. Polaris submarines are ready in the Holy Loch, our troops are in West Germany and we've armed the Federal Republic against the Soviet—"

Latymer broke in irritably. "Is there much more of this homespun philosopher's speechifying, Shaw?"

"No, sir, that's about the lot—"

"Good. Have you actually joined the Communist Party yet, Shaw?"

Shaw grinned tautly. "I'm sorry, sir. I was merely quoting Rudintsev. The reason I gave you all that was because I wanted you to see what makes Rudintsev tick, and why I believe him, why I don't think he's a traitor. He sounded absolutely genuine and sincere—and I do believe him."

"H'm." Latymer lit a cigarette from a slim gold case. "Now tell me this: why doesn't Rudintsev go to his own Government with his yarns about a *coup?*"

"I went into that, sir, naturally. He can't do that, because he doesn't know for sure whom he can trust. The only man he can really be sure of is his own Minister, and it was he who got Rudintsev to talk to me." He added, "I rather gather the Minister wants to go on living, and since the thing's timed for when he's over here, the present outlook is cloudy."

"How did he get to hear of all this in the first place?"

"Rudintsev's in touch with certain elements, sir, men with liberal views. Some information leaked through to him from these people, but he admits he doesn't know the whole story by any means. I asked him how any *coup* could succeed in a country like Russia, and he just said it had been done be-

17

fore and it was dead easy when you had the M.V.D. be-hind you."

Latymer looked up sharply. "These hoodlums've got the secret police in their pockets, have they?"

"Apparently so."

"Then that'll make it bloody nearly impossible to get any reliable information. Now—what's this blow, as you call it, to be?"

Shaw shook his head. "Rudintsev didn't know that, sir. All he could say was this: although it's going to do a hell of a lot of damage to the British Isles, and to a lesser extent to the Continent as well, it won't in fact have the appearance of an act of war."

"Why not?"

"They've got to respect the neutrals and the uncommitteds. World reactions, Rudintsev said, are still important, even to the extreme militarists. Also they don't want to bring the United States in if they can help it."

"It's to look like—what, then? An accident?"

"That's what I gathered, sir."

Latymer let out a long breath. He asked, "I suppose he offered no proof whatever of all this?"

"None at all, sir." Shaw added rather diffidently, "Just his . . . well, I can only call it his sincerity."

"Ha bloody ha!" Latymer said with heavy sarcasm. "My dear Shaw, you're going soft in the head!"

"I don't think so, sir." Shaw leaned forward again, earnestly. "Look, sir. There *was* a bit more homespun philosophy, as a matter of fact. If you don't mind listening to it, it may make you see it the way I do. May I go on?"

"Yes. But be brief."

"Yes, sir. Well . . . he went on a bit more about humanity. This may sound naïve, but—he had a humanist look about him, sir. He spoke of the effects of nuclear war. He said that personally, having been much in the West, he didn't necessarily share his leaders' fears of Western hostile intentions. He said that, like the Russians themselves, we were simply frightened. He said he was seeking to prevent a terrible tragedy, not only involving us but in the long run his own country too if the extremists should gain and keep power. Then he said that there are many people inside Russia who see things in much the same way as he does, some of them even more so. Intellectuals mainly, people who still think for themselves and whose thoughts are not controlled by—"

18

"And the man himself, Shaw? Didn't you say he was a Party Member and a convinced communist?"

"Yes, I did." Shaw hesitated. "Somehow I got the impression that he wasn't quite so convinced as he said, though. To that extent, and that extent alone, I'd agree he may have got his wires crossed. I'd say he's had a shift of beliefs, maybe as a result of what he's told me about. Anyway, these people, these liberals for want of a better name, sir—they don't like the way things are shaping and they realize that Russia can't always be in the right, so they tend to disbelieve what they read in their papers, even in *Pravda*—perhaps particularly in *Pravda*. And they have a deep horror at the mere thought that the world may go up in a mushroom-cloud one of these days. What they want to see is *peaceful* Soviet expansion, and they believe it can be done. Then he said something else—after I'd asked him what he expected us to do about his story." Shaw hesitated, choosing his words. "He suggested that if we tried what he had failed to do, that is, to find out what the threat is in concrete form and then take steps to prevent it, sabotage it perhaps, then these liberal-minded men and women would actually help us."

Latymer's eyebrows went up.

"God bless my soul, Shaw—you didn't believe that, did you?"

"Well, I don't know, sir. Could be possible—don't you think? He said that if we succeeded, Russia, the real Russia, as well as the West, would have reason to be grateful both to him and us."

"Us? Naval Intelligence? He suggests we actually handle it right through ourselves, does he?"

"Yes, sir. He said it wouldn't be easy—"

"No! Did he?"

"—but that Russia isn't as impregnable as is popularly supposed. There's spies in plenty inside the frontiers—we know that's true, sir—and many of the people are illiterate and stupid and a determined man can go a very long way, at least in normal circumstances. He admitted it would be more difficult just now."

"Very perceptive of him. Now then: this blow is to fall during the Conference—right? So we've got thirteen days in which to get something done . . . five days before the Soviet man gets here, and eight while he's actually in London." Latymer puffed at his cigarette, staring across the room. "I think the first thing to do is for me to see Comrade Rudintsev myself."

"No, sir." Shaw was definite. "He's quite firm that he won't repeat tonight's work. It's far too dangerous for him, and slipping away from his Embassy tonight was risky enough."

Latymer nodded. "He's got a point. But am I expected to alert the Government on your version of what he said? Use second-hand information?"

Shaw grinned tightly. "We're always doing that, sir. I've got by quite nicely on tenth-hand stuff before now."

Latymer splashed more brandy into his glass and nodded. "True, true. . . . Now, look, Shaw. I'm not doubting your assessment of the man. All Russians aren't like the big bears put on show to impress the West, I know that. But I don't like this. Rudintsev's a big name himself—not one of those you hear much about, but still high up in the Kremlin's confidence. If *he* doesn't know the whole story, how the ruddy hell are *we* going to find anything out?"

Shaw shrugged. "It'll need a lot of luck."

"Luck!" Latymer's shoulders twisted irritably. "By God, Shaw, words fail me!" He blew out a long, hissing breath. "Damned if I can believe all this, you know. To use a Foreign Ministers' Conference as cover, and perhaps blow up their own delegation—that's going a little far even for Eastern extremist hoodlums."

"It's a nice easy way of getting rid of some of the legal Government, sir. But there *is* something that's just occurred to me, I'll admit. There's this British naval squadron paying a goodwill visit at the same time as the Conference—"

"The Leningrad visit?"

"Yes, sir. The Russians themselves suggested it, didn't they?"

"They did indeed. The invitation came from the Russian Defence Ministry in the first place, and once it was official we accepted with alacrity. Why?"

"Well, sir—isn't it rather fishy? I mean, why should they invite a British squadron right to their own doorstep when the balloon's due to go up? I know I'm talking against myself, as it were, but it is a point."

Latymer scratched his jaw reflectively. "Did you take it up with Rudintsev?"

"I'm sorry, sir, no. I'm afraid I—"

Latymer said sourly, "Forgot all about it—what? Every one forgets about the British Navy these days—even, it seems, its own officers. However, I think it's only a minor point. If we can accept the one—and mind you, I'm not saying I have

—we can accept the other. Damn it, one aircraft-carrier, an obsolete training-cruiser and a handful of frigates . . . the whole ruddy Navy steaming in wouldn't make 'em lose a wink of sleep these days, let alone our poor little flag-showing effort! If anything, it could be just another blind, neatly arranged by one of the V.I.P. extemists in advance." He sighed and added, "I wish to God we could get hold of some more precise information before I stick my neck out in Whitehall. I'm bound to get it run over otherwise." Suddenly Latymer came bolt upright in his chair and jabbed a finger towards Shaw. "Now look here. I've a nasty idea that the whole of this *could* be designed precisely to panic the West into starting something and thus give Russia a cast-iron excuse to counter-attack—an excuse that couldn't be bettered however hard they tried. Just think of it, Shaw— the West on the warpath on the eve of the Conference—a ruddy *Pravda*'s delight—d'you see what I'm getting at?"

"Of course, sir, and I've considered that. It's not the right assessment, though, I'm sure of it."

"Just how sure are you?" Latymer stared at him, right into him, the green eyes narrowed dangerously all at once.

Shaw asked, "How d'you mean, sir?"

"Listen and I'll tell you." The voice was harsh, almost hectoring now. "If all this is true, I've got to alert Whitehall immediately. Half the Government will leap out of their beds. 'Stand by to repel boarders' will go to all commands as an essential precaution. The whole blasted country will gear up for war the moment that signal goes out. And all because of you, Shaw. It's obvious this could be the most perilous situation we've ever been in, any of us, in our lives, and it's how it's handled right from the start that may decide the issue in the end. Now—there are two courses of action open to me, Shaw. One, tell the bigwigs to play it down on the grounds that it may be an Eastern trick. They'll do what I tell them all right, and if I tell them that, they'll lap it up. No one wants trouble just now. Two, I tell them it's highly dangerous, that it's most probably true. Then they'll fly into a very natural tizzy and at once we'll be on a war footing with the woolly minded lunatic fringe howling the odds that the Government's warmongering. Since United States bases in the U.K. will be involved automatically, it also means getting the Pentagon to line up every available missile on the communist bloc so that they can be blasted right off the map the moment there's a hint of trouble. And—don't you see—once the Russians get wind of that, the whole thing

21

blows right up into a war anyway! A nuclear war from the start. Shaw, you've got to hoist this in: any mistake on your part—in your assessment of Rudintsev is what it boils down to—may start off something that we'll never be able to stop this side of the hereafter." His eyes glittered beneath the thick white brows. "Well?"

Shaw met his stare. He said quietly, "I'll back my judgment, sir. And I'd say that our defences *should* be made ready now, whatever the risk involved." Then he added, "Can't we get the Prime Minister to try to alert the Moscow Government, sir, and get all this confirmed?"

"The thought did flash through my mind," Latymer said bleakly, "and it flashed right out again. If Rudintsev doesn't know whom to trust, how the hell would we? And even if we happened to contact the right people by some stroke of luck, I doubt if they'd believe us. They'd say we were stirring something up and sidetracking the Conference before it started. So that won't wash. And now I've got just one more question: do you believe Rudintsev enough to go into Russia yourself and find out what all this is about?"

Shaw hesitated only for a second, then he said, "Well, sir, someone's got to go, and at least I speak Russian!"

Latymer went on staring at him for nearly a minute, his face expressionless. Then suddenly he heaved himself to his feet. Crossing the room he picked up the hush line and after a moment he said, "Chief of Special Services . . . get Captain Carberry's home number." There was a longish pause. "Carberry? Rub the sleep out and get round to the office. Yes, at once. There's a hell of a lot of work you can start on right away. Before you leave, ring through to the Private Secretary to the Minister of Defence. Warn him I'm going to ask the P.M. personally for a meeting of the Cabinet and the Chiefs of Staff as early as possible tomorrow morning. . . . What? Oh, to hell with precedent! And I'm bringing Shaw whether they like it or not. I'll leave it to him to convince the powers-that-be of something that's going to make the Prime Minister's hair curl."

THREE

It was lunchtime before the Cabinet meeting broke up next day and immediately they were free Latymer and Shaw drove almost in silence along Whitehall to the Admiralty. Back in his office Latymer rang through to his secretary and demanded sandwiches and coffee to be sent in for two and then he faced Shaw across the polished shagreen top of his wide desk.

He said abruptly, "Well now, Shaw, I'll just put you in the picture as to what went on after they'd done with you—and by the way, congratulations on the way you put it across. You certainly convinced them." Lighting a cigarette, he passed the box to Shaw. He went on, "The Prime Minister summed the situation up admirably. Of course, it was a stroke of luck that he'd met Rudintsev a couple of times in Moscow."

"I gathered they didn't hit it off very well, sir?"

"True, and they only met officially—but the P.M. does agree fully with your estimate of the man, that's the point, and he thinks he's only too likely to be perfectly genuine in what he says. Anyway, he's going to proceed on that assumption and make preparations to meet any situation that may arise from now on, pending what we can dig out in the meantime. We're aided by the fact that some members of the Cabinet are personally very suspicious of Russia anyway and haven't taken quite the optimistic view of the Conference that the Press and the public generally have. I don't need to stress that the P.M.'s a very worried man, in fact the whole Cabinet's got the wind up now—and so have I, I don't mind telling you. Some of them wanted to cancel the Conference and the fleet's visit, but the P.M. won't have that and he's sticking tight. I agree with him. He's already been on the line to Washington and they agree also. His view and mine is that any cancellation would not only tell the other side that we're on to something, but it would also play right into the hands of the Eastern bloc by showing us up, however wrongly, as not wanting to get round a table and talk peace."

"Quite, sir. As usual, Moscow has us where they want us—even a rebellious junta. In any case, they'd soon find another opportunity to do what they want."

"Precisely." Latymer sat forward. "Now, here's a summary of the action we're taking. All the armed forces are going to get an immediate but limited alert—that includes N.A.T.O., by the way. It'll just be a question of bringing all missile launching-sites and all airfields, both fighters and long-range conventional bombers as well as the V Force Vulcans, to immediate readiness and getting the big I.C.B.M.'s armed with their nuclear warheads. And of course there's the Early

Warning Stations, for what a four-minute warning's worth —just time to get your trousers up, I've always thought! Some troops and ships will be moved into defensive positions and there'll be some aerial activity, but so far as the public's concerned it'll just be a case of routine exercises. There's no question of mobilization—wouldn't help much anyway in a nuclear attack. It's not vast numbers of men we want these days, after all."

Shaw asked, "How long will the public accept the 'exercise' eyewash, sir?"

Latymer shrugged massively. "We live on hope so far as that's concerned—with any luck, they'll take it for long enough, and I think we can keep 'em happy. It's the ruddy Press that always stirs things up, and this time the P.M.'s giving the Press boys his personal attention!" He grinned. "He's tough when he needs to be. A Government directive will go out and the Official Secrets Act quoted at the editors. Everything will be heavily censored and any editor who passes anything out of place will end up in Brixton Prison. You won't see a damn thing that really matters in the newspapers," he added grimly, "you can take that from me."

"That," Shaw said, "is something! But what about any Russian agents? It won't be long before they spot what's going on, surely?"

"There lies the biggest danger, I admit, but we can't have the defences other than in a state of instant readiness from now on—as you said yourself last night. Suppose, for instance, they get to hear back in Moscow that Rudintsev's talked—they might go into action right away. Security measures will be rigorously tightened up right throughout the N.A.T.O. countries and all ports and airfields will have an extra watch clapped on 'em as of now. M.I.5 and Scotland Yard have already been alerted on those lines, and it'll be the finest net you ever saw. There will also be extra monitoring to pick up any unauthorized radio transmissions. If necessary we'll put out a yarn that all the precautions are intended solely for the security of the Foreign Ministers. That'll go down nicely. In any case, remember this is the nineteen-sixties, Shaw. At least in the early stages, war today doesn't involve wholesale troop movements and most of the preliminaries to the pressing of buttons on missile sites can be done very unobtrusively. The visible flap won't last long. And now . . . ah, come in, Clarice. Welcome indeed!"

Shaw turned, caught an aroma of hot coffee and saw

Latymer's Clarice Larkin coming in, prim and precise as ever. The secretary put the tray down in front of Latymer who sniffed appreciatively and said, "Thank you, Clarice. You've been quick."

"I'd already warned the kitchen staff, Mr Latymer. I thought you'd want something."

"You're a thought-reader." Latymer reached for a sandwich.

She almost blushed with pleasure; Shaw looked at her with sympathy and understanding. She was a tough bird, but she'd have done anything in the world for her unresponsive chief. As she went out of the door she said, "I'm glad you like them, Mr Latymer." She hesitated for a moment and then disappeared.

"Admirable woman, quite admirable," Latymer said absently between mouthfuls, "but sexless." He pushed the tray forward. "Get started on this lot while I talk. There's a lot to get through."

Shaw nodded and took a sandwich, poured himself and Latymer some coffee.

"I needn't point out that you haven't much time available, or that Russia's a big country to cover." Latymer took a gulp at his cup. "A B.O.A.C. flight leaves London Airport for Vienna at 2100 hours tonight. You'll be on it. Carberry will hand you your ticket later."

"Why Vienna, sir?"

"Because there's always the chance that our man there may have picked up something by the time you get there. You know what Vienna's like. Carberry will have been in touch with him already—he's had a busy time since I rang him last night, has Carberry. But the real point is that we hope our man'll be able to ease your passage into Russia by—er—various unorthodox routes, and believe me, that's far less tricky than if *we* tired to get you in direct by sea along the Baltic coast. So you'll check in at the Hotel Metropole and our man'll contact you there."

"Right, sir. Do I gather I break through the Curtain, then?"

Latymer said crisply, "I'm afraid so, yes. The matter's far too urgent to allow any delay now, and you know how long the Soviet takes to issue visas. That precludes sending you out as a harmless soap-powder flogger or what-have-you. Nevertheless, you'll be provided with a passport, fully visa-ed by Carberry's forgery section and with the proper frontier-stamps in it as if you'd entered Russia via Czechoslovakia, in the Uzhgorod region. Uzhgorod's an open town, and though it's in a closed area and you wouldn't be allowed to circulate in the actual area around the city, you'd be able to travel direct from Uzhgorod to anywhere in the open area beyond—which is what you will have done if you're asked. Remember that even the Russians themselves can't all travel about freely inside the closed areas. You can use that passport if you're questioned inside Russia, which you will be—you do not of course use it to cross in, I need hardly say, and where you do actually make the crossing doesn't matter in the least. Now, your passport will be a foolproof job and it'll satisfy anyone checking it—except possibly two groups of people. One, the frontier-guards, the checkpoint personnel on whom you'll have gathered I'm not prepared to risk either it or you—you'll have a much better chance through the back door. Two, the M.V.D. themselves inside Russia. All I can say is, keep well to leeward of those bastards. They're hot stuff and they'll sniff out faked documents at half a mile if they actually rope you in for questioning."

"What about snap checks, sir?"

"Liable to happen almost anywhere—roads, trains . . . but I'm hoping you'll skip through them. Don't take any unnecessary risks, however. If the M.V.D. should decide to grill you, you've had it, Shaw. So—watch your step twenty-four hours a day."

Shaw grinned. "I will, sir, don't worry!"

"Now—cover. You're Peter Martin Alison, representing W.I.O.C.A.—which in case you don't know it is the Workers' International Organization for Cultural Advancement. It's akin to the British Council—you know the sort of thing. As their name implies, they're international in structure and they've got agents in pretty well every country in the world, and a really big set-up in Russia. That background gives you excellent scope for moving about the Soviet Union, especially as the Russians have a very high regard for the organization—they really are dead keen on it and pay it tremendous respect, every one does, from highest to lowest. You need to be a deep pink politically, of course, but you *don't* need to be particularly cultured—and I'm not being rude. For all I know, you're bursting with erudition. However, your particular line will be literature and what I'm saying is, the average well-read man, which you are, can get by very adequately. Well now—you'll contact the W.I.O.C.A. office in Moscow. They, along with the Embassy, will have been warned about you—that's to say, a man called Chaffinch,

26

who's the British bigwig in W.I.O.C.A. out there, will know about you, but as far as the rest of the staff are concerned you're the genuine egghead, Peter Alison, out from home to get to know the boys. If you really don't know much about our great literary heritage and the current best-sellers, remember the broad rule-of-thumb: best sellers are mainly in the brackets sex, sodomy and sadism. Right?"

"Yes, sir. What about reporting back?"

"You'll have one of Carberry's latest gadgets. A neat little portable transceiver which looks like, and in fact is, a battery shaver, complete with aerial in the flex. It has a very special opening mechanism and no one but you will be able to get inside it, short of smashing it. Small, yes, but it's got enough range to reach Moscow from almost anywhere inside Russia —Carberry will give you all the details later. It will be arranged, by the way, whatever the Foreign Office has to say about it, that the Embassy will retransmit anything you send and pass it directly to me immediately. If we want to call you, we'll transmit at 2300 hours Moscow time. You'll keep a listening watch at that time whenever you possibly can. Once you've found out what the threat is, tell us at once of course, but meanwhile go ahead and sabotage it if you can. You see, taking into account that it's all to look like an accident, it's pretty obvious that some kind of new weapon is involved in this thing rather than a military operation as such—and secret weapons are susceptible to sabotage." Latymer paused. "Now, Shaw. Both you and I realize quite well what's involved in sabotage. It's highly dangerous to put it mildly, especially where nuclear devices are involved. I won't say any more about that, but believe me, I regret having to send you on this job. However, I'll be relying on you to give me the picture as fully as possible via the Embassy—and when you've done that I'll guarantee to raise heaven and earth to help you. There may come a point when the only course for survival will be to send in the V Force Vulcans with their skybolt missiles—I don't know, and it'll be up to you to guide me on that. Understood?"

"Yes, sir."

"Right. Now, seeing we've got a fleet going in later, I'll pave the way with the Admiral just in case you want to contact him for anything, but as far as getting yourself out of Russia when the time comes is concerned, I wouldn't advise actually trying to sneak aboard his ships in Leningrad —or offshore either. They're hot, along that coast." Latymer glanced at his watch. "Well, Shaw, I've another appointment with the Chiefs of Staff in ten minutes, so I'll have to throw you out. Report back here to Carberry at four o'clock and he'll fill in details about background and so on inside the Curtain, and also hand you that passport—and brief you about our imaginary Peter Alison's home life, and such W.I.O.C.A. activities as you might need to know about." He got up and came round the desk, and placed a hand heavily on Shaw's shoulder. His face was stiff and concerned as he said gruffly, "Good luck, my boy—and look after yourself. I don't want to lose you and I'll expect you back in this room with a whole skin as soon as you've unearthed this thing. And just remember, won't you, that the smallest thing you can pass back to me may be vital for God knows how many millions of us. . . ."

The defensive measures were already getting into gear. Not one minute was being lost.

As the Piccadilly Line tube-train rattled Shaw westward beneath Hyde Park Corner for Baron's Court, a convoy of Army lorries rolled up Constitution Hill carrying a Guards' detachment from Wellington Barracks. That detachment had been trained in missile-launching and behind them came a vast vehicle from the back of which protruded the long blunt snout of a mobile rocket-launching platform. The workaday crowds looked with casual curiosity at this contraption, scarcely giving the troops themselves a second glance. Two or three small boys displayed more detailed interest and that was all. The whole procession had been forgotten as soon as it had moved on. Those people didn't realize, and if Shaw was successful they never would realize, that the signals that were responsible, among other things, for that detachment's journey, had gone out scarcely one hour before from the War Office and the Air Ministry and the Admiralty, on the personal authority of the Prime Minister. Those urgent, top-priority and most secret signals had gone to all naval, military, and air commands and they read: *Exercise Repel Boarders. Stand by for action alert.* And in isolated sites widely dispersed about the British Isles from Kent and Sussex and Hampshire up to Inverness and Sutherland and the Outer Hebrides, the long, menacing fingers of the missiles were by now lined up on their targets thousand of miles away. In the Clyde, officers of the Unites States Navy were already watching while the Polaris-carrying submarines were fully stored up for long patrols and in all respects made

28

ready for sea. Within hours those submarines would proceed, for all the public would know, on just one more exercise, but this time they would not come back until the flap was over; and their journey would take them out through the Cumbraes and beyond Arran and Ailsa Craig, north round the Mull of Kintyre or south past The Rhinns and the Mull of Galloway, there to submerge and proceed to their action-stations, the firing-positions from which their searching weapons could when necessary flash their way into the Eastern land mass. There was as yet four days to go before the arrival of the Foreign Ministers but the West was not going to be caught with its pants down.

That night Shaw was driven in a fast, closed car down the Mall for London Airport. Feeling for the Webley .38 in its shoulder-holster, he looked out at the ordinary sights of London and her people. As always in the early stages, he had been gripped by his old feelings of inadequacy; he knew he would rise above them later on, and he knew too that he had to bring this job off if it was the last one he ever did in his life. Failure must not even be considered. He was still looking out of the window as the car swept past the Palace. This was a journey he knew well; it seldom varied when he was starting an assignment that involved an overseas posting. But this time, since it involved a penetration of the Russian enigma, it was subtly different.

FOUR

The telephone in Shaw's luxurious bedroom in the Hotel Metropole buzzed into his subconscious and when he lifted the handset a voice, speaking English with a Viennese accent, said, "Mr Alison?"

"Speaking." He was wide awake at once.

"Good morning, Mr Alison. I apologize for telephoning you so early, but I am to inform you that Herr Prakesh's car will be at your hotel at ten o'clock."

"Right, I—"

There was a click in his ear and he jammed the receiver back. Prakesh was his contact. He rubbed the remainder of his sleep from his eyes and stretched, flexing his muscles. He had checked in at the Metropole in the early hours, tired and edgy after the flight and a concentrated session with Carberry at the Admiralty. Sleep hadn't come for a long time, for he was conscious all the while of the shortness of days. It was a pity, he felt, that he wouldn't have Debonnair's assistance this time—for one thing he was very fond of the girl and for another she would have been invaluable if he could have left her to nose around in Vienna after he had moved on . . . her former Foreign Office background meant that she could be trusted by Latymer and because of her training and experience she had often been useful in the past. On the Gibraltar job, for instance, she'd been with him nearly all the way, and she had given him very valuable help in the early stages of the assignments that had led him, at other times, to Australia and West Africa. Currently, however, she'd been sent out to Australia herself on a job for her bosses in Eastern Petroleum —damn their eyes! But they, after all, paid the girl her magnificent salary, so he could scarcely tell them what to do with the job. . . .

A moment later he pushed the sheet right off and put his feet down into thick pile. Walking over to the window he stepped on to a balcony and looked out at the city. Below him, Vienna was waking up to another day and everything looked ordinary and calm; this old city had seen so much trouble in its time, had only started to settle down when the occupation forces had been withdrawn in 1955. Now, like the rest of the world, it deserved its peace.

Turning away with a faint breeze ruffling his hair, Shaw returned to the room. He went into his bathroom and had a shave and a steaming hot bath. After that he felt fine but, as always, he disliked the waiting period. He could never get properly settled down until the action started. When he was dressed he rang for breakfast, which was brought up to him by a pretty, dark-eyed waitress who looked him up and down, provocatively and with frank approval. At his request she laid a table for him out on the balcony. He enjoyed the crisp rolls and excellent coffee and when he had finished he sat back with a cigarette and listened to the faint street sounds coming up to him, and sniffed the keen Austrian air appreciatively.

This was the calm before the storm, was almost certainly the last time for many days that he would be able to sit about and luxuriate like this.

He was going to make the most of it.

At 9.45 he rang down to reception and said he was expecting a car to call for him in fifteen minutes and he would be in the lounge. Then, after taking routine precautions with his gear, he went downstairs and settled himself behind a newspaper in a comfortable chair until he heard himself being paged. He got up then and went across to the reception-desk and found a blue-uniformed chauffeur waiting for him, cap in hand.

The man asked, "Herr Alison?"

"Yes."

"I am Herr Prakesh's chauffeur, at your service, Herr Alison."

Shaw nodded and the man turned about. Shaw followed him across the foyer and down the steps, casually but with his right hand inside the lapel of his double-breasted grey suit, all ready to slide round the butt of his Webley, as the chauffeur opened the door of a big black Mercedes. You could never be sure of anything in this game. Inside the car he saw a monkey-faced little man grinning at him, a dark little man in a city suit and a high white collar. He let his hand fall to his side then; Carberry had shown him a photograph and he recognized Wolfgang Prakesh right away.

Prakesh said, "Ah, Mr Alison. How nice to see you. Please get in."

Shaw smiled back at him and climbed in, sinking into soft upholstery. The chauffeur shut the door and ran round to his glass-enclosed compartment. As the Mercedes moved out into the stream of traffic the little man said politely, "I hope you enjoy your stay, Mr Alison. I thought perhaps you would like a drive on a fine morning, to see something of our countryside before you begin work."

"Very kind of you, Herr Prakesh."

Prakesh reached up and flicked a switch on a small microphone hanging from a hook in the car's bodywork. Then he said quietly, "We have much to talk about, I am sure, and you may speak freely here. We are entirely to ourselves, that is why I decided it would be better to meet you here rather than in my office or my home. I have just switched my chauffeur off and he will hear nothing until I want him to." He added, "Private as we are, I shall continue to address you as Alison, so that you will grow accustomed to the sound of it—if you will forgive me for the suggestion, which no doubt I scarcely need to make. I have heard much of your great experience. . . . And now tell me: how is my old friend in Whitehall?"

Shaw grinned. "Very well, Herr Prakesh."

"But worried?" A keen glance swept over him.

"Very. You know, of course, exactly why I'm here."

"Oh, yes. I had a cypher from headquarters, a very full message."

For a moment Shaw was silent, thinking about his companion. Carberry had told him that Wolfgang Prakesh was a banker of repute. As such as he was invaluable, for he had business contacts among all the European communities and in all the capitals—and he was known to have others also, men who were not exactly business contacts at all. He had first come within the orbit of Latymer during the war. At the start he had been interned, having been caught in London by the outbreak of war, but very soon he had been able to give excellent proof of where his sympathies lay and indeed he had been able to give very practical help to the Intelligence services. After the war, when he had returned to his native Vienna, he had agreed to continue this help and to become one of the Outfit's world-wide network of part-time agents.

Now, as though reading Shaw's mind, Prakesh said, "I am here to help you, yes . . . please ask anything you wish."

"Thank you—I shall." Shaw glanced out of the window as the Mercedes, crossing the Danube, headed north-eastward out of the city, then he turned to Prakesh again. He asked, "Bearing in mind what I've come for, have you any fresh information that might help?"

Prakesh shook his head regretfully, pursing full lips. "None. I am sorry. The news came to me as a complete surprise. There have been no hints, no straws in the wind—and there have been none since."

"That's not surprising, I'll admit. This thing's obviously being handled with kid gloves." He frowned. "What puzzles me is how they can get away with it. I mean, it must in its very nature be something really big, and there are any number of Western agents inside Russia at this very moment—yet not one of them has reported a thing, so far as we know. I don't see how they can keep any sizeable project quite so hushed up, particularly from their own people."

Prakesh said, "Remember you are dealing with Russia, Mr Alison. They have a long history of intrigue behind them, they are plotters by nature. Also, do not lose sight of the fact that something else may be being used as cover. That is very important."

"Yes, of course—I'd considered that. But we've no information of *anything* new going on."

"Ah, but perhaps it is something that is not new. Forgive me. I am merely speaking my thoughts aloud, Mr Alison."

He leaned sideways as the Mercedes took a bend at speed. "They may be nonsense, but. . . ." He shrugged.

"On the contrary, anything you say may be a big help," Shaw told him. "It looks like being the toughest job I've come up against." He hesitated. "Herr Prakesh, I'd like your honest opinion. You know the whole story so far as we know it ourselves. Do you believe it?"

Prakesh pulled at his upper lip. "Do I think the Eastern powers are hatching something?"

"Yes. The extremists, not the Kremlin itself."

"Quite, yes. I gathered that the Russian Government is not involved directly." The banker was silent for a moment after that, frowning to himself. Then he said slowly, "The East is always hatching something, my friend. Perhaps even more so when they appear to be friendly. You may have noticed that every friendly overture is quickly followed by a drop in the temperature of the cold war? I see no reason to doubt that the principle remains exactly the same this time, even though it is potential revolutionaries that we are concerned with rather than a government as legally constituted. That makes little difference to the fundamentals of the Eastern mind. Also, Rudintsev himself has an unusual reputation, a reputation of straight dealing, and I do not think he would be party to any kind of double game. Yes—I believe it to be true. Always I have thought that one day the East might try something like this, some sudden blow, and as you are aware, there has recently been much testing of nuclear weapons. This may have some bearing on what Rudintsev spoke of—these extremists may in some way be using the resources of the Soviet, the proper resources, to twist them to their own ends."

"Could be. Certainly our people have been worried about those tests, though not in this particular connexion—so far, anyway. You see, so far as we know, they've only been trying out bigger and better H-bombs, nothing more unusual or newer than that."

"Ummm . . . *so far as we know*, Mr Alison."

Shaw looked at him quickly. "How d'you mean?"

"Only what I say." Prakesh screwed up his face thoughtfully. "They may be trying out something very new under cover of the H-bomb test-firings. A kind of—if I may use an old-fashioned phrase—a kind of secret weapon."

"Yes . . . that's what the Chief said, as a matter of fact."

"Then I believe he may be right. There could so easily be such. These extremists could perhaps be intending to use this new weapon, or to force the legal Government to use it, whereas the true intention of the Kremlin may be not to use it but rather to have it in reserve only."

Shaw nodded. "It's a line of thought. But from a practical viewpoint, what form could such a thing possibly take? Haven't they already thought of everything, every possible kind of horror? Surely it's only a question of size and degree these days?"

"I am not an expert in such matters," Prakesh confessed, shrugging. "But there has been much increase in fallout recently in North Russia, in the Laptev Sea region, and the island of Novaya Zemlya has seen much activity, I am told. Also the Barents Sea, where they carry out the underwater tests, between Spitzbergen and Novaya Zemlya." He broke off, sighing deeply. "It is a puzzle, Mr Alison, but you will solve it, never fear."

Shaw was silent after that as the Mercedes sped on, swallowing the miles. The city and suburbs were well behind them now and they were running through fields with men and women, happy-looking peasants, at work. A little later they drove beneath the shade of some tall trees and then the car started up an incline. When they reached the top Prakesh flicked his intercom switch and spoke to the driver, and the car slowed and stopped. Shaw looked down at rolling green country interspersed with clumps of trees. A calm scene under a clear blue sky flecked with tiny white streaks of cloud, no more than cotton wisps against the deep blue. A fresh wind blew from the south-west, cool from its passage across the snows of the high lands. Shaw said quietly, almost involuntarily, "It's beautiful, Herr Prakesh. Really beautiful. I'm glad you brought me out here."

Prakesh gave a faint sigh, looking troubled. "Let us hope," he said sadly, "that nothing ever comes to spoil it. You know, of course, that my country is ultimately concerned in this as well as yours. If war comes, then an independent Austria will not long survive."

Shaw gave a bitter laugh. "What country will, in the long run, Herr Prakesh?"

"Precisely!" The little banker nodded vigorously. "Therefore we should now discuss the next point, which in fact is the first priority: how you are going to get behind the Curtain, Mr Alison."

"Ready when you are."

Prakesh spoke again to his driver and the Mercedes turned to head back into the city. Shaw looked out once again at the distant prospect of fields and woods and hills. The land he was going to was grimmer, harder, full of menace. He would feel almost nostalgic about this last peaceful scene, this sight of the Austrian plain in sunlight.

As they went along Prakesh told Shaw that he was to leave Vienna that night by train for Indsbach on the Austro-Czech border. Outside Indsbach he was to meet an English-speaking Hungarian named Istvan Gorsak. Gorsak would know nothing of the purpose of Shaw's journey but he would see him across the frontier into Czechoslovakia and thence into the Soviet Union by means known at present only to Gorsak himself. Gorsak, Prakesh said, never gave anything away in advance and he was very much a rough diamond; but Shaw could have every confidence in him and was not to worry. Prakesh handed Shaw a bulky package containing, he said 7,500 Russian roubles in mixed notes; Gorsak would provide any local currency he might need as far as the Russian frontier and Shaw would of course be able to get more roubles from the W.I.O.C.A. office in Moscow if necessary. The full instructions for making contact with Gorsak were lengthy and had to be repeated back until Shaw was word perfect; and he had to memorize a map of the Indsbach are. So it was not until the car was once again crossing the Danube into Vienna that the little man sat back and relaxed.

When the banker dropped him outside the Metropole Shaw went straight up to his room to chuck his things together. But first of all he examined everything carefully, noted that his grip was still locked and intact, as were his drawers. The shaver-transceiver was safe in its case. Nothing had been touched.

FIVE

It was a comparatively short journey to Indsbach—little more than seventy miles by rail.

Shaw arrived there at eleven o'clock that night. For the time being his appearance was somewhat altered. Before going aboard the train in Vienna he had spent some time in a washroom at the station together with his grip. When he came out again he was no longer the well-dressed W.I.O.C.A. man who had driven only that morning in a Mercedes with a respected banker. He was a workman now, in soiled corduroys and a zipped leather windcheater and heavy, clumping boots. And it was in this temporary disguise that he left the train at Indsbach and, following his memorized instructions, set out on foot, still carrying his grip.

It was cold, with a hint of rain, and there was a chilly wind blowing dust and scraps of paper along the road as he came out of the station and turned to his left.

He picked up his bearings quickly. Ahead of him now was the railway bridge. He climbed the steps slowly, not hurrying at this stage, making for the other side of the track. An old woman passed him, a peasant, her seamed face half concealed behind a filthy brown shawl, stained with the grease of ages. She smelt of poverty, she carried its inescapable aura with her; she scarcely glanced at Shaw as he brushed by her. Down the steps into a dingy street of sad little dwellings he went, saw the smoking fingers of the scattered factory chimneys, heard in the near distance the nerve-racking scream of a circular saw biting into timber. Somebody was working a night-shift. The factories looked small, and Indsbach itself was a small place; the station was on its outskirts. Few people were about at this hour, but the occasional vague shadow flitted by across the street, outlined in the few fitful lamps, hands in pockets and heads sunk into thin, ill-clad shoulders. This place was a far cry from Vienna in spirit and it gave Shaw the shivers; possibly it was too close to the grim reality of the frontier for gay hearts and carefree spirits—these could not survive the frightening emanations of slavery and conquest from behind the Curtain. No doubt all frontiersmen throughout time had lived in uncertainty, but in this part of Europe they existed right under the shadow, the shadow of what might come at them swiftly and without warning from a mere few hundred yards away. Across the little town Shaw could see the loom of the floodlights at the frontier-post, could almost fancy he heard the stamp and ring of metal as heavy nailed boots and gun-butts smashed into concrete.

He made his way along, still unhurriedly, stopped after a while to light a cigarette and look cautiously behind. All clear.

He walked on again.

The rows of mean little houses gave way now to dispersed cabin-like dwellings, isolated and ramshackle buildings. A little farther on the metalled road came to a sudden and inglorious end, as though, on this side of town, the roadmakers had wearied of their task and had just given up.

Shaw trudged on along a country road, rutted and rough, and he was soon into open country with Indsbach, cut off short like an amputated limb, two miles behind him.

It was midnight now and he increased his pace.

Another half-mile and he reached a crossroads. Taking the left-hand turning, he walked on for another fifteen minutes, his eyes straining through the blank darkness. Some distance off, he began to make out the scattered lights of a village—the village for which, in the unlikely event of his being questioned, he was supposed to be bound.

Then, two hundred yards or so farther on, he saw the loom of trees, tall and dark against the night sky—the start of a thick belt of forest. He went on carefully, feeling a strange fluttering in his stomach, a wateriness. There was something about the silent Austrian night, alone there beneath a starless, overcast sky, that reminded him, incongruously enough perhaps, of oldtime fairy stories, of Grimm and his monsters and his distressed princesses, and the ogres and giants of folklore, the witches who changed men into dwarfs or animals . . . he laughed at his fancies and went on, but there was still the feeling of being submerged beneath a thousand years of bloody, turbulent history. Soon he had reached the first of the trees, had come beneath their whispering high branches which locked together across the road above his head, forming a black and continuous cavern.

Except for the faint stirring of the wind in those trees, and his own footsteps, there was utter silence.

Shaw licked his dry lips, and began whistling.

It sounded incongruous, eerie, even fearful in that place. *"Land der Berge, Land am Strome. . . ."* The notes, somewhat flat, of the Austrian national anthem went out into the still air and Shaw walked on, slowly. He had gone almost a hundred yards between the two halves of the forest when he heard the response. The cry of an owl—once, twice. Shaw now whistled the Blue Danube Waltz. He kept this up for perhaps fifteen seconds and then he stopped, and at once the owl's cry came back at him. Three times, then a pause, and then twice more.

Then silence again, utter and profound.

Shaw had stopped on the roadway now. The owl's cry had come, as he expected, from his left. He judged that he was abreast of it now, and that it was not far off in the forest. He moved into the lee of the trees and watched, looking up and down the road. He allowed five minutes but nothing moved, and then abruptly he swung round. Stepping between

37

the trees, he plunged into the forest, felt twigs and brush-wood snap beneath his boots. Small night-animals scurried away from his approach, something furry and yet slithery scuttled across his feet and there was a whimper as he jerked his heavy boot. Ahead of him the owl called again and he moved on, feeling his way blindly in the pitch darkness, branches, whipping across his face stingingly. Prak-esh had warned him not to use his torch. His legs caught in the undergrowth and in roots and fronds so that he tripped constantly as he did his best to home on to the owl's inter-mittent cry. He could move only slowly. He cursed the case he was carrying as the branches time after time seized it and he had to stop and free it, wasting the hurrying minutes. The owl's cry had an impatient note now; once when it came he had to alter his direction a little. But it was only some ten minutes after he had entered the forest that the resistance of pliant branch and twig and the hard rigidity of the tree-trunks seemed suddenly to break and he realized that he was on the edge of a clearing.

A moment later a blinding light shone full into his face. His body jerked with the sheer suddenness of it and he shut his eyes. It didn't check with Prakesh's warning . . .

Then a rough voice hissed in English, "Still, you. Quite still. I have a gun."

Shaw kept perfectly still and said nothing. He heard crunching footsteps then and heavy breathing and then he smelt the strong acid of a man's body-sweat as the torch came nearer. Foul breath swept his face. The torch was lowered from his eyes then and he was able to make out a big, coarse man with a black beard. This man was glaring at him surlily and in his hands he carried an old-fashioned Sten gun lined up on Shaw's chest. That Sten might be old-fashioned, but it looked well kept and highly dangerous.

The man asked softly, "Alison?"

"Right. You're Istvan Gorsak?"

"Your papers first."

"I think not. I want—"

"Your papers. Come." The muzzle of the Sten dug into his ribs. "I take no chances. I will shoot."

Shaw breathed hard; he couldn't argue with that Sten. He reached into his windcheater and handed over his forged passport. In the light of the torch the man flicked over the pages, glanced keenly at Shaw's face, and handed the pass-port back. Then he said, "So. I am Istvan Gorsak, yes. It is good that you 'ave got here."

"Then we agree on something. Well—now you know who I am, you can put that gun away, can't you?"

The man shook his head stubbornly, looked angry. "No. You have a gun." It was a statement rather than a question.

Shaw said, "Of course I have. What did you expect me to carry—a parasol?"

"Give it to me."

"Look here, Gorsak—"

"Give it to me." The Sten was pushed into him again and he saw the finger tightening on the trigger. "At once, friend. If I am to help, you must obey. I give all the orders."

Shaw's mouth hardened for a moment and then he shrugged and let out his breath in irritation. He would have preferred some other guide than this suspicious, heavy-handed peasant. He said, "As you wish." He reached into the windcheater and brought out the Webley .38 and handed it over. Gorsak took it without a word and thrust it into his belt. Then he lowered the Sten and swung the sling across his thick shoulders.

He said shortly, "Now come."

The light snapped off and the darkness was blacker than ever. Shaw sensed the man turning and then heard his command, "Your hand on my shoulder."

Shaw reached out, felt the hard muscles beneath his hand. This man was built like a gorilla; Shaw hoped he wasn't on the same level of intelligence. Gorsak moved across the clearing, Shaw holding on to his gigantic body. In a few moments they were back in thick forest again, but Gorsak found his way unerringly, making away from the Indsbach road along which Shaw had come.

Half an hour later Gorsak stopped. Over his shoulder he said curtly, "Wait here. Do not move."

He went forward, slowly and cautiously, almost soundlessly. Then Shaw heard him calling softly in his own language, and then a woman's voice came back in answer. Shaw hadn't expected a second person, let alone a woman. He heard Gorsak mutter something and soon after that the Hungarian was back beside him. The man seemed to have cat's eyes, for he hadn't used the torch. He hissed, "Come. My woman Gelda tells me the road is quite clear. Keep silent. We shall see no one, I believe, but if we do, I talk—not you talk." He jerked the Sten and when he spoke again he sounded as if he was grinning. "Or maybe this talk, yes?"

Gorsak went forward again then and within half a minute they were out of the trees. The road was still clear and in the fitful moonlight as the clouds moved Shaw could make out the woman, Gelda—a wide-mouthed, husky young gipsy woman with swelling breasts, going towards an ancient vehicle which once had been a bus, drawn up out of sight from the road. As they came nearer Shaw looked at its gaudy sides covered with peeling paint and at the windows, bare of glass mostly and filled in with what looked like plywood or even cardboard. Ancient, decayed posters flapped from its bodywork. It looked as though it was used as a cara-van—very likely Gorsak was also a gipsy, like the woman. Gorsak gestured Shaw to get into the front. Gelda climbed in beside him on the wide seat and then Gorsak heaved himself up, grunting, behind the wheel. The decayed old bus started up with a roar and a rattle which sounded to Shaw as though it must be heard in Indsbach itself, but Gorsak was quite unperturbed. He drove out into the road, his biceps bulging hard against Shaw's body as he swung the wheel hard over, the vehicle lurching heavily over the bumps. He headed then, so far as Shaw could judge, away from the direction of Indsbach, making southward. A light rain began to fall, spotting the windscreen.

Shaw looked sideways at the Hungarian. In the faint light from the dash he appeared ugly and brutal, with an almost brigandish air. Despite the chill of the night he wore only a dirty check shirt with rolled-up sleeves, below which his arms were like tree-trunks—hard, dark brown, knotted, thick-ly covered with hair, as were the backs of his enormous, stubby-fingered hands, hands that looked as though they could strangle a man with ease, break his neck in seconds. Black hair sprouted through the open neck of the shirt and from his ears and nostrils. On the other side of Shaw, the woman was dark and voluptuous, with promiscuous lips and high cheekbones and an arrogant nose. There was an ani-mal smell about her body, earthy and crude. Her hair was jet black, in daylight might have a bluish sheen, and it was half concealed beneath a gaudy headcloth. Small golden ear-rings pierced her lobes. Shaw didn't much care for the look of either of these two, but he would have to make the best of them. Wolfgang Prakesh must know what he was about.

After a while Shaw asked, "Where are we going to cross the frontier, Gorsak?"

"You will see." The tone was surly and unhelpful but Shaw persisted.

He asked, "Surely if we go much farther south, we won't be on the Czech border at all?"

The glances of the man and woman seemed to meet across him and Gorsak laughed. He said, "We do not go into Czechoslovakia. You have been told that I come from Hungary?"

"Yes, but I thought—"

"Do not think from now on. *I* think. Only Gorsak think. You are nothing. Do only as Gorsak say. Indsbach. . . ." He shrugged massively. "Was only a false trail, Indsbach— just in case of accidents. Is better so. Gorsak prefer to cross into Russia through 'is own country."

Shaw nodded. It made sense right enough, though he had decidedly understood from Prakesh that they were to go by way of Czechoslovakia. He said, "All right, I get you. You know best."

Again Gorsak laughed. "Good. You are wise, friend."

"How are we going to cross?" Shaw asked.

"The usual route. The frontier post at Carovác."

Shaw came bolt upright. "Over my dead body!" he snapped. "We can't possibly do that. I've no papers—at least, none that I can use at any frontier post, and I only know a word or two of the language—"

Gorsak broke in savagely as he swung the bus round a bend. "Who knows best his own country? Who knows best what can be done in Hungary and what cannot? You—or Gorsak?" He seethed for a while, muttering and grumbling to himself, then calmed down. "Do not be foolish, friend. You will not need to worry. We shall get through . . . eh, Gelda?"

Gelda smiled and moved her body against Shaw's. In halting English she said, "Trust Gorsak. Gorsak know what he do. Often he go over."

"Is right. I go through on business—plenty, plenty times."

Shaw had to be content with that. He was committed to Gorsak now and they all knew it. But he didn't like any of this. He saw no prospect whatever of evading a search by the B.A.C.S., the Hungarian Security Police. They wouldn't miss a trick any more than the M.V.D. He was more and more worried as the ancient vehicle bounced and rattled along the wet road, south for the Hungarian border. Meanwhile he was uncomfortably aware of Gelda's closeness and of her breath, hot on his face, and of the way she was thrusting her tight, hard breasts against him whenever she leaned across to speak to Gorsak. There was a time and a place for everything, Shaw thought, and this wasn't it. Besides, he told himself with a faint grin, any more of this

41

and Gorsak might get jealous! He didn't care for the thought of a jealous Gorsak. Gelda had all the appearance of a nymphomaniac, but no doubt Gorsak was more than equal to that and wouldn't appreciate any help.

When the first faint streaks of dawn lightened the eastern sky Gorsak broke a long silence, speaking in Hungarian to Gelda. Gelda nodded in reply and once again her body moved hard against Shaw as she turned towards Gorsak. A little after, Gorsak pulled the bus off the road and stopped. He jumped down, landing on soft earth wet with the recent rain.

"Out," he said brusquely to Shaw.

"What for?"

"Do as Gordak say." A huge hand reached in, took Shaw's upper arm, and squeezed. The grip tightened painfully until the forearm swelled and throbbed with trapped blood. Gorsak pulled Shaw close to his heavy, bearded face. He grinned. "O.K.?"

Shaw's eyes were blue ice and he had to use every effort of his will to stop himself smashing a left into Gorsak's face. But he said evenly, "All right, Gorsak. I said you knew best. That stands. But I only hope to God I'm right. And I've just an idea that you and I are going to fall right out before long." He climbed stiffly out of the bus, saw Gelda coming round the back, giving him a lascivious look and rather more than a glimpse of her body. As he glanced at her, almost in unwilling fascination, he sensed Gorsak moving, but he was a fraction too late. A huge bunched fist took him just above the ear. He staggered and fell, dazed and caught right off his guard. He saw the two of them looking down at him, Gelda with a curious mixture of emotions in her dark face. Maddened with pain and rage, Shaw struggled up and went for the Hungarian. Gorsak stood like a rock, taking blows as they came through his guard without a flicker, and then he simply reached out and grabbed the collar of Shaw's windcheater. Pushing Shaw backwards, he propped him against the side of the bus and slammed his fist into his face. The back of Shaw's head hit the bus with a cracking jerk and he felt blood spurting from his cheek where the skin had split. Two more blows came in rapid succession, followed by a couple of short, vicious jabs to the body and a knee in the crotch. He went down in a heap, dazedly pulled himself to a sitting position. They watched him as he lurched to his feet like a drunk, bent almost double with pain, and then Gorsak came in again and finally. Shaw's head seemed to part from his neck and then he passed out in a blinding flash of coloured light.

Gorsak stepped back and looked down at him. He said, "Gelda, strip him and rub his clothes in the mud. I will help." Together they bent and, helped by Gorsak, Gelda stripped Shaw naked. As she began to tread his clothing into a muddy heap, Gorsak picked Shaw up and carried him into the back of the bus, where he put him down on a sleazy bunk.

Gelda came in then and he said, "The leaves."

Gelda went over to a box under the second of the two bunks, and came back with a handful of oily leaves. She wrinkled up her nose and said, "They stink. I am sorry for him."

"No time for pity, Gelda. Rub him all over, but not the face. Leave that. He is brown with the sun, and it would not take, over the bleeding."

Gelda nodded and got to work. She kneaded the dye into every part of his body and gradually his skin darkened. Then they dressed him again in the muddy clothes and lay him down once more on the bunk. He was still flat out. Gorsak slammed the door and he and Gelda climbed back into the front and Gorsak took the bus back onto the road and drove on for Carovác and the frontier into Hungary—and the Iron Curtain.

SIX

Shaw came round slowly and painfully after having been out for a long while and when he did so he felt the bus still jolting and rattling beneath his bruised, muddy body. The jerking motion racked his head and he felt a wave of nausea. His face was stiff, his jaw ached abominably, and his whole body felt as if it were caked with blood. His flesh was bruised, pulpy. He lay there on the filthy bunk for many minutes before he found the strength to lift his head. When he was able to do so, he twisted round and saw Gorsak and the woman in the front. He must have made some small sound for Gelda looked round and then turned to Gorsak and said something to him in Hungarian.

Gorsak jerked the bus to a stop and climbed through to the back. Standing by the bunk with Shaw's Webley in his hand, he looked down, his dark eyes searching the agent's face. After a moment he said, "Gorsak is sorry, friend."

"Sorry!" Shaw tried to sit up, but fell back heavily, his head splitting and another wave of sickness racking him. He retched agonizingly. Then he saw the Webley and said bitterly, "You bastard. Just tell me something, Gorsak—is Prakesh behind this?"

Gorsak grinned, showing broken yellow teeth. He sat down on a packing case and said, "Yes, friend, he is."

"Where are you taking me?"

"To Russia."

"I see." Shaw tried to struggle up, but Gorsak reached out and pushed him down firmly.

Gorsak said, "Now I joke no more. I am sorry. We take you not *into* Russia, but simply to the Russian frontier, as arranged."

Shaw stared at him. "What? D'you mean——"

"What I have said." The man was grinning still. "You are now inside Hungary, friend, and Gorsak has kept his promise. You are thinking Gorsak is a double agent, but not so. To prove, you may now have back the revolver."

He handed the Webley to Shaw.

"Well, I'll be damned," Shaw said wonderingly. "So that beating-up . . . was it all part of the cover, Gorsak? How did you work it all?"

"It was easy—and much, much the best way. It meant that you would not be called upon to speak in a tongue that you do not know. You were my brother-in-law, who had come into Austria with me on business of his own. You had made unwelcome advances of love to my woman, and Gorsak had been forced to deal with you. The security policeman on the frontier post at Carovác came to look at you in the back and he laughed very much when he saw you. That, he said, is the kind of thing that should happen to men who advance love on other men's women, and I agreed. It is not needed, perhaps, to say that this man, an N.C.O., is a good friend of mine . . . if he had not been, he would have looked a little harder and checked you more thoroughly with the papers. This also was part of the plan—that we should cross the frontier while this man was on duty."

Shaw nodded painfully. "Did you mention . . . papers, Gorsak?"

"Yes!" Gorsak's eyes gleamed oddly. "My brother-in-law's papers. He came through with us not a week earlier."

"Did he indeed?" Shaw looked hard at Gorsak. "Where is he now?"

"Not your business, friend." Gorsak's heavy, bearded face leered down at him and he heard Gelda give a throaty gurgle of laughter. Then Gorsak went on, "But I will tell you all the same, for I am so sorry for hitting you so hard! You understand, I did not like my brother-in-law." His face darkened savagely, cruelly. "You English have a proverb, no? Kill the two birds with one stone. My brother-in-law's body lies in the forest where we met. You understand, yes?"

"I understand all right! You're a tough nut, Gorsak. Well, I—suppose I ought to say thank you."

"There is not need. It is enough that I am able to help. Gorsak hates many people, not alone his brother-in-law, that is why he does this work." He got to his feet, looming larger than ever in the confined space. "Now we must get on—but first, Gelda will attend to you."

Gorsak went away. Shaw lay back and closed his eyes and then Gelda came into the back of the bus with a pannikin of clear, cold water. They had stopped, she told him, where a stream ran along beside the road. She gave Shaw a refreshing drink of water and then bathed his face free of blood. Her hands were surprisingly gentle.

The cold water did him good and after a while Gelda said comfortingly, "The marks—not bad. Many bloods all gone. Gorsak know how, where to hit so not mark long time. Not show, all gone, day after this day."

"Well, that's good. I suppose I've got a nice pair of black eyes all the same."

"Eyes . . ." She bent to examine his face and he felt the nearness of her again. Hot breath swept his face. "Eyes . . . iss blue. Pretty. I like."

There was a gust of laughter from the front and Shaw, smiling, said, "Better cut out the flattery, Gelda. I don't want to end up like Gorsak's brother-in-law!"

Gorsak called something in Hungarian then and Gelda, smiling back at Shaw, said, "No black eyes. Face some swollen, soon go. Eyes quite O.K."

When Gelda had finished with him she gave him a drink from a bottle. It tasted like some rough form of brandy and after it he felt a good deal better, though when they started up again the shaking he got racked his head badly. As Gorsak drove off, he said they were already through Moson-magyaróvár and heading south-east for Gyor where they would turn off for Budapest.

45

They stopped for meals en route, pulling off the road while Gorsak made a fire and Gelda prepared some food and cooked it. It was mainly a very sustaining vegetable soup which she provided, a soup made from what they could find in the fields, and once there was a rabbit which Gorsak, with his gipsy skill, was able to catch bare-handed. The Hungarian preferred eating this way to stopping in any of the towns and villages for a meal at a workers' eating-place. This was partly due to his gipsy blood, but also partly to caution. The fewer the people who saw them together, he said, the better it would be for him if anything unfortunate should happen after Shaw was across the border—a hypothesis which Shaw found peculiarly depressing. So Gorsak made the fires and Gelda cooked, and when they sat down for that first meal in the open Shaw found the Hungarian much more forthcoming than he had been on their first meeting. He had mellowed and was no longer suspicious and surly. Perhaps it was the fact that he was back in his own country, perhaps it was because his part in the mission, with the first obstacle behind him, was soon to be over—for he would not cross into Russia with Shaw.

"How *do* I cross?" Shaw asked, biting hungrily into a vast hunk of black bread. "And talking of that, I've been meaning to ask you . . . why didn't you tell me back in Austria how you meant to get me through Carovác?"

Gorsak smiled and said simply, "You said I was tough. I am, friend. By God, I have to be. But there are times . . . let me put it this way: I wished for obvious reasons to make your beating-up look very convincing. If you had known what I was going to do, you would not have defended yourself properly—and I could not have made a good and thorough business of it." He added with an incongruous touch of virtue that made Shaw smile inwardly, "It is the way Gorsak is made—you know?"

"H'm . . . what about your brother-in-law?"

"Is different." Gorsak's face darkened, the dangerous look returning. "I told you. My brother-in-law was my enemy, so I slit his throat." He gestured accordingly, with a sharp knife which he had used for skinning the rabbit. "You, now—you had done me no harm. There is a difference."

"For which the Lord make me truly thankful," Shaw murmured, grinning. "But suppose I'd come round at the frontier? I couldn't have backed your story about Gelda then, could I?"

"Gorsak hit good." He struck himself boastfully on the

chest, his eyes gleaming. "I knew you would not come round. But if you had, I would have hit you again, very hard, in the natural course of my indignation. You understand? And now, all that is in the past. We must think for the future, so listen carefully, friend." Gorsak put down the pot from which he was drinking soup, and fumbled with a filthy pipe. "We shall be across Hungary by about nine o'clock tomorrow night, allowing for as many stops as we shall need. We could do it quicker, but this is not wanted, so we shall not go too fast. We make for the frontier town of Khamchevko, where arrives at nine-thirty-five the express from Budapest on its way to Smolensk in Russia. This express, which you will catch after I have bought you a ticket for Smolensk, stops at Khamchevko for the frontier check out of Hungary—the railway-station is itself the frontier post for the train passengers. Now, friend." Gorsak leaned forward, closer, speaking softly although they were in open country miles from any human habitation. "The station is built across the actual frontier, and half of it is in Hungary and the other half in Russia. A stout barrier across the platform at each side, with much barbed wire and electrification, and armed guards, divides the station in two. When the trains pull in, they pull only so far as this barrier, and all the passengers are made to disembark under guard. The train is then searched and when it is empty it pulls ahead, beyond the barrier, to the Russian end. Into Russia, you understand. Then it stops again, and waits. The people go through the combined Hungary-Soviet checkpoint where their documents are most carefully examined. Once they have passed through, they are free to board the train again. Naturally, if there are many passengers, this process takes some time, but normally the train moves on at midnight. You understand?"

"I'm with you so far, Gorsak."

"Now, here is the interesting thing. If one extends a line sideways into the station buildings from the barrier, one finds that the frontier between Hungary and Russia at this point runs precisely between the Hungarian men's urinal and the Russian women's lavatory." Gorsak gave a deep, coarse chuckle and nudged Shaw hard in the ribs. "Odd, yes—but true—and very fortunate, friend, because at the present, due to some reconstruction in progress of which I intend to take advantage, there is a long, high gap at the top of the wall, a gap through which you will be able to pass easily. Had it not been for this, we would have had to find another way, which would have been more dangerous——"

"And this isn't?" Shaw was incredulous. "Surely the authorities have taken precautions?"

"Yes, they have. As I understand it, this is what they do: On the Hungarian side, an armed guard stands inside the men's urinal. On the Russian side, another armed guard stands, but outside and not inside, since the compartment is for the use of women. The only exit opens into the already guarded platform. Now, I shall accompany you into the Hungarian side, and together we shall deal with the guard. Then I shall give you a hand up to the gap. After that, it is for you to deal with the Russian guard on the other side when he comes to investigate any sound. This will not be easy, yet neither will it be impossible. Also, friend, it is the best I can offer."

"Sure? I don't like it, Gorsak. I'd much rather take a chance on getting through the wire somewhere well away from a town or a station."

Gorsak shrugged. "Certainly—if you wish to die! For myself, I do not. That wire is heavily guarded, very heavily guarded with men and guns and dogs, and many searchlights sweep it continually from the watch-towers—continually and to a great depth of cleared ground on either side. I assure you, there is not one chance." He stared at Shaw and added ominously, "I would not be anxious to take part in such an attempt."

"Yes, but this is madness, sheer goddam lunacy——"

"Listen." Gorsak leaned forward, stubbing a thick finger at Shaw. "I know—you do *not* know. I have never said it will be easy. But it is the only way. I got you through Carovác, yet you did not believe that I could do that. You must take my word that I can succeed again—or I shall not help you."

Shaw's teeth came together, hard. Then he said, "All right, Gorsak. But there's one hell of a lot of snags your way, you know." He hesitated. "Suppose both lavatories are full at the time? Suppose the cubicle in the women's side is occupied when I drop through?"

Gorsak grinned. "Excellent! The woman will cry out, the Russian guard will come in for you to deal with him—and there you are!" He made a stabbing movement with his knife. "Nothing could be better."

"That's all very well," Shaw objected. "If the whole place is full of women, I'll never get away with it. And what if I'm seen coming out of the women's lavatory?"

Gorsak said, "Always a man needs luck when doing some-

48

thing that is dangerous. Luck we shall have, you and I. We shall succeed, but we must go carefully and await the right moment. That is the point. Always there is a right moment. This time I believe it will come just before the express is due to pull out, while the guards are more relaxed, more bored, more thoughtful of going off duty—and the bladders of the passengers already emptied. There will be plenty of time, you understand, and we must judge our movements prudently."

Shaw grunted. "Well, let's suppose I do get away with it. I just walk along the platform and go aboard the train?"

"That is right. You take your place with those whose papers have been checked."

"Uh-huh. And suppose there's a snap check on the train?" Shaw asked sardonically. "My passport's stamped for the Uzhgorod region, which means I've got to be a long way from the frontier before I can survive a check. And what happens when they find the guards—the ones we've dealt with, by which of course you mean the ones we've killed?"

"Yes, that is what I mean. They will not find them until the train has pulled out, friend. I promise you I shall begin a diversion to ensure that. When they do find them, then they will have the train checked again at the next stopping-point, and all the passengers will be held—but you will no longer be aboard, which is why you need not worry about a snap check either. Approximately one hour out of Khamchevko, the train will enter its first tunnel, a very long one which runs beneath the Carpathians. For some way before the tunnel, the train runs up an incline, and just before entering the tunnel this incline becomes steeper, and the train slows almost to a stop. When it slows, you will get down on to the track. You should be able to do this very easily, for the train is never so full that a man cannot be alone in a corridor for quite long enough. After that it is up to you—but I would advise you to continue through the tunnel itself and make for the rail-town of Petroslav and there get on another train for Moscow. I have here a map, which you must study and impress upon your mind." As he reached into his pocket he added, smiling, "It sounds hard, friend. It is very easy! Whatever I said earlier, it is easy . . ."

"Oh, sure it is, like falling off a log." Suddenly, Shaw laughed. "It has its attractions, I admit. Into Russia by the lavatory wall. . . ."

They pressed on, rattling and banging and clanking across

49

Hungary, Gelda sharing the driving with Gorsak. Gorsak was firm in not allowing Shaw to drive—he must, the Hungarian said, rest all he could and later on he would be glad of it. They skirted Budapest, made across country for Hatvan and Gyöngyös, nearing the frontier. At times Gorsak sang in a deep bass voice, songs of old Hungary before the days of communism, and now and then Gelda joined in with him, though she didn't know the words of many of the songs that Gorsak sang so nostalgically. She was plainly very much in love with Gorsak despite a big difference in their ages, and there was, Shaw found, something attractive in the man's personality; no doubt the girl responded to that. And there was no doubt about his guts. Shaw had begun to like this man who was risking so much to help him and the West and once, while Gelda was asleep in the back and he was sitting alongside Gorsak in front, he asked him tentatively how his country was managing under the communists.

Gorsak stared moodily ahead for a while, concentrating on the road, and then he said morosely, "Ah, the communists." He gathered spit in his mouth and ejected it viciously onto the floor of the bus. "Me, I always hated them, even before the Rising. There are many, very many, in Hungary who hate them too. We shall never forget the Rising. How can you forget that? Friend, they killed my little son." His voice was harsh, grating, coldly savage now. "I saw him, my little son—spitted like a sucking pig on the bayonets. I was powerless to help. They held him on the bayonets over a fire. . . . mercifully, he died quickly. And he was only three, friend. As for my other children and my wife, I do not know to this day what happened to them. Shall I tell you something else, friend?"

"Go on, Gorsak."

"It was my brother-in-law who told them where my family was. And my wife, friend, was blood of his blood, flesh of his flesh! Can you begin to understand? My brother-in-law did not know I knew, you see, and I waited my time. As I said earlier—there is always a right moment for everything if you wait for it. Do you understand now?"

"Yes," Shaw said quietly. "I understand now, Gorsak. I'm sorry."

Gorsak gave a harsh, humourless laugh. "Do not be sorry. That is over now—the agony. Gorsak must be constructive. Gorsak puts it out of his mind and concentrates on the fight itself, the fight against the communists. But every now and then he remembers, and whenever he begins to think that after all, perhaps, a soft and easy life would be better for him in his later years, he hardens his heart again."

"That's natural. But why don't you leave Hungary? You say you're often in Austria. Why not stay there?"

"Because I can fight communism more effectively from inside. They do not know my feelings, you see. As far as they are concerned, I believe their story, expressed to me with much sympathy, that it was the mobs of Imre Nagy who killed my family. I work along with them—and I fight them. You know what I mean. Some Russian soldiers die in an ambush, some Party members are blown up when crossing a bridge. I and my friends have always got away so far. Gorsak is lucky. Always Gorsak is lucky."

"For heaven's sake," Shaw said, "don't say that just yet!"

Gorsak gave his booming laugh and reached out to put a hairy arm round Shaw's shoulders. "We are going to succeed. I feel it in my bones."

"You're risking your life for me, Gorsak. Why do you do that?"

Gorsak shook his head. "Not for you. Against the communists. That is what urges me—the harm I can do *them*. I am quite ready to die for my work, and I have an idea that your journey is of much importance, though I do not know what it is and neither do I ask."

"I was wondering if you would, Gorsak."

"No. For our own sakes, Gelda's and mine, no. The truth drug, if ever we are caught, is what you would call a bastard, friend."

They drove on in silence for a while. It was night now, and the sky was clear of the rain of the night before. The moon shone down ghostlike on the Hungarian Plain, where Attila's hordes had passed centuries ago, pillaging and burning their way across Europe from their capital city of Buda. Attila the Hun . . . and his kind of rule by fear held sway once more in these unhappy lands, though in a less obtrusive way, perhaps, so that people outside were able to close their eyes and their consciences to what went on. It didn't concern the Western peoples—yet.

Soon after that Gelda woke up and Gorsak handed over the driving. Shaw sat on with her for a few minutes. She seemed to enjoy driving, her big capable hands managing the heavy vehicle with ease. They chatted a little, making heavy weather of the language problem, and then he got up and climbed into the back. He switched on his shaver-transceiver just before 2300 hours calculated at zone-time for Moscow, and listened for a transmission from Latymer. Dead on time his call-sign came through and was followed by a brief coded message: *Fleet's visit altered from Leningrad to Moltsk*. That was all; he had never heard of Moltsk and the message meant little to him—but he was surprised and somewhat perturbed. Why an alteration in plans now—and why ask the fleet to what must be an insignificant minor port? A calculated insult? But why bother—if the end was as near as Rudintsev had suggested? He worried around the point for a while, got nowhere, and then he turned in, taking Gorsak's advice to get as much sleep as was possible in between the Hungarian's gross snores and the attentions of the bedbugs.

At nine-fifteen the next night Gorsak—who had already passed Shaw the brother-in-law's papers as a last-ditch and probably vain precaution—announced that they were within five kilometres of the frontier and indeed Shaw could already begin to see the lights of Khamchevko ahead.

In the back of the bus, he got his suitcase ready and made certain his prepared passport was there, also his Russian money. Then he checked his gun. His hands were clammy and he was on edge as the moment of action approached, his stomach-nerves playing up on him badly, though he knew that once he was inside the station he would be all right. The bus went on slowly now and they didn't speak. Soon they were driving along dark, mean streets, streets only dimly lit and, like those back in Indsbach, almost empty. Shaw shivered. Only a few hundred yards away now lay the heavily-guarded Russian frontier, and the M.V.D., and the grilling-rooms, and the Siberian forced-labour camps waiting for agents who got caught. There was a terrible brooding fear over the place, a fear from which one couldn't escape. It was everywhere, it pervaded everything like an insidious disease, an infection of the state, an effluence from Russia. It was the fear of the jackboot, the firing-squad, the visit in the middle of the night, the bloodbath—the whole regime of terror and brutality which the Stalin era had brought and which could not be eradicated all at once. . . .

Gorsak said suddenly, "Here is the station."

He shifted gear and swung the vehicle slowly left into the approach, up a slight incline, and then stopped. There were some people, peasants mostly, going with their pitiful bundles into the station. A heavy lorry ahead of them disgorged a line of sick-looking men wearing handcuffs and chained together, and Gorsak said quietly, leaning on the wheel, "Deviationists. This happens most nights. They are being

52

sent into Russia—to learn the truth!" He laughed cynically. "They will not come back, of course, even when they have learned it, poor devils." Then he added, "I knew about these people, naturally. They can be useful to us to-night—you will understand later."

Sweat broke out on Shaw's body, though it was a bitterly cold night, as he watched that line of hopeless men shuffling wearily into the station. Thin, starved, white—they were shivering in their wretched clothing. Then he stiffened as he heard a distant rumble in the air, a rumble that came nearer. . . . Gorsak said in a low voice, "Here she comes. Do not get out until Gorsak tells you."

"Right." Shaw felt for the Webley; it gave him some comfort. He heard a deep-toned, clanging bell in the distance and soon he saw the fiery glow of the great engine approaching from the south-west, heard the clanking of carriage wheels on metal and then saw a blurred line of light from the steamed-up windows. The Budapest-Smolensk Transfrontier Express was pulling in for checking. A steamy smell, raw and damp and hard, came down to them as the long train clanked and jangled to a stop inside the frontier, and then they heard the hoarse shouts, the orders driving the passengers to pile out onto the platform, orders coming crisp and menacing on the cold night air. Shaw moved restlessly, but Gorsak sat there without moving a muscle, waiting, waiting. He put out a hand to Shaw after a while. He said quietly, "Not yet, friend. Patience. We must wait until the checking is well started."

It was almost two hours later when Gorsak glanced round and nodded. He climbed through into the back and rooted about in a wooden crate, brought out a voluminous cloak which he threw on to his body with a large gesture almost of defiance. Then he picked up the old Sten, concealing it in the folds of the cloak.

Looking at Shaw he said curtly, "Now we go. Do exactly as I tell you from now on, without question." He went to the front of the bus and took Gelda in his arms, kissed her passionately on the lips, his hands feeling for her body. Then he jumped out quickly. As Shaw, about to follow him, took Gelda's hand, he saw how pale her dark face had become and saw, too, the sparkle of sudden tears in her eyes.

He said, "Don't worry, Gelda. I'll do my best to see that nothing happens to him."

Her voice was breaking. "You are the one only. Gelda will

not speak blame. Must is that *you* pass." She was trembling now. "God be with you."

He squeezed her rough, work-hardened hand, the hand that was too old for a young girl. He couldn't find anything to say.

He jumped down and followed behind Gorsak, carrying his grip. They went through the cold night up some steep steps and Shaw looked through into the Hungarian ticket-hall. It was a dreary, depressing place with peeling paintwork and old posters faded and yellow with dirt and age; a deadly cold draught blew through, as though it had come straight off the bitter Siberian plain. At the door Shaw turned and looked back at the old bus with its gaudy sides and its boarded windows. It was semi-derelict and it stank and it was bug-ridden—but it had made a brave endeavour and it had brought him a long way and it looked remarkably like home at that moment.

They walked on into the ticket-hall and as they did so a man in uniform came through from the platform, slamming a gate behind him. The uniform was that of the Hungarian Security Police and the man had a Russian Simonov semi-automatic carbine slung from his shoulder. He glanced coldly at Shaw and Gorsak and went on through into a waiting-room where they heard his voice coming back to them in a bullying shout and a moment later two old women and a man came into the ticket-hall shivering with cold and terror.

Shaw followed Gorsak to the ticket-window and the Hungarian bought a ticket for Smolensk. Half a minute later the two of them were out on the platform where the passengers were lined up, patiently shuffling through the Hungarian-Russian checkpoint. To their left a sign said, in Hungarian: MEN'S URINAL.

Casually, they joined the tail-end of the slow-moving queue. Gorsak's big voice boomed out jovially, telling Shaw to enjoy his visit to Smolensk.

SEVEN

The express was not particularly full and by the time Shaw and Gorsak joined the queue on the platform it had shrunk to little more than thirty people. But the frontier guards and security officials were not hurrying themselves; the check of documents was being carried out with thoroughgoing efficiency, and all the callous grimness and autocracy which Shaw had always associated with armed frontier checkpoints was there in strength.

A bitterly cold wind swept the platform, stirring up spirals of dust and blowing grit along the empty section of the line—the express had pulled along to the Russian end of the station some time earlier—and scraps of paper swirled along the concrete. Gorsak huddled massively in his cloak, clutching the Sten beneath it. Shaw shivered, despite the thick leather windcheater which was zipped right up to his neck now. Breath steamed in the air beneath the station lights, there was still the harsh smell of train and sordid travel, of poverty. The queue moved on very slowly. Stamping their feet against the cold, then shuffling forward a pace, they were patient, apathetic, scarcely speaking—though here and there a child cried with sheer tiredness and a baby howled its hunger thinly into the night and was pulled tighter into its mother's shawl. A few people ate sandwiches or fruit, or gnawed at hunks of black bread, or drank from flasks and bottles. It was a depressing scene; it was depressing that these people were so obviously used to this kind of thing nowadays, that it seemed to have become, to all except the very old, perhaps, an accepted part of life like eating and drinking and going to work, so that they had ceased even to wonder about it. For so very many things you had to stand in line and have your papers looked at by a man clothed in the authority of uniform, a man who always looked as though he were about to spit in your face and arrest you, but then thrust the papers rudely back in your face—if you were lucky.

Gorsak and Shaw waited. The suspense, the feeling of imminent disaster, of being on the razor's edge, was intense as they got nearer the control-point, and at last there were no more than a dozen or so people ahead of them and a handful behind who had entered the station after them. Shaw felt the slight pressure of Gorsak's hand on his arm and could just catch the Hungarian's whisper close to his ear: "Now, brother. You first."

Shaw gave no sign of having heard but he yawned, shivered, beat his arms across his chest and then excused himself to his "brother-in-law." Picking up his handcase he left the queue casually and moved across the platform to the men's lavatory and pushed the door open. He walked in, feeling the fear in his bowels. Inside, a squat, tough-looking Hungarian trooper was sauntering up and down, a Kalashnikova sub-machine-gun in the crook of his arm, its chromium-plated barrel glinting in the harsh light of an unshaded electric light bulb overhead. He looked bored and indifferent and he took no notice of Shaw. Shaw looked around quickly. There was only one cubicle and it had its door standing open— empty, thank heaven—but there were three men standing at the urinals and Shaw's hopes hit rock-bottom. He hadn't liked this from the start and here he was, as he had anticipated, up against a check already. He couldn't possibly start anything with three customers and a sentry around. But perhaps the others would go and still leave him with time enough . . . glancing up as though vaguely, he looked at the unfinished repair-work in the long, thick wall, the dividing wall which he had to cross, looked at the gap high up in the bare concrete. On the ground, building-materials were stacked in one corner, ready for the next day's work, and it looked as though another couple of days would finish the job.

When two of the other men left Shaw breathed easier.

Just after they had gone the door was jerked open again and Gorsak came in, muttering to himself and blowing on his fingers. Somehow or other he had managed to give his ruddy, bearded face a drawn and pinched look, and his teeth chattered. It was very convincing.

He glared at the sentry and said wearily, "Good evening, comrade. You are fortunate to be inside! The night is cold, so cold. . . ."

The man flexed his knees tiredly and gave a wide yawn, showing broken and blackened teeth. He said, "You can have my job, comrade, whenever you like. Me—I prefer the fresh air." Disinterestedly his gaze followed the third customer, who was leaving now and buttoning his clothing as he went. The man pulled the door open, shouldered it aside, and as he disappeared onto the platform Gorsak gave a low moan and leaned his full weight against the door. He put a hand to his head and allowed his body to sag.

He muttered faintly, "My head, oh, my head . . . comrade! I am sick."

The sentry came forward reluctantly. "What is it, then?" He added contemptuously, "Can you not stand the cold? Are you so old that your blood is thin and poor?"

Gorsak muttered, "Old enough. It is cruel, this wind. Cruel. I . . . am sick. It is my head. Get help, I beg of you."

He groaned again, holding his stomach now, his hands sliding towards the concealed Sten. The sentry muttered something under his breath, his face tightening in exasperation. He said sourly, "If you will move your body from the door, I will call someone."

Gorsak nodded weakly and the sentry came nearer. Gorsak began to move away from the door and then, straightening in a flash, let the folds of his cloak fall apart. The sentry looked right into the muzzle of the Sten, saw Gorsak's eyes steady above it, red-flecked, murderous, determined. Before the sentry had time to make a sound Gorsak's left hand shot forward, striking like a snake, went round the man's neck, squeezed, and pulled him close to the big, hairy body. Gorsak wedged the Sten between his knees and took the man's head in both hands, letting go his stranglehold on the neck. The head seemed to vanish in those enormous rough hands. As Shaw ran forward he saw Gorsak give a hard downward pressure and flick his wrists to the left so that the head seemed to jerk round, sightless and staring like a doll. Then he gave a sharp right-hand twist, his knuckles standing out white, and there was a small snapping sound. The sentry slid limply to the floor of the urinal. Bending, Gorsak grasped the body by the shoulders and, putting all his huge strength into it, he shook the man like a rat, his eyes gleaming like a madman's. The head lolled horribly, falling about like a lump of lead jerking on a string. Gorsak still kept his rump hard up against the door.

When he had made certain the man was dead he snapped at Shaw, "Quick, friend! The bolts."

Shaw ran across and pushed the big bolts through into their sockets at top and bottom. When he turned round again Gorsak had already carried the sentry into the single cubicle and had dumped the body on the floor. The big man went in himself and locked the door from the inside and then dragged himself over the top of the partition to land with surprising lightness on the floor. The whole business had taken no more than sixty seconds. Gorsak grabbed Shaw and pushed him over towards the dividing wall. There he braced his body against the concrete and held out his hands, cupped together to form a step.

He said, "A foot in my hands. Quickly. We must hurry in case the locked outer door is remarked upon." He was sweating like a pig now. "You must chance if there is a woman on the other side, and if there is, you must turn her to your own advantage, friend. Now—please."

"Thanks for everything, Gorsak——"

"*Now!*" It was a savage hiss.

Shaw gave a tight grin and clapped Gorsak on the shoulder. Then he put his foot in the big man's hands. He sprang upwards, aided by a powerful heave from Gorsak, and got his fingers on the edge of the gap. Gorsak gave him a final push, chucked up the grip which Shaw caught neatly, and then turned away and made quickly for the outer door on to the platform, the Sten concealed once again beneath his cloak. Then, as Shaw balanced his body on the ledge ready to drop, he heard a high scream and, looking down, saw a woman's terrified face staring up at him, a hand to her mouth.

He swore viciously.

He was conscious of a fervent hope that if the scream had been heard on the platform, then Gorsak would have heard it too—and would start up his own diversion as promised . . . and then in a split second he had dropped, his shoulder grazing painfully down rough concrete until he landed in the narrow space between seat and door. He was almost on top of the woman, a middle-aged woman who looked like a housewife. Steadying himself he jerked out his Webley and pressed it into her stomach, hard.

He hissed at her in Russian, "Quiet. The sentry will come now. You are not to say anything or I shall kill you."

Keeping the gun lined up on her, he slid the silencer on and then flattened himself behind the door. Already there was a commotion outside, the Russian sentry's boots clumping across the floor. Reaching out, Shaw slid back the lock and waited. A heavy, urgent hand thumped on the panel and a man's rough voice demanded, "What's the matter there?"

There was a moan from the woman and then the door was pushed open. Shaw heard the sentry's heavy breathing as the man stared in stupidity at the woman, not sure what was going on. Shaw stood ready. There was a pause and then the sentry's face came farther round the door and he looked right into Shaw's eyes. As the mouth opened Shaw fired, point-blank.

The expression seemed to freeze into astonishment and the eyes went dark and sightless. Then the face crumpled and broke, and the blood came. It spurted and welled in a red river, a gush coming from the boneless cavity that had been the mouth, another from the back of the smashed skull. The man crumpled at the knees, his shattered face and head arcing down towards the woman. Her mouth opened but she made no sound. Then she swayed, in a dead faint. Shaw caught her and eased her on to the seat, then grabbed the sentry's body and pulled it right inside the cubicle. Picking up the man's gun he shut and locked the door, fearing at

58

any moment to hear some of the frontier-guards move in from the platform. Even if no one else had heard the woman's screams, it couldn't be long now before the absence of both sentries, and especially the Russian one who should be out there on the platform, was noted. Luckily, the silence in Shaw's immediate surroundings seemed to indicate that all the other cubicles were vacant—and probably, with the express almost ready to leave, no one else would come in. Empty bladders all round, as Gorsak had suggested. So far, so good. . . .

Just then the shooting started, a distant burst and then a nearer one in answer.

It was, he fancied, just outside the station on the Hungarian side of the border. Gorsak—making his promised diversion! He'd timed it beautifully—maybe he'd seen someone going for the door of the lavatory on the Hungarian side. There was a rattle of automatic fire—that old Sten in action —drawing farther away. Then there were cries, and more gunfire came from nearer at hand, the Kalashnikovas pumping out their hundred rounds a minute. This was followed quickly once again by the now more distant Sten. Shaw fancied he heard the thud of bullets smacking into concrete near by, then there was a scream from the station entrance and a few moments after, thankfully, he heard—or was almost certain he heard—the outlandish rattle and clank of Gorsak's pathetic old bus, beating it away from the station flat out, and then the firing stopped.

Precisely ninety seconds later, with the Hungarian end of the platform still in total uproar and a bell clanging furiously on the Russian side for the Smolensk passengers to board the train which was about to pull out of the trouble-spot a little before time—for, as Gorsak had so obviously intended, the shooting had been taken as an attempt to rescue the handcuffed prisoners whom Shaw had seen entering the station earlier—a tall figure left the Russian ladies' lavatory.

This figure was dressed in a Russian frontier guard's greatcoat, a greatcoat which was a little on the short side for him. The coat was tightly buttoned to the neck and the man had a Russian steel helmet on his head. A Kalashnikova sub-machine-gun was slung from his shoulder and in his left hand he carried a suitcase. On his right arm he half-carried a woman who looked as if she had been taken ill, a woman who whimpered and muttered something about the train for Smolensk which she must at all costs catch. The

Russian soldier uttered rough but kindly assurances. All eyes were on the area of the shooting, so no one bothered to look at these two—at least, not close enough to notice that the Russian's boots and trouser-bottoms were not of the regulation pattern—and thus unremarked they made their way to the nearest coach of the Smolensk Express where the "sentry" helped the woman aboard. He swung himself up after her and banged the door shut behind him. Faces still stared fearfully out of the train's windows, but the owners of those faces made way respectfully, ingratiatingly, when the "sentry" pushed along behind their backs, with the woman in front of him. The two went along the corridor and then the "sentry" thrust the woman into an empty compartment, shut the door very firmly, and pulled down the blinds. Out in the corridor the passengers—miserable, haunted people many of them, in poor, threadbare clothing—whispered amongst themselves. The unfortunate woman was under arrest for some misdemeanour, some transgression of the Soviet's many complicated laws—or possibly even for being involved in the shooting, who could tell?

There was a shrill whistle.

The station bell stopped its clanging and there were shouts along the platform, and then a deep roar of escaping steam and the sound of pistons turning over and wheels racing on steel rails until the great engine got its grip. Then there was a jerk and a bump and a moment later the locomotive moved ahead, easing the Budapest-Smolensk Transfrontier Express smoothly, slowly, out of Khamchevko inexorably into Russia.

In his compartment Shaw mopped at his forehead, which was beaded with sweat under the heavy steel helmet. He could only hope that Gorsak and his Gelda were really clear and away now. Of one thing, at least, Shaw was quite certain: Nothing of this night's work would ever come out through either of them. Gorsak would never be taken alive by the communists nor would he allow Gelda to be. He knew too much about communist methods for that.

The express gathered speed, rocking and swaying out of the borderlands, flying on through the night for the passage of the Carpathians, its great deep-toned bell clanging out at intervals like a knell, a sound of doom, sparks streaming back along the wind from the hurtling footplate's inferno.

Now and again, whenever he heard footsteps clumping along the swaying corridor, Shaw let the blind fly up and, propaganda-wise, showed his head and shoulders to the curious, the sentry's Kalashnikova much in evidence. The curious didn't linger, but looked away quickly and passed on. Gun and uniform carried a lot of weight inside Russia and for the time being Shaw was extremely glad of it. He was quite safe now and would remain so until the express neared the tunnel under the mountain ranges and, on meeting the steep part of the incline, he had to jump for it.

There was still the woman, however, and Shaw knew quite well that a live witness in the form of this woman could wreck anything that Gorsak might have achieved by his drawing-off tactics.

But he couldn't kill her.

He had to put his whole faith in his own speed after jumping off the train—and he knew that in fact he had a pretty good chance.

He looked again at the woman, sitting crying quietly in the corner opposite him, her eyes on the Kalashnikova as if hypnotized by the wicked-looking weapon. Leaning forward he said kindly, "Cheer up, Mother. I'm not going to hurt you. But I'm afraid I'll have to tie you up for a while."

She didn't say anything, just sat there looking back at him, her dark eyes wide like pools of black ink. As the train, travelling very fast now—touching eighty was Shaw's guess —rushed on through the night deeper and deeper into Soviet territory, Shaw reached into his pocket for a clasp-knife. Cutting away at the blinds on the outer windows, he soon had them in strips which he knotted together. He tied the woman's hands behind her back, securely, then cut a further length and looped this around her ankles, hauling them tight together, and led the other end over a steam pipe beneath the seat. She would be immobilized now until the train stopped. There was no reason why anybody should look into the compartment after he had gone, but a wedge might help . . . Shaw took a couple of cartridges from his own gun and opened them gingerly with his knife. Pouring away the powder, he slipped the bullets into his pocket. Then he sat back and waited, with the Kalashnikova across his knees.

Some time later the train's rattle changed its tempo, slowing down. Shaw got up again then and securely gagged the woman with some of her own clothing.

Then, once again, he waited.

It seemed to him a long wait. Then at last the express began to climb more slowly, the motion becoming more and more laboured. They had reached the steepest part now.

61

Shaw got up, murmured, "Good luck, Mother!" and went out into the corridor, slamming the door behind him. The corridor was empty. Bringing out the lead bullets from his pocket and using the butt of his Webley as a hammer, he tapped them quickly and efficiently into the jamb of the sliding door where they wouldn't easily be seen. When he tried the door, it was jammed solid. Carrying his case, he walked ahead to the exit door at the forward end of the coach. As the train snorted almost to a halt at the top of the gradient, he opened the door. He waited until the train had started to gather a little speed again and then he got down onto the step, his case in his hand. Hooking two fingers round a metal grip in the coachwork, he shut the door as quietly as he could and then he jumped outward and forward.

He hit the track with bone-crunching force, close to the tunnel and between high banks of rock. He rolled over and over, half a dozen times. As he struggled to a sitting position, dust-covered and winded, the end carriages of the long express went on past him, the engine well into the tunnel now and filling it with its reek as it chuffed on for Smolensk, the lights from the rear windows where people were still awake throwing flickering shadows on the side of the track. When the train had passed him, he got up and stepped on to the rails behind it, watching its tail-light fading into the distance, beneath the great craggy overhang of the mountain. Then he walked on ahead into the tunnel's mouth, flicking on a torch which he had taken from his case, shining it on foul, slimy walls.

He had to clear the whole long length of this Carpathian tunnel before daybreak—and before the Smolensk Express made its first stop, also at daybreak, and that woman began talking.

He was on his own now, all right.

EIGHT

Only two trains—one up, one down—passed Shaw during that walk along the tunnel and he was reasonably certain he hadn't been spotted from either of them.

The up train had come along comparatively slowly and Shaw had been able to get off the track into a working recess in time. He had covered his face with the Russian's greatcoat and all had been well. As for the down train, no one would every have had a chance to spot him from that. It had come down upon him with its great bell clanging, clanging violently . . . the huge engine racing at him out of the darkness, enveloped in steam and smoke and flying sparks, thundering along the track. That time, Shaw had been no-where near a recess. When he had heard the approaching racket and felt the shudder and shake of the rails, he had simply crouched right down and clung to the up rail until the monstrous whirlwind had passed in its steam and uproar and high, racketing din. Its terrible slipstream had torn and ripped and flayed at his body as the blur of lights had flashed past at something like ninety and he had been battered, deafened by the din, scarcely able to think for some moments after it had ceased.

Then—filthy dirty—he had scrambled up and walked on into the evil stink of fumes and the whirling dust and grit which filled the whole tunnel and tore at his throat and near-ly choked him.

He stumbled along altogether for three hours and when he emerged thankfully into the open and took a deep gulp of fresh air into his clogged, tortured lungs, the sky was still dark and a steady drizzle soaked into his clothing. Tired and stiff, colder than ever and hungry, he slumped to the side of the track a little way farther on, clear of a deep cutting, and eased his aching feet and leg muscles. A little later he pulled himself up again and looked around.

Not far off he could make out a hump of ground. He made his way up the slope towards it in order to reconnoitre; he couldn't afford a proper rest yet, had to get clear away from the railway line as fast as he could before he could let up in any way.

He found that he was looking out over a valley.

Seeing Gorsak's map in his mind's eye, he searched through the darkness for signs of a road running through the valley, and after a time he fancied he could see a faint lightening of the blackness, a long thin streak which could well be that road. After some ten minutes this was confirmed when he saw headlights moving along it, flickering off the track into scrubby undergrowth and trees. Then, a little later again, he saw away in the distance a few widely dispersed lights—probably in the homes of families already waking to a day's work. It was still too dark for him to be certain of whether he was looking at a town—there had been one on the map—or merely a few scattered cottages, but whatever it was he would do well to avoid being seen in any kind of community too close to the railway.

Within the next two hours the express would reach its first stopping-point inside Russia and then the search would be on.

Meanwhile, that road offered hope.

Half an hour later Shaw's wishful thinking had materialized in the form of a small closed van which had come along that road.

Shaw, wet through by now although he was hidden in a clump of trees near the road, had carried out an eminently successful ambush on that van, aided once again by his uniform and the Russian's chromium-barrelled Kalashnikova. Afterwards he had left the driver and his mate stone cold in those same trees and he didn't see any reason why they should be discovered for some time yet.

The uniform greatcoat was now concealed in the back of the vehicle and the "sentry" had vanished under a resumption of the windcheater and the corduroys, which made admirable garb for a van-driver. He drove on through the town which he had observed earlier—it was just a small country township—and, once on the other side and putting mile after mile between himself and the railway-line to Smolensk, he came to a crossroads and turned left for Petroslav as Gorsak had advised. The rain had stopped now and it was almost daylight. It was a long drive into Petroslav but Shaw took it flat out, easing down only once or twice when he spotted an oncoming vehicle ahead—there was no point in drawing attention to himself by appearing to be in too much of a hurry. If he could make the rail-centre of Petroslav quickly, then he fancied he would be quite far enough from the area of likely search for him to show himself.

When he was a couple of kilometres short of the town, he caught sight of a stretch of water to his left; it looked like a large lake, and it gave him an idea.

Easing his speed, he turned up a rough track to the left of the road, bumping and lurching heavily over the uneven ground, until he was on the shore of the lake, and under cover of thick bushes and trees. Switching off the engine, he stripped off all his clothes and had an invigorating swim which washed away all the filth of his night journey through the tunnel. After this he dried out in the climbing sun and a light breeze and then he dressed himself in clean clothing, putting on the grey suit. The uniform and the windcheater rig he secured tightly round the Kalashnikova and then he threw the whole bundle far out into the lake.

It went in with a splash and, with the weight of the sub-machine-gun, disappeared at once.

Shaw climbed back into the van, turned it, and drove again down the track to the road, turning left for Petroslav and driving at a normal speed now. Soon he was in the maze of streets, approaching the centre of the town. He pulled into the roadside in a busy street, switched off the engine, and got out. Leaving the van without looking back he set off, carrying his grip, along the street until he was well away from the vehicle. Then, and only then, did he ask his way to the railway-station, speaking in Russian.

He felt, as he walked off briskly towards the station, that he hadn't done too badly so far. But, when he reached the station, he found that the M.V.D. had mounted one of their checks.

NINE

They were standing at the barrier between the ticket-hall and the platform—two sallow, grim-faced men with revolvers at their belts, backed up by a couple of troopers of the Red Army with Simonov carbines, and Shaw was conscious of their eyes watching him all the time he was buying his ticket through to Moscow. The booking-clerk asked to see his papers and he pushed his British passport through to the man, who seemed perfectly satisfied.

He took Shaw's roubles and issued a ticket.

Shaw approached the barrier, whistling flatly between his teeth, his eyes watchful but his face calm. He smiled at the stony faces and asked with casual interest, "Do you always guard the railway-stations like this?"

The men stared at him and one of them asked, "English?"

"Why, yes! Name of Alison. I'm on the staff of W.I.O.C.A. It's all here." He handed his passport over and the man took it.

The Russian said, "W.I.O.C.A.?" There had been an immediate change in the attitude of both the M.V.D. men; they seemed to have relaxed a little and Shaw realized that Latymer had been dead right when he'd talked of the respect the Russians had for the workers' organization. But it wasn't altogether an open sesame, for the first man stuck his fist forward, holding up Shaw's passport, and demanded, "Mr Alison, where did you enter the Soviet Union?"

"Through Czechoslovakia. I was checked in in the Uzhgorod area."

The man grunted and opened the passport, looking keenly at Shaw and studying the photograph. It seemed to satisfy him. Then he leafed through the document, glanced at the visa and the entry stamp for Uzhgorod so neatly made by Carberry's forgers.

He said, "That is in order." He glanced down at the entry once again and said, "You entered Soviet territory three days ago. What have you been doing since then, Mr Alison?"

Keen eyes looked into Shaw's and he shrugged. "Getting here—that's all. I wanted to take it slowly, and see all I could."

"This is your first visit to Russia?" The man could see that it was the first for some time anyway, by the absence of any other Soviet stamps, and Shaw nodded. "How did you come here, Mr Alison—to Petroslav?"

Shaw said, "By road. That was the best way to see the country, I thought."

"No doubt. What did you see—which way did you come?"

"Mukachevo, Beregovo, Khust, Bolekhov."

"And now you go to Moscow?"

Shaw said politely, "That's the general idea, if you'll let me through."

"You may proceed, Mr Alison." The M.V.D. man handed back the passport and stood aside. "I hope you will enjoy your visit to the Soviet Union's great capital city."

As Shaw walked away he felt the stickiness in his palms. It was to say the least of it unlikely that an English W.I.O.C.A. man, decently dressed, fully documented, properly checked in via Czechoslovakia, able to detail his route, would be connected in the strait-jacketed official mind with a fracas at Khamchevko in Hungary, with a Russian-uniformed man who had tied up a woman on board the Smolensk Express, or with the windcheater and corduroys of Gorsak's "brother-in-law." Nevertheless, he felt he had had a pretty benevolent slice of luck to get through the M.V.D.

As the Moscow train pulled out a little later he felt fully confident that he had covered his tracks adequately, though there would be some wonderment in official quarters, perhaps, when the abandoned van was found. It would be a long shot to connect it with him, however—and, as always, dead men told no tales. He had no qualms when, during the journey, his passport was examined once again in a snap check by armed guards aboard the train. Undoubtedly W.I.O.C.A. was a big help.

On arrival in Moscow early next day Shaw made his number at the W.I.O.C.A. office, which was in an impressive building not far from the British Embassy. He was shown up immediately and ushered into the office of the man called Chaffinch of whom Latymer had spoken. Chaffinch was a pleasant, chubby man of around fifty with a pinkly bald head—a man who looked as if normally he would smile a lot, but who was far from happy now. He and Shaw talked for some minutes about how London was looking and about Shaw's impressions of Russia so far, and Shaw sensed the man's nostalgia, his consuming anxiety, his fears perhaps for a family in England. Then Chaffinch said quietly, "I know all about you, of course, Commander. There's someone else who's been expecting you and wants to meet you, so we won't talk real business till he gets here. Excuse me." He picked up a telephone and said, "Get me the Embassy, please, Miss Pullman. Mr Hart." After a short wait he said, "Ah, Hart. Those books have come—the ones you asked for. Yes. Good—then we'll expect you as soon as you can make it."

He hung up, his hands shaking and his face puckered with worry. Only a few minutes later there was a knock at the door and a messenger showed in a tall man in his late thirties with thin, sandy hair and a bow tie. He had rather cold blue eyes and the suave, well-polished look of a diplomat. Chaffinch introduced him as Hart, but no mention was made of his function within the Embassy.

Hart, who seemed the efficient sort but under an assured manner was as worried and nervy as Chaffinch, got down to things right away. Pulling up a chair he said, echoing Chaffinch, "We know all about you, so you needn't bother with any explanations." He gave Shaw a straight, hard look. "I suppose I don't need to tell you that it's highly irregular for our people to be mixed up in your sort of game, Shaw. We've only agreed to come into this as a result of great presure from top sources—and because of the extreme gravity of the situation. But you'll understand, of course."

"Yes. Your part in it is only unofficial—I know that. By the way . . . have you gathered how I got into Russia?"

Hart said, "As a matter of fact—yes. We do gather things one way and another, but let me repeat, that doesn't make us into agents."

"Quite. But I'd like to know how you assess my chances of keeping in the clear."

Hart pursed his lips. "It's hard to say. I gather the trail's very confused. You and Gorsak handled it very nicely between you——"

"You know about Gorsak, then?"

"Of course," Hart said evenly.

"Did he get away, he and Gelda?"

"I can't say, Shaw." Hart gnawed at his bottom lip. "Personally I'd think it doubtful, but at any rate he clearly hasn't talked. You'd better pray he doesn't—and so had the rest of us! You're in the clear for now, but the Russians aren't fools. You mustn't bank on them following your false leads for long."

Shaw said, "I'll be watching out—don't worry! Now—what about the actual job, Hart? Have you anything new to offer, any leads at all?"

"As a matter of fact—yes, I have." Hart paused, lowering his voice instinctively even in this room. "Some news came through only this morning . . . certain of Russia's top nuclear men have left Moscow again after being sent for, urgently and at short notice, to take part in high-level talks in the Kremlin."

Shaw felt his mouth go dry. "Any idea what about?" he asked.

"None. Officially we don't even know there *were* talks. There's been a heavy security screen around the whole thing, a heavier screen than anything I've come up against since I've been in Moscow. Nevertheless we have reason to believe it wasn't the official Russian leadership that was involved, but the other people."

"The extremists?"

"Yes," Hart said briefly, lighting a cigarette. "That's right——"

"Have you heard much about that business—the proposed *coup d'etat?*"

"Not much. I believe they're working up to a take-over all right, and it could come any day now, but no one knows a damn thing for certain." He blew a trail of smoke, flicked his cigarette nervily towards an ashtray. "As a matter of fact, Shaw, if it hadn't been for Rudintsev, we would never have suspected anything—but since we heard about that, certain other past events have dropped into their slots, d'you see——"

"What about the people, the ordinary people, here in Moscow?"

Hart shrugged. "It's all quiet on the Moscow front. Perhaps too much so. At any rate, no one suspects anything at all so far as we know. Well now—those talks I mentioned. The nuclear men concerned have *not* returned to their normal appointments, but are believed to have turned up, the whole bunch of them, in the naval port of Moltsk."

"Moltsk?" Shaw frowned. "That's funny . . . by the way, where is Moltsk?"

Hart gave a brief grin. He said, "I can't say I'm surprised you don't know the place, but I'm going to suggest you get there as fast as you can. It's in the Kola Peninsula——"

"Murmansk way?"

"No, it's on the Barents Sea certainly, but nowhere near as far north as Murmansk."

Shaw said reflectively, "The Barents Sea. . . . That's where there's been a lot of nuclear test explosions lately, isn't it. D'you think that's what these physicists are concerned with?"

"Not in a direct sense, no." Hart frowned. "To my mind this doesn't quite fit—but there's something else, something that I feel is rather more significant when you start to think about it, and it's this: Our ships—the goodwill squadron, you know—they're not going to Leningrad after all. They're going to Moltsk—by special request of the Russian Defence Ministry."

"I know," Shaw said in a puzzled voice. "I heard that direct from my chief—the changed plans, I mean. I didn't know who was responsible for it."

"Did it surprise you?" Hart looked at him intently, his facial muscles twitching. "It did me, I confess."

"Well," Shaw said slowly, "I'm surprised at *any* alteration of plans at this stage. They'll be due very soon, won't they?"

"They're due to go alongside the outer mole in Moltsk at 2 P.M. on the 24th."

"Uh-huh. . . . I don't quite see the connexion between this and your nuclear chaps, all the same."

"There's no direct connexion, so far as I can see, but I think the whole thing's very odd. You see, I'm sure the physicists haven't gone to Moltsk in connexion with the test-firings, and if I'm right on that, it means there's something else to take them there, take them direct to Moltsk. Something brand new. Now, it occurs to me that the fleet's visit there instead of Leningrad *could* be a further blind—d'you follow?"

Shaw nodded. "Could be . . . but go on."

"Well now, if it's a blind, then it could also be a *lead* in a kind of inside-out sense. I mean—let's assume for the moment that this threat *is* centred on Moltsk, or at any rate on the Barents Sea area in general. Now, to divert a British squadron there could be an excellent way of in effect *distracting attention away* from the area, from whatever is going on behind the scenes—a simple precaution taken just in case there should be a leak in the meantime. D'you agree with that?"

Shaw said, "It makes sense, certainly. No one would imagine there could be anything hush-hush going on just around there, not with British naval units being, in theory at any rate, able to report back on what they saw. . . ." He hesitated, then asked, "Can you tell me anything about Moltsk itself?"

"Oh well . . . let's see." Hart screwed up his eyes. "It's a typical naval port. Nothing much in it really except for the dockyard. Pretty grim, I'd say, from its geographical location—I've never been there myself, by the way. Damned cold, though being clear of the White Sea it doesn't freeze up at all—the port's open even in winter, and at this time of the year you might even say the sea's swimmable-in, if you're a Spartan. There's pack-ice in the far north of the Barents Sea, of course, later on in the year, but that doesn't touch Moltsk. It's by no means an important place, even to the Navy, except for the fact that they've been drilling for oil in the sea-bed somewhere around that way. Been at it for years, building various constructions off shore——"

"Successfully—or not?"

"Very much not." Hart laughed cynically. "Don't know why they waste their time."

"Do Russians ever waste their time?"

Hart lifted an eyebrow. "Do I take it you think there may be a connexion?"

"I don't know yet." Shaw pulled thoughtfully at his chin. He'd had Moltsk on his mind ever since getting that message from Latymer and now he was beginning to feel something crystallizing, though he couldn't possibly have said what it was . . . just a hunch coming to the surface and that was all. Hunches couldn't always be neglected, though. A good hunch could sometimes be worth months of patient, painstaking investigation which so often proved merely misleading and frustrating—and, this time, speed was everything, was absolutely vital; already the days were passing rather too rapidly for Shaw. He said, "I've an idea you're dead right, Hart. Moltsk could certainly be worth a visit."

"I'm sure it would be." Hart leaned forward anxiously. "I know I could be looking at this the wrong way—it could be a kind of double-bluff and all the time Leningrad's the right place, but I don't think so somehow. It would be much harder to keep anything dark in a place like Leningrad. I might also add that I don't think you'll get very far in Moscow anyway, not unless you can find out exactly who the extremists in the Kremlin are and then get to work on them, but—"

"But that'd take a damn sight too long! I've got to go straight for the best possible bet now, and I agree that the juxtaposition of those nuclear experts and our fleet looks like being just that. I'll give Moltsk a looking over, anyway. What's the best way of getting there—train, plane, road?"

Hart said, "Train undoubtedly. Faster and safer—too many checks on the roads, and there's no plane for Arkhangel'sk, which is the nearest airfield for Moltsk, for some days."

Shaw nodded. "Right, I'll be guided by you." He swung round. "Mr Chaffinch, have you an office in Moltsk?"

"More's the pity—no. I'm sorry."

"H'm. That's awkward." Shaw rubbed his chin. "Is there any reason, any completely convincing reason, why a W.I.O.C.A. man should go there, then? I've got to have cover."

Chaffinch shook his head doubtfully. "You might be able to say you were looking over the possibilities of setting up an office in Moltsk, I suppose——"

Hart interrupted. "There's always old Godov."

"Professor Godov?" Chaffinch's eyebrows went up. "He's very much out of things these days. He's a very old man, and anyway——"

"Yes," Hart said urgently, "but couldn't Shaw pay him a visit? He's by way of being your Grand Old Man, isn't he? It'd be natural for a W.I.O.C.A. man out from home to go along and make his number with the G.O.M., wouldn't it?"

"Yes, certainly—you have a point there," Chaffinch agreed, looking happier. "I wonder. . . ."

"Who is this Godov?" Shaw asked.

"Well, as Hart says, he's our Grand Old Man. A charming old gentleman, an old-fashioned liberal—and not too happy with the regime, actually. He's been a big name in W.I.O.C.A. right from the start . . . and, you see, he lives not far from Moltsk, in what one might call splendid isolation!" For the first time Chaffinch's anxious face creased into a tired half-smile. "You see, he incurred official displeasure some years ago, when he deviated from the Party line in one of his books. He was banished from Moscow as a result and sent to his childhood home near Moltsk. It's in a kind of swamp, I believe, rather a dreadful place really, on the Kola Peninsula north of Ponoy. All that was some time ago, as I said, and he's considered harmless enough now—he's over ninety, after all, and I expect he's somewhat senile. But he's still very much alive, and I agree with Hart, he could be a good enough excuse for your going to Moltsk. Very fortuitous indeed."

Shaw nodded. "Sounds all right," he said thoughtfully. "Look, Mr Chaffinch. When I spoke to Rudintsev back in London, he told me that a number of people inside Russia think along the same lines as he does." He gave Chaffinch a résumé of Rudintsev's remarks. "Now, you say Godov's not happy with the regime. Do you think, then, that he could be considered as a possible Rudintsev sympathizer?"

Chaffinch shrugged. "I really couldn't say, but I would consider it a possibility, I think—yes. Rudintsev's right, there are many people who do feel like that. As for Godov . . . well, of course, he's never really toed the line all his life. He got up against the Czars in the first place, I believe. Mind you, I haven't seen him for years, or even heard from him, so I really can't say what his views are now. In any case, whatever his sympathies may be, I can't really see him being the least actual use to you—beyond his value as an excuse for your visit."

"You never know how people can help if they really want to. He's well worth contacting, in my opinion. Would you fix me up with a letter of introduction, Mr Chaffinch?"

"Why yes, certainly. I'll see to that right away."

"Thank you. And Hart—would you radio my chief in London, tell him I'm going direct to Moltsk as soon as possible?"

"Yes, I'll see to that. By the way," Hart added, "I'd advise you to be very careful in Moltsk. Like all the Kola Peninsula except Murmansk and Iokanga, it's an open area, but being a naval port it's naturally full of naval men and also a considerable number of Red Army personnel seem to have moved in over the last few months. And even though it's open, they've had restrictions on aliens' movements in part of the area for some years. That's why it's always been hard for anyone to get much reliable and useful information out of the place, of course." He added more encouragingly, "You'll find W.I.O.C.A.'s a good password on the whole, though, even where there's no office—at least you'll be a highly respected official, and that's always useful!" Hart stood up. "As soon as you've got something to report, call us up. We'll be keeping a constant if highly unconstitutional listening watch, but don't overdo it, of course. We don't want them to home on to your transmissions. And don't expect us to acknowledge anything. Just repeat any message twice through and leave it at that. Once we've got it, you can rely on it that we'll retransmit at once to London." He held out his hand. "Good luck, Shaw. Remember time's desperately short now. We'll be relying on you."

The train for Arkhangel'sk, whnce he would go on to Moltsk by ferry, did not leave until late afternoon and so Shaw arranged to meet Chaffinch for lunch—Moscow, Chaffinch said, was full of eyes and ears and it would be a good thing for the two of them to be seen together in public, just in case some of those eyes and ears were in touch with the Kremlin—and meanwhile he did some sight-seeing around the capital, letting the Russian scene sink in. He spent part of the morning visiting the great red granite bulk of the Lenin Mausoleum amid the crowding spires of Red Square; he looked in at the waxen corpse of the leader in its sarcophagus, saw the mouth of the dark subterranean tunnel through which the dishonoured corpse of Stalin had gone on its final journey to a grass plot on the Kremlin wall. Not having been in Russia before he couldn't make any comparisons, but the general impression he got was one of complete normality. The streets were austere, the people poorly dressed, the women in the main frumpy and frowzy-looking, but there were no signs of alarm, or of jubilation, or of tenseness. Hart was probably right; nothing of coming events, of any attempt to seize the supreme power behind the scenes, had leaked out here in Moscow. No wonder London hadn't known anything. . . .

One pointer that didn't fit Shaw's impressions came when he met Chaffinch and the W.I.O.C.A. man remarked quite casually that there seemed to be many more police about that day . . . and Shaw recalled what Rudintsev had said about the M.V.D. being in with the extremists.

When lunch was over and they were sipping at coffee and liqueurs, Chaffinch coughed a little and then said quietly, almost diffidently, "I don't want to sound . . . mawkish, Alison. That's not my way, and I know quite well that you're doing everything you possibly can. But . . . well, I'll come right out with it. I've got three children at school in England. Alan Hart's got two, and his wife's back there at the moment as well. It . . . er . . . it's rather a worry."

And that, Shaw thought bitterly, looking at the man's haggard eyes, just about put it in a nutshell.

He was already extremely worried about the shortness of time left, and then, as he went to the station for his train, he saw the newspaper placards:

FOREIGN MINISTERS ARRIVE IN LONDON.

Even though the Conference date had been constantly in his thoughts, that still gave him a jolt.

TEN

Hart had been absolutely right in one thing at all events. When Shaw arrived in Moltsk two days after leaving Moscow—and after surviving another snap check on the train and yet another on the night ferry from Arkhangel'sk—he found that the place was full of uniformed men. Oddly for a naval port, it was in fact the Red Army that appeared to predominate, and the majority of the men seemed to belong to artillery and technical units.

Shaw decided to walk from the ferry terminal so that he could become familiar with the layout and character of the port as quickly as possible. It was, he found, a dreary, windswept place of grey and ugly buildings, utterly unwelcoming. The people looked miserable, haggard, pinched with the cold of that biting wind. The civilians looked as though they hadn't enough to eat, though the troops and sailors certainly appeared fit and healthy. Those civilians crept about like dogs, as if they were on sufferance and might at any moment be kicked into the gutter by a bellicose officer.

It was a curiously remote and cut-off feeling to find himself in this northern Russian port. Moscow, even the train journeys, had been different. Moscow was the capital and all capitals were to some extent cosmopolitan. Moltsk was not! Moltsk was Russian grimness, Russian austerity, Russian gloom personified. A brooding fear hung over the place. One could imagine the effect, the alarm, if an Englishman were to speak to any man or woman among these depressed crowds; and one could also imagine Moltsk in winter, under a couple of feet of snow.

Shaw gave a shiver and walked on more quickly, saw the naval dockyard area away to the east, where the streets sloped to the sea. There were a few masts and funnels visible over the tops of buildings, and a number of vast, towering cranes, and the smell of salt water. That—and, except for the muted street sounds, for there was surprisingly little traffic, an uncanny, spine-chilling silence.

It was as though Moltsk was waiting for something to happen, as though the port was some hibernating juggernaut biding its time to strike. Shaw had an instinctive and very strong feeling that he'd been right, that he was pretty near the heart of things now.

Approaching his hotel he could see the name ahead in big letters. Chaffinch had booked a room for him at the Nikolai, by telephone from Moscow. He had apologized for the accommodation; and when Shaw arrived there he found that the place, though large enough, was little better than a one-star pub in its air of dinginess and its lack of amenities. Yet it was pretty full, and staying there were a number of junior officers of the armed forces, Red Army captains and below mostly, and a bunch of civilians who seemed to be fraternizing a good deal with the Army, talking quietly and earnestly in corners. These civilians must be from Moscow; they looked subtly different from the Moltskites, less repressed, fully accepted by the military. Shaw formed the notion, without any real evidence to go on, that they worked side by side with the Army.

There was little doubt that something was going on in Moltsk, and when Shaw filled in the detailed forms at the reception-desk and produced his passport he got the unspoken impression from the clerk's harassed manner that it had all been stepped up in the last day or so—which might explain why nothing had come through earlier to suggest that Moltsk might be the centre of this mysterious threat. Shaw didn't like the atmosphere at all, but, on the chance that he might pick up something useful, he went into

75

the lounge just before lunch and pushed through a boisterous bunch of young officers towards the bar, where he asked for a vodka. He spoke in Russian; but as he did so, he felt a hand fingering the cloth of his suit and then he was smitten heavily between his shoulderblades and a voice said loudly, "English?"

Shaw turned and looked into the grinning face of a young captain of artillery, all epaulettes and gilded high collar, a young man who seemed to have been hitting the vodka bottle rather hard. Shaw smiled back politely and said, "Yes, I'm English. You speak the language?"

"Sure do. Guess I was a year in America, as Assistant Military Attaché in our Embassy in Washington."

Shaw laughed, crinkling the flesh round his eyes in sudden amusement. "Correction. You speak American!"

The young man roared with laughter, slapped his thigh and translated loudly to several others near by. There was a general laugh and Shaw found that he was the centre of a vodka-swilling group of officers. The man who had first spoken seized his hand and began pumping it. He roared, "Say, what do you think of Moltsk, Englishman?"

"I've not seen much of it yet, Captain."

"Menikoff. Captain Menikoff."

"Fine, my name's Alison, Peter Alison."

"Al—i—son. I have it. Alison, you will have a drink."

"Thanks, but——"

"I insist!" Captain Menikoff pushed through to the bar and slammed his own glass down on it. "Guess we don't see many limeys around here!" Grinning broadly he interpreted his own remark and again there was a bellow of appreciative laughter. The Russians, Shaw decided, were easily amused. "Why have you come to Moltsk, Alison?"

"To see one of our people." Shaw took the drink which Menikoff passed to him, twirled the stem of the glass in his fingers. "I'm on the staff of W.I.O.C.A."

"So?" Menikoff put his glass down. "I am interested in that, Alison. I have seen your fine libraries, your exhibitions of books and of beautiful paintings. I envy you, Alison."

Curious, Shaw reflected, the respect the Russians had for culture when it was directed at the workers. They rated their artists and writers far higher than did England hers, and yet at the same time they were a military-minded nation—not that that was necessarily incompatible . . . after all, one of England's finest field-marshals was said to have carried a book of poetry with him into battle. He asked lightly,

"Why do you envy me, Captain Menikoff? Does the military life not satisfy you?"

"Oh, but certainly it does," Menikoff answered quickly. "Possibly I use the word envy in a wrong sense." He hesitated, seeming at a loss to explain, then went on with a boyish naivety, "But I congratulate you because you are in Russia—and envy you because you are an intellectual—and I congratulate you again because you are at this moment in Russia and not in . . . England. . . ."

He trailed off; there was a sudden silence, and he went very white. He didn't say any more and Shaw wondered what he had meant; could be his English at fault—Menikoff wasn't really as fluent as he liked to think—or on the other hand he could well have been on the verge of a vodka-inspired indiscretion. Shaw lifted an eyebrow, quizzically. "Why so?" he asked.

Menikoff shrugged uncomfortably and said, as though repeating a lesson, his boyishness gone now, "Our country leads the world, Alison, that is why. Intellectually, militarily, in all spheres. Soon we will lead other worlds as well, following in the footsteps of Gagarin and Titov and the others. You understand? Nobody can hope to surpass the Soviets, even to rival their great achievements. . . ."

Shaw listened in growing boredom to the spate of propaganda. The buzz of conversation had started up again now; Shaw tried to lead Menikoff back to what he had said earlier but the man had taken a grip on himself and was thoroughly wound up. Nothing would stop him. One or two of the others joined in and Shaw talked generally, exercising his Russian, but he soon realized that he wasn't getting anywhere and had already had too much vodka for his liking; and he escaped to the dining-room.

As he ate, he went on thinking about Menikoff and the more he thought the more he felt that those remarks had been leading somewhere. That sudden silence, and then an end of Menikoff's exuberance. He frowned, lit a cigarette as he waited for the next course—waited interminably for the next course. *If* the secrets were penetrating down to captains' level, then it pointed to two things: One, Russia was nearly ready, was right on the brink of starting something; and two, it shouldn't take him long to ferret out what that something was.

It had better not.

After lunch he got the reception-clerk to call a car and he

77

was driven out of Moltsk openly to Professor Godov's home. This was inland, some thirty kilometres north-west of Moltsk, and two kilometres from its nearest population centre—the tiny cluster of dwellings which made up the isolated village of Emets.

It was in bleak, grim country across which the winds blew right off the Arctic Ocean from the Pole; an almost terrifying land of flat plain and dreary swamp and little vegetation beyond low shrubs and moss, for they were north of the forests that covered the southern tip of the Peninsula. This was barren tundra which in winter would remain under snow and ice for months at a time. An utterly oppressive place in which to live, a place inhabited only by nomadic huntsmen and fishermen, apart from the few small communities like Emets itself. Godov, Shaw thought, must be a genuine hermit, a cranky recluse, to live in such a place . . . but then, no doubt, an old man of his years wouldn't want much more out of life than to be left alone in peace and tranquillity—and after all this region had been his childhood home, and Chaffinch had told him that Godov was a true son of the people even now. Moreover, he was probably still regarded as being to some extent in exile even though he was now considered harmless. It was a fitting place to be in exile, all right. And it must have been some childhood!

But the house, when he reached it at last at the end of a long, stone-built track off the road beyond Emets, was biggish, with great thick walls to keep out the bitter wind. At one time it could have been a farmhouse—if ever they had such things up here on the fringe of the Arctic Circle. It had the same barren, bleak look that its surroundings had, indeed it seemed nearly to merge into the landscape in some curious way; but, once he had tugged at a rusty bell-pull and an old woman, seamed and wrinkled and dressed in black from head to foot, had unhooked a chain and opened the door to him, a sense of comfort and well-being struck him immediately; and warmth, on both the mental and the physical planes, came out to meet him.

The old woman's beady eyes stared at him unblinkingly and she asked, "Who are you, and what do you want?"

"My name is Alison, and I come from friends of Professor Godov in Moscow. I have a letter." He passed it over to her. "If you will please give the Professor this?"

She took it suspiciously, reaching out with workstained fingers. "The Professor has had no warning."

"I am sorry for that."

78

"Your business . . . is it important?"

He nodded. "Yes. If you would——"

"The Professor sees few people these days. Nevertheless, I will see. You will wait, please."

She went away, leaving Shaw to kick his heels in the stone porch. He glanced back at the hired car, where the driver, whom he had told to wait, was hunched gloomily over the wheel, staring out at the monotonous landscape. The old woman was back within a minute and smiling now, her lined face puckering. She said, "The Professor will see you. I must ask you not to tire him. He is very frail."

Shaw promised, "I'll remember. Don't worry."

She turned away and led him down a long passage and into a room at the end. It was a cosy room, not large, with a good carpet on the floor, and its walls were filled with bookcases overflowing with learned volumes. On either side of the fireplace were tall inset cupboards, like gun cupboards. There was a cheerful fire flickering in the grate and, although the comparatively short Arctic daylight of early autumn was not yet over—this region was not far off the Land of the Midnight Sun and its converse the midday night—a red-shaded oil-lamp was burning on a table. Beside the fire, in a big armchair, sat a tiny old man with very bright black eyes and a high, domed forehead thinly topped with scanty white hair.

The eyes, shrewd and penetrating, twinkled at Shaw but Godov didn't say anything at first.

Shaw heard the door shut behind him, gently. The old woman had gone. He went towards the fire and said, "Professor Godov?"

The old man inclined his head slowly, in an old-world gesture of courtliness. In a thin, high voice he said, "Yes, I am Godov, Mr Alison." His English was precise but hesitant, as though his knowledge of the language had been good but was now rusty. "It is kind of you to come all the way from Moscow to see an old man."

"Not at all, Professor." Shaw spoke cheerfully but respectfully, as befitted a staff member talking to the Grand Old Man. "Yours is an esteemed name in the organization——"

"Ah—in the organization!" Godov coughed a little, and Shaw heard the phlegm whistling and heaving in his thin chest. "Not, I fear, in the files of the Party, however."

Shaw smiled. "So it has been said, Professor. But that is not my business . . . and I couldn't come to Moltsk without calling on you."

"Then you did not come expressly to see me?" The black eyes glittered at him, almost mockingly.

"No, sir," he said. "Not exactly."

The old man nodded again and smiled thinly. He said, "Please sit down. And let me express my regret that my housekeeper, Anna, left you in the cold."

"It doesn't matter in the least." Shaw sat on the opposite side of the fire, in another big old armchair with cosy wings. A feeling of well-being came over him, a sense of finding himself unexpectedly in friendly and comforting hands. It was a feeling that he didn't remember ever having had before while actually on an assignment. Nevertheless he wondered, having got here, exactly what he was going to say. His principal object in coming had been, of course, to establish himself, in case anyone in Moltsk should investigate him, as a genuine W.I.O.C.A. man; to give himself, as it were, an alibi. He could scarcely say this—and yet he had a curious inward feeling all the time that the old man knew; he could see that the brain was alert enough still. Meanwhile Godov, with a kind of innate kindliness and politeness, put Shaw at his ease and started the conversation by speaking of people he had known in W.I.O.C.A. and of the work that he himself had been, as he put it, privileged to do for the organization in his time; which fortunately was so long ago now that Shaw had no need to pretend to any intimate knowledge of any of it. He was able then to talk of Chaffinch and of the current affairs of the Moscow office as told him by Chaffinch himself, and the old man seemed to accept him without question—although there was still that odd feeling that in point of fact Godov had, in some mysterious way, seen through him. Whatever the frailty of the body there was no senility in the mental state; and no one would get far if he tried to fool this old gentleman.

Then, suddenly, the Professor changed his tack.

He said, "I have visited the West. England, France, America. That was many years ago now. France I loved, perhaps more than the other countries, but yours is a great country of genuine liberal ideas and I much enjoyed—much enjoyed—the time I spent in London." He seemed to be looking back into the past, sadly. "I addressed the British Council as well as W.I.O.C.A. Also the Royal Society of Arts. They were all very kind, so very kind. Yes, I loved it all." He paused for several moments and then said, "It is sad that wars come to change it all. Do you not agree?"

"I do."

"But you, your country I mean, she is as much to blame as us. Do you agree with that?"

Shaw said cautiously, feeling his way, "In some respects, possibly. Suspicion breeds suspicion, and preparations breed counter-preparations. It seems to me that no one has ever tried reducing the world's temperature . . . instead we have threat and counter-threat, retaliation, vengeance, national prejudice and pride and propaganda, and no one knows where he stands."

"Aha, you are right, my young friend, very right! You have a thinking mind, and it is surprising how few people have that. The recipe for the thinking mind is never to believe anything that is written in the newspapers, of course, not to be a mere echo of other men's opinions. As to what you have said . . . when one does not know where one stands, one becomes apprehensive and aggressive and by stages, logical stages, the mind drifts imperceptibly towards war. When the national mind accepts the mere idea of war, then war becomes inevitable sooner or later. I tell you this: Your country should have heeded your great Montgomery. Excepting only Churchill, there has been for many years past no person in all your country of his stature—and our people trusted him as they trust no one else from Britain. Remember, Mr Alison, that he spoke of disengagement, of ending this terrible suspicion with the borders manned by armed men facing one another with steel and hatred across the frontiers. He wished to end provocation, but no one would listen, preferring instead the sabre-rattlers and the old, outdated panoply of pomp and power which should have been swept away when the war ended."

The old man sighed deeply and Shaw felt that this was where he had come in; Rudintsev had spoken along these lines. Godov went on, "Ah well . . . we, like you, are largely bluff—or we have been so far. But in these times bluff is clearly most dangerous. One does not bluff with a match in a powder-magazine."

"No." Shaw's eyes narrowed. "Professor, you said your country has been bluffing *so far*. Did you mean anything special by that?"

"Did I say that?" Godov chuckled. He put up a thin white hand, laced with the swollen bluish veins of great age, and rubbed slowly at his eyes. He said, "I would call that a leading question, Mr Alison, and hardly, perhaps, one that should be addressed to a Soviet citizen, even an exiled Soviet citizen, by an Englishman. You are most indiscreet."

"I'm sorry."

Godov chuckled again. "Nevertheless you have asked it, and in my own way I shall answer it. I am an old man, and I am not afraid to speak my mind." He was silent again for some time and then he said, "You have not, I gather, been long in Moltsk—but you may have formed some impressions already. What are they?"

Shaw hesitated only for a second and then he said, "Bad, I'm afraid, Professor."

"In what way?"

"It's hard to be exact. The place is . . . well, one might say buzzing with something. The people I've spoken to have all been perfectly friendly, but——"

"To whom have you spoken?"

Shaw gave a shrug. "Not many people, I admit. The hotel staff, and a bunch of Army officers, that's all so far. But their attitude struck me as strange in a way, because I'd always thought Red Army officers in particular would be rather more circumspect in their relationships with Westerners."

"So they have been, until the last few days, at any rate in Moltsk. Certainly there are few Westerners in the port, but those that are there have been avoided so far as possible in case the M.V.D. should become interested. This, I understand, has indeed changed in the way you say. Now, you may ask how I, an old man, know this. I shall tell you. I have a . . . very dear friend, a young woman, who comes often from Moltsk to see me. Almost every day, when her work permits. Also Anna, my housekeeper, and Josef, an old servant who now acts as the man about the house and also drives my car—they go often into Moltsk on my errands. Sometimes I still go myself for the drive and to sit in the big hotel and watch the world go by, you understand? All my life I have been observant, also I have trained myself to interpret, rather than merely read, what is in the newspapers. The mention of a thing here, the omission of another there—and so on. You will understand, I am sure." The black eyes, diamond-bright, glittered at Shaw. "Thus I form my own conclusions, rather than accept at face value . . . what I am supposed to accept. Now, Mr Alison, this is what I want to say to you: The air is friendlier for one reason only, and that is—it no longer matters now."

Shaw stiffened, felt a shake in his hands. "I see. Why do you think it no longer matters, Professor?"

Godov smiled. "We are on dangerous ground, Mr Alison.

Even what I have already said would be considered enough to send me to Siberia."

"Yet you said it, Professor." Shaw's voice was urgent, hard. "Can't you say a little more?"

"You wish me to say things against my country?"

"Professor, let me ask you a question in reply to that." Shaw leaned forward. "Are you content with your country's leaders, and do you like the way things are going?"

Godov didn't answer right away, though his bright eyes never left Shaw's face; then he said slowly, "I am known not to be a convinced communist, and I realize that my reputation must already be fully known to you. So I can be honest. I do not like my country's leaders, neither do I like the way things appear to be going. But I do not believe that it is the wish of our leaders that they should go that way. Our Government wants nothing to do with war, of that I am convinced. But there are pressures—you understand?"

"I think I do. Professor, tell me—what do you think is going to happen?"

Godov laughed gently. "My dear Mr Alison, I have no idea!"

"No? I think you have, Professor."

"You do?" The black eyes surveyed him sardonically. "And if I have? How do I know I can trust you?"

"You don't," Shaw said frankly. "But is it really likely I'm going to go to the M.V.D. and tell them what you've said? Do you think I'm an M.V.D. spy?"

"Scarcely that!" The eyes were twinkling now, and merry. "You have a good point! No, I am quite sure you would not do that, Mr Alison, though I formed the impression—call it an old man's perception if you like—that you have not come to Moltsk simply on the business of our organization. Is that not so?" He paused, still looking hard at Shaw. "Come now. We are men of the world, you and I. And I am a liberal —not a communist. I believe we can, after all, trust one another?"

Shaw sweated and his face hardened. Almost unconsciously his hand slid inside his double-breasted jacket, then he withdrew it again shamefacedly. Godov, however, had seen the gesture and interpreted it. He said calmly, "Yes, Mr Alison, you could shoot me and Anna and Josef very easily and no one in the Party would mourn us, and your secret would then be quite safe. But I feel certain you will do no such thing. Men like you do not shoot down the old—and in any case it is quite unnecessary. I believe you know that, in your heart, or you would not have come to me. I, like you, am not likely to go to the authorities with any tales. The mere fact that an agent of the West—yes, you may look horrified, but I say that—an agent of the West had contacted me would be the very signature on my death warrant. You see, I dare not take the least overt risk with the Party. I have powerful enemies in Moscow, who would swing their authority against me the moment they saw their chance."

Shaw said hoarsely, "But if you reported me, that would wipe out the past, not increase the risk, wouldn't it?"

Godov shook his head. "You do not know my country. They would be grateful for what I had done, yes—but they would put me out of the way afterwards, just in case. I know that very well, and I have no wish to die unless by dying I can be of some positive help. But leaving that aside, Mr Alison, I wish you no harm. On the contrary, I am perfectly willing to help you in such ways as I can, if you will give me your assurance of one thing."

"And that is?"

"That you intend to bring no harm to my country or her innocent people, but only to prevent what I believe to be a very terrible thing, a tragedy."

Shaw said, "I'll give you that promise willingly, with one proviso: That, in doing what I have come to do, it may be necessary to cause some loss of life."

"That I understand, and I must accept it. It is unavoidable."

Shaw nodded and then asked, "And now—the tragedy you spoke of. What is it, Professor?"

"In concrete terms, I do not know. I only suspect certain things, you understand." The old professor tapped his fingers on the arm of his chair. "But I believe that the great tower, apparently so innocent, where the oil-borings are, contains the seeds of that tragedy——"

"What tower is this?"

Godov said, "It is built in the sea, where the first borehole was sunk. It has been there for some years. This tower stands up from the water, an enormously wide shaft, to the north of Moltsk, almost due east of here. It is surrounded by other towers, much smaller, which are linked with a kind of steel mesh, a boom you would say perhaps, to keep shipping away. Now, yesterday the friend of whom I spoke came to see me . . . she has a cousin, an officer of the Red Army, a major recently posted to the area, who works on that tower. She tells me that it is being used as a store for nuclear devices, a deep store in case we are attacked, so that we can continue our retaliation even after heavy saturation by the inter-continental ballistic missiles. I have heard that there are indeed deep nuclear stores all over Russia, genuine ones —but in this particular case I do not believe the story."

"Why not?"

Godov shrugged. "Because if it were true, they would never have allowed the story to leak out so openly. My friend's cousin would not speak of it for one, he would have more regard for his life. No—they use that story merely as a smoke-screen, Mr Alison. Therefore I say, look for what you seek in that great tower. And I trust you will use every endeavor of which you are capable to stop the plans of these people." The old man's voice shook now. "Mr Alison, I am loyal to Russia and I love her. That is why I wish you well. These men who would put pressure on her leaders do Russia no good service and in the long run nothing but evil can come of their designs. Unfortunately I am old, and can give you no practical help, but"—he shrugged again—"my hopes and prayers will be with you."

"Thank you, Professor. I appreciate that." Shaw added hesitantly, "By the way . . . I suppose you wouldn't give me the address of your friend? I—er—think it'd be helpful to have a word with her."

"Yes, I will do so," Godov said at once. "Indeed, I was going to suggest that myself. She will wish to help if I send you to her, that I know. She has been cruelly used by the communists, and she shares my views. She can be completely trusted. Go and see her, Mr Alison. Her name is Triska Somalin, and she is a doctor . . . she lives at 1736 Arkhangel'sk Street, which is not far from your hotel. You will tell her that I have sent you." He paused. "Better—I shall give you a letter. But remember, Mr Alison, that her cousin, Major Igor Bronsky, is a zealous communist and a dangerous man, which is why I am certain he would not have talked even to Triska except to help in laying that smoke-screen. Nevertheless, if you are clever and patient—if there is time for that now—then you may find ways of eliciting some of the truth from him, perhaps through Triska." He lifted himself slowly from his chair. Shaw got up and went over to help him and the old man added, as they went slowly towards a desk, "Be of good heart, Mr Alison. Your cover is good and it will hold—to all except me! You need not fear."

Driving back into Moltsk with the Professor's reiterated assurances of any help he could give him, and the letter for Triska Somalin in his pocket, Shaw reflected that what Godov had told him was mere conjecture; but it sounded good sense all the same. A little way after Emets, he stopped thinking about Godov when he noticed a road leading off in a north-easterly direction just opposite what looked like an old wartime pill-box. He leaned forward to speak to his driver. He asked, "Is there another way into Moltsk?"

"There is."

"Can we go that way? I'd like to see all I can while I'm here."

The man said shortly, "It cannot be used. The road runs through the closed military area." His voice was surly and unhelpful and it finished the brief conversation. Shaw wasn't going to risk being shopped to the M.V.D. as the Englishman who had shown too much curiosity about the military area. And that military area, he suspected, included the tower and the oil-drillings.

ELEVEN

"Dr. Triska Somalin?"

"Yes, that is my name."

The girl was attractive and had a nice figure—that was Shaw's first impression.

Tall and dark, with black hair curling over her ears, and direct brown eyes, she was far from being one of the crowd of drab, depressed women that Shaw had seen in the streets, though her clothes, certainly, were as dowdy and utilitarian as the rest. There was a look of strength and self-reliance in her face and her bearing, though just at this moment she was looking at him with a guarded reserve which he found perfectly natural. A peal at a doorbell in Moltsk no doubt had many possible interpretations—and even more so had the sudden appearance of a stranger on the threshold; yet there was no perceptible trace of fear, indeed she gave the impression that all fear had been purged out of her, that she had already been through the worst that Man could offer.

This was a young woman who wouldn't be rattled, who could be trusted in an emergency.

Shaw had just come up to the tenth floor in the skyscraper-like block of utilitarian flats and pressed the bell, and she had come to the door and looked him up and down, waiting for him to speak first.

He said, still speaking in Russian, "It's quite all right, Dr Somalin. Professor Godov asked me to call and give you his good wishes."

"Professor Godov?" She looked at him sharply then; her tone was sharp too, though the voice was as attracitve as the girl herself. "He sent you to me?"

He smiled, seeing her instinctive disbelief, her feeling that this was a trap of some kind. He said reassuringly, "I came down from Moscow to see him. I'm in W.I.O.C.A., by the way. He gave me this."

He passed Godov's envelope over and she opened it. Pulling the letter out she read it quickly and then, catching her breath in sudden relief, she said, "Yes, it is all right, Mr Alison. Please come in."

"Just a moment." He put a hand on her arm as she turned away into a tiny square hall. "You're alone?"

"I am alone, Mr Alison."

He nodded, and followed her in. They went across the hall into the sitting-room. This was a small, bare apartment with few signs of the kind of comfort that Godov enjoyed out in the wilds. The floor was covered with a dullish composition like cheap linoleum, the one window looked out over the concrete jungle behind the block of flats; there was a single bulb cheaply shaded and hanging from the centre of the ceiling, and an electric fire set in one wall gave out only a feeble heat. Triska Somalin asked him to sit on a plush-covered chair and, drawing up another to face him, offered him cigarettes. She watched him as he lit one, still not at ease with him, still with an air of reserve and bewilderment, waiting for him to make things clear to her. Her face was a little flushed now and she sat with her arms folded in her lap, leaning towards him so that he caught her faint, elusive scent.

He said quietly, "I had a long talk with Professor Godov this afternoon."

"There is nothing wrong?" There was sudden fear in her face.

"Wrong? Not with Godov. He's perfectly well." Shaw blew a long trail of smoke. "But he's worried."

She seemed to disregard that. "He says little in the letter except that he would like me to help you, Mr Alison. You yourself have told me you are a member of W.I.O.C.A., and this he confirms." She hesitated, pushing a strand of hair back from her forehead. "Do you wish help in that connexion—you have some questions, perhaps, about our medical research centre?"

"That's where you work, Dr Somalin?"

"Yes."

"I see. It's not that, though."

"No? Tell me, Mr Alison—what did Professor Godov say about me?"

He smiled at her. "Just as little as he seems to have said about me. Except that you were a good friend of his."

"A good friend . . . yes, that is true." There was a curious look in her eyes and she, too, smiled faintly, inwardly. "We have talked much together. I am very, very fond of him, and I respect him greatly."

"And you share his views?"

She answered cautiously, "I did not say that."

"I know you didn't, but——"

"But *he* did?"

He nodded, looking at her hard. "Yes, Dr Somalin, he did."

"I see." She hesitated, biting at her lower lip uncertainly. She looked away from Shaw into the glowing bars of the electric fire. Then she said in a low voice, "I accept you as a friend, Mr Alison. If Godov sent you, then I can talk to you. Yes, I will admit that I share his views. But I am just a woman, Mr Alison. I do not know what I can do to help you—or indeed what kind of help you want."

"Perhaps you could give me some information," he said.

She looked him straight in the eyes then. "Please tell me the truth," she said. "Tell me why Godov sent you here."

Shaw inhaled smoke deeply into his lungs. Godov had said this girl was absolutely all right and Godov himself had already guessed why he was in Russia anyway. Nothing could be lost now that was not already in jeopardy if things went wrong with Godov, and if the girl was to help him, then she must know the full score and no holding back. So he said, "Godov told me of some great tragedy that he believes to be building up, here in Moltsk, something that affects my country, Dr Somalin. Can you tell me anything about this?"

She had gone very white and he noticed the shake in the fingers that held her cigarette. She said, "This is dangerous. I think you must tell me a little more. Is that not fair, Mr Alison?"

"Quite fair." He took a deep breath. He had to take a big chance now and had to force the issue with this girl; time was desperately short and there was no knowing when he might be connected with the shooting back at Khamchevko railway-station. He said, "I am a British agent, and I'm here to stop this thing taking place. Godov already knows this and I'm in his hands—and yours now, Dr Somalin."

She had taken it perfectly calmly, reacting well to what must have been the cruel shock of hearing that she was now sitting in a room with a British undercover agent, that she was now in the most terrible danger; that she would die if anything went wrong thereafter. But her trust in Godov was absolute, as his was in her, and she wasn't going to weaken, to back out of anything or let the old man down. She simply said, very quietly, that since Shaw had told her honestly and openly what his job was, she in her turn wanted to tell him as much as was relevant about herself. Then, her lips trembling just a little, she went over to the window and looked out for nearly a minute; and then she turned away and went back to her chair, and spoke with her head bent, not looking at Shaw.

It was quite a short story and perhaps, except in one particular, unremarkable in present times. Triska Somalin had been married to a Czechoslovakian lawyer and she had been deeply in love with her husband. Violently opposed to the communist regime in Czechoslovakia, he had been one of a small group of dedicated men and women working, like Gorsak in Hungary, against the State. He had been bowled out in the end and he had been third-degreed in Prague in an attempt to make him reveal the names of his group. He was not a strong man physically but in spite of all they could do in an attempt to break him, he had refused to say a word and one day he had simply died while under intensive questioning—died, Triska had assumed, as the result of being beaten-up and from the lack of sleep and food. This, Triska told Shaw, was little more than routine, the kind of thing one had come to expect in Czechoslovakia, and she was not the only woman who had lost her husband in such a way. But the manner in which the news had been given to her was not routine and was a refinement of cruelty that Shaw found almost unbelievable. Triska had been told nothing of her husband's death until one night a thundering knock had come on the door of the flat in Prague in the small hours. When she pulled on her dressing-gown and opened the door, stiff with terror, four men dressed in black had pushed their way in and she had seen that they were carrying a coffin. They placed the coffin on the floor of the hall and then left without speaking a word to her. All the rest of that night Triska had sat by the coffin, alone, knowing perfectly well what it must contain, and during that vigil a coldness had crept into her heart and also a great hatred for her own country, the country that had brought its ideologies and methods to Czechoslovakia. Though, because she was a sensible young woman with her life before her, she had done her best to forget subsequently, that hatred had remained with her and had even grown, grown and crystallized and hardened into a set intensity of purpose to fight the communist regime if ever she got the chance.

Godov, she said, knew this.

She was a Russian citizen by birth and, to her own surprise, no obstacle had been placed in the way of her return to her own country after two whole days of grilling by the security police in Prague, though she was told that any application to visit the West would be automatically refused thereafter. No explanations were given when she was released but Triska had a muddled idea that they might have been attempting to show the Czechs that they had the magnanimity to soft-pedal the widow of a self-confessed traitor—as they made her husband out to be. So she had come back to Russia where she had reverted to her maiden name and she had retained this iron resolve to revenge her dead husband in whatever way was open to her. Godov, she said, had done his best to talk her out of her hate, but he had seen in the end that she was never going to weaken.

And now it appeared that he had put an instrument into her hands, insofar as he had sent Shaw to her.

Shaw interrupted there. He said, "This thing that's going to happen isn't an act of your Government, Dr Somalin. Someone's going to take over in the Kremlin, or so we understand, and they'll be the ones who'll carry it through."

She shrugged indifferently. "It is all the same to me, they are all communists."

"You'll help me, then?"

"Yes, I shall help you if I can," she said. "It is not only because of my husband, Mr Alison. Before I was married I visited Britain with an official party of students. I so much liked what I saw, Mr Alison. The freedom, the leisure, the fact that your students did not have to spend their free time, as so largely our students have to, attending indoctrination classes and lectures on some current ideology." She made a gesture of anger. "Me, I love my work, I love to feel that I am helping to heal and not destroy—but I resent having to spend much time even now in listening to the set pieces glorifying Soviet medicine for purposes of propaganda." She leaned forward, spoke intensely. "Such propaganda, and such vile lies, when it is the Soviet that threatens the world with nuclear destruction and wholesale slaughter, rather than give it healing. Mr Alison, I hate nuclear armaments! I have seen so many of the results."

"*You* have?"

"Yes!" Her lips were white. "From the tests in the Barents Sea, and on Novaya Zemlya. The fallout . . . men become sick when things go wrong."

"Do things go wrong?"

She laughed harshly. "Of course—very often! The papers do not say so, and I am sure you in the West do not get to hear of it, but I know, I and my colleagues. They bring the victims to our centre sometimes."

"For cure?"

"Certainly, if possible. But chiefly for—experiment. We are working on the total cure for all diseases caused by radio-active fallout—leukaemia, various other forms of cancer . . . you understand? It is right, of course, that we should find these things out so long as the world has these horrible, de-grading weapons—but to use these men as guinea-pigs, as rats . . . it is terrible, horrible. To have to experiment to cure a man-made disease, do you not see?" There were tears in her eyes now, and her hands shook uncontrollably. "It is not unknown for men to be forcibly subjected to radiation, when there is no series of test-firings in progress. All this is why I hate the thing that has brought you here, the terrible thing which I, too, believe is going to happen——"

"Why do you believe that?"

She said, "Because Moltsk has been full of rumours for the last twenty-four hours. There is nothing definite, but our people seem to sense that shortly Russia is to be world-powerful. This must suggest something terrible, to bring such a thing about."

"How shortly?"

She hesitated. "I have the impression that it will be very soon. Moltsk is becoming an uneasy place. There is a change in the atmosphere. It is a feeling of terrible anticipation, of joy, which I myself find shocking and unholy."

"Are the people behind all this, then—are they reacting as if they approve?"

She said sadly, "Yes. In many cases, yes. As for the others—they have to approve. There is no alternative other than Siberia. They will not criticize, not even to one another in their homes. But even so I believe there are in Russia many, many people who share Godov's views and mine."

Shaw asked suddenly, "Your cousin? He doesn't share them?"

"Ah—so Godov mentioned him, did he?" She laughed, and it was a scornful sound. "Igor, my cousin, is an extrovert, and a militarist, and an excellent communist, all the things that I am not, or Godov. We have many arguments when I cannot contain myself—he uses my flat when he is off duty—but even he does not know entirely how I think."

"Does he know about Godov—that you are friendly with him, I mean?"

She gave him an odd look. "Oh yes! He does not approve, Mr Alison, but I do not let my cousin run my life for me! As it is, he laughs and says the old man is harmless, that Moscow has his measure and he is too senile to be a danger now—so, you see, we do not disagree about him too violently." She added, "But of course I shall say nothing to Igor about your visit."

He grinned at that. "Just as well not to! By the way—how long are we safe here now?"

"From Igor? A long time!" She grimaced. "He is out with a woman, and he will not be back to-night. He will appear for lunch tomorrow, late and full of vodka. Then he will go on duty for twenty-four hours from four o'clock in the afternoon. This is how he has divided his time for the week he has been here in Moltsk—women, drink, duty. Nothing else. He is an animal."

Shaw nodded reflectively. "He's working on that tower, isn't he, on the oil-drillings—or I gather it's in use as a store now. Can you tell me anything more about it?"

She said, "A little, perhaps. Igor is in charge of a large body of engineers and men of the artillery who are working there. I do not know exactly what he does, but you are right that it is being used now as a store, that tower. I believe that it has been used so for some time, but the news has come out since the last day or two only. I can tell you little else . . . except that when the borehole was first sunk there were genuine oilmen working on it to send down the first cutting-head, but when that had been done and no oil appeared, other men, scientists and engineers, came to widen the original small shaft, and to build the tower over it. And now the soldiers are there, you see. All of them have had training in the handling of nuclear devices, which possibly is no more than natural when they are putting such devices in the store . . . but I confess I am sceptical about that store, and I have told Godov so."

"So am I, Dr Somalin. I've asked myself why a tower should be considered as a safe store. Unless it goes very deep and can be well sealed off, but even then. . . ." He paused, running his hand along his chin thoughtfully. "No, there's a damn sight more in that tower than meets the eye."

Shaw left the flat soon after, determined to get into the military area as soon as he could. He had just said good-bye to Triska Somalin and she had shut the door, and he was making for the lift, when he saw a big man in uniform bounding up the stairs. Some sixth sense made him sink back into a cross-passage where he could watch and not be seen, and a few moments later he heard the man thumping on Triska's door. Then he heard her say sarcastically,

"Well, well. What's gone wrong with your plans, Igor?"

Shaw didn't catch the answer but the man sounded savagely angry. Evidently cousin Igor's woman had failed to come up to scratch. Shaw congratulated himself on having got clear of the flat just in time. Major Igor Bronsky certainly looked a dangerous character, with a white, sadistic face and a strutting manner.

Shaw came quietly out of hiding, found that the lift was out of order, and went down the stairs fast.

TWELVE

Shaw went back to his hotel first and equipped himself with his torch and a pair of binoculars which he concealed under a loose raincoat. After that he went out and walked down Arkhangel'sk Street again, casually smoking a cigarette, on the look-out for a parked bicycle. Triska had told him she had a small car of her own but he felt that a car anywhere near the military area would invite unwelcome attentions to say the least of it. On the other hand a bicycle could easily be hidden or disposed of when necessary, and since Moltsk seemed to be full of bicycles he would be reasonably inconspicuous.

He found one leaning against a building farther on in a quiet, dark street and he wheeled it out into the roadway and mounted it. As he pedalled away he reflected that if he was unlucky he might be pinched for stealing but it was doubtful if such a minor affair would merit any police action before he was back and had ditched it again.

He went rapidly along the road to the north that he had taken that same afternoon to Godov's house, until, just short of Emets, he reached the road leading north-eastward to the sea. Turning off along here he went on cautiously, keeping well on the look-out for anything on the road ahead. Farther along, climbing some rising ground to the crest of a seaward-stretching slope, he saw the floodlights ahead, the heavily guarded, double-banked wire fence, and the pole-barrier thrown across the road with two armed men walking up and down behind it. In rear were groups of low huts, probably billets and offices for the troops. Along the shoreline he could see what he took to be banks of rocket-launchers and there were also two turrets of heavy conventional guns. Beyond—a long way beyond and well out to sea—was a vast blaze of light, a blaze like artificial daylight which lit up the flat top of a thick projection rising sheer out of the sea like a sawn-off lighthouse.

The tower.

Chucking the bicycle down on the verge Shaw lifted his binoculars and studied that tower. From it a pier ran shore-ward, reaching the beach to the south of the pole-barrier, a wide pier that seemed to carry a roadway and sidewalk. He could also make out the ring of smaller constructions which carried the protective boom around the main erection.

There was a prickling sensation in his scalp as he watched, and a gnawing uncertainty. He had found the tower, but what was he going to do about it? Use his transceiver to warn Latymer, give him an exact position so that the bombers could be sent in, or the missiles, to blow it sky-high? That would hardly do; bombers and missiles would be an act of war, which would play right into the hands of these people. Short as the time was now, he must not send anything approaching an action-signal until he had found out exactly what that tower contained, exactly what it was there for, and then, perhaps, and only then, if indeed it contained the threat which was so extreme that nothing could be made any worse by an act of war, they could send the missiles in. Meanwhile there was so much conjecture about all this, so much that was really sheer, unsubstantiated hearsay. That

94

tower could be perfectly innocent for all Godov and Triska had said; the soldiers working on it might indeed have had nuclear training—but so what? Might they not simply be blasting to get deeper, in order to extend the place as a store?

He foreshortened the range of his binoculars and stared ahead at the shore beyond the barrier. After a while he saw three more objects in line with the tower, three round pill-box-like constructions, one in the sea and two on shore. They were similar to the one, well outside the military area, that he had noticed briefly that afternoon on the way back from Godov's house. He frowned, rubbed a hand along his jaw. What could they be for? Possibly some sort of defensive position—and yet pill-box strategy was dead nowadays, dead and buried.

But those three inside the military area must serve some useful purpose, or they would have been dismantled long ago. . . .

He lowered his glasses. He wasn't doing any good here, and certainly he couldn't pass that barrier. Somehow or other he had to get out to the tower itself, making his way by sea, and have a look around inside it. He laughed to himself, cynically, bitterly. Offhand he couldn't possibly have thought up a more impossible task to set himself, but it would have to be done—unless, perhaps, he could get Major Igor Bronsky into a nice, quiet spot and threaten to blow his guts out if he didn't tell him just what was going on? But then even Bronsky, assuming he could be believed under threat, might not know the whole story. If he wanted that, he would have to get himself a general. There was no time to mess about with the small fry now.

Frowning in black anxiety, he was about to get onto the bicycle again when he heard the racket, distantly, on the road behind him. He swung round in alarm, saw the lights turning shoreward off the main road from Moltsk . . . the distant headlamps of many big lorries swinging round across the barren, swampy land. Quickly he pushed the bicycle over the verge so that it was hidden by the mossy overhang of the raised metal road-surface and then he crouched down flat beside it. Soon after, the roar on the roadway increased as the heavy convoy approached up the rising ground. As they took a slight bend he saw them clearly: ten-ton lorries, one after the other, never-ending.

They were close on him now and he ducked right down. Dust swirled over him, stones and grit flew over his body, as wheel after wheel crunched by close to his head. Some of the lorries were crammed with troops, some with civilians, while others were full of wooden crates of varying sizes. The shouting sound of roaring song came down to him from the troop lorries, men bawling out the words of the Soviet's national anthem at the top of their voices: *Soyuz nerushimy respublik svobodnykh. . . .*

They sounded extremely het-up about something; there was some curious quality in their voices, some quality which England had very likely had in the days of the Crimea and the Boer War, which Germany had certainly had in 1939. It was a kind of baying hysteria, terrifying in its implications.

Shaw counted between thirty and forty vehicles and after they had all roared past beyond the barrier he allowed ten minutes in case there was another convoy behind; and when the night remained still he scrambled back onto the road. Beyond the wire the troops had spilled out of the lorries. Some were unloading the crates, others were getting aboard smaller trucks, light vehicles, which as they filled were heading up one by one under the control of a beachmaster for the roadway along the pier to the tower.

How could all this possibly be going on without the knowledge of the central Government in Moscow? Or didn't even these troops know the full score, was there—there must be —some genuine but actually unwarlike purpose for which the tower was officially being used?

The nuclear-device storehouse?

Must be. Quite genuinely—and the extremists could in effect be making use of what was already there. Back in Vienna, Prakesh had said something along those lines, now he came to think of it. *But how were they making use of it?*

Getting onto the bicycle he pedalled back to the Moltsk road. When he reached the turning he stopped by the pill-box, shoved the bicycle onto the verge again and went across towards the stubby concrete structure gingerly, for the ground to the west of the main road was largely swamp. He was able to keep to a fairly firm track, however, and he reached the pill-box with no more mishap than muddied boots. It was a wide, squat affair, very thick, and was almost identical with the last-war British pattern except that its firing-slots (as he took them to be) were rather higher, just about on a level with the top of his head and below a kind of detached mushroom-top, also of concrete, held firmly in stanchion-like steel uprights. Nothing about it to attract attention or interest, except possibly as a war relic and not a very dramatic one at that.

But it was going to be worth a closer look.

Shaw heaved himself up, getting a grip on the edge of one of the slots and using his feet to give himself leverage on the rough concrete wall. His hand slid on thick grease as he grasped one of the stanchions. There was plenty of clearance between the top of the wall and the mushroom-roof, and, reaching out with his torch, he could estimate the great width of the wall itself. It must have been a good eight feet thick all round—and it was practically solid, with only a central hole of perhaps four feet across.

So—it was no ordinary pill-box after all!

Shaw pulled himself onto the top of the wall and, still using his torch, edged towards the hole. He found that it was more of a shaft than just a hole. Down the middle of it ran a thick metal rod which was fitted into the mushroom-top and was screw-threaded for something like two feet of its length. He squirmed farther forward and then gave a sudden exclamation as the beam of his torch, dipping into the shaft, showed up more of the construction. The centre of the pill-box, the tube or shaft, was lead-lined; and so was the base of the mushroom-top, as he saw when he looked up. And it seemed very much as though the screw rod could be used to wind down that top, which in effect must be a lid, a lead-lined lid to seal off a lead-lined tube.

Interesting. . . .

He reached down with his torch, looking directly into the tube shown up by the beam of light. There was a stuffy smell, an indescribable smell of over-used, foetid air blowing past his head and ruffling his hair. The torch was a powerful one but its beam flickered away into nothingness, totally dark, blank space. That tube was deep all right, had been sunk right into the earth. Frowning in puzzlement Shaw went on peering down the beam. After a while he detected a very faint and distant whirring sound funnelling up to him eerily and he realized that somewhere down there in the bowels of the earth there was an electric fan blowing air up the shaft . . . an extractor, expelling foul air from somewhere below.

So that was it!

This was an air-shaft, part of a breathing system.

What was it all for?

This was the fourth in the chain of pill-boxes leading shoreward. It could be assumed that they were all like this

97

one. It seemed likely that there was a tunnel, then, leading inland, and he was now looking down into it via that airshaft. This, of course, *could* fit with the storehouse theory still; it would indeed be more likely that a tunnel rather than the tower itself was the store. The tower was just the entrance —but why build it out at sea? And why all these lead linings? And again—why, if the secret was coming out about a store, didn't they also talk about the tunnel? There must be a reason for that somewhere. There was something here that was more sinister than just a store.

Shaw shook his head in bewilderment, pulled himself up to a crouching position. There had to be some logical answer here, but he couldn't see it yet. He went on staring down the shaft and at first he didn't notice that the fan had stopped and the central rod was turning, turning very slowly . . . it was only when he felt the gentle but irresistible pressure of the huge concrete block on his shoulders that he realized, with a thrill of utter horror, that the lid was coming down between its greased stanchions, that he was about to be wound into the two layers like grain on a millstone, squeezed flat, his body pulped and then wrung dry between the two even massive concrete sections.

THIRTEEN

As the gap began to close, as the slabs came slowly together, Shaw felt blind horror. The mushroom-top was pressing him down now, irresistibly, uncheckable and monstrous, an awful force which he could not fight. There was no time for him to scramble clear now, to reach the edge and drop down. Long before he could squeeze and wriggle through that narrowing gap the two halves would have come flat together.

There was only one thing to do.

Dragging his body forward, scraping along the rough concrete, he got his hands firmly on the central rod as it turned and he plunged down into the darkness of the shaft itself, head first, turning on the rod. He slid down quickly, felt his feet clear the concrete, got a grip with them on the rod. Just as he did so the rod stopped turning, the mushroom-top hit the lower section of the pill-box with a dull boom, a thud which echoed eerily down the shaft. In pitch darkness and stifling heat, Shaw hung upside down, the blood pounding and swelling in his head until he felt that it must burst. Hanging on to the rod with a grip as tight as death itself, he let his feet come clear, taking all his weight on his hands. Groping around with his feet, he felt for the sides of the shaft, found them, braced his legs out sideways, and shifted the grip of his hands. Then he swung his legs downward, came head up, and gripped with his knees tightly on the rod, hanging like a monkey on a stick but, at least, the right way up now. Thankfully, he felt the blood leave his head. He felt a good deal safer now, but it was only a comparative safety. He knew that he was caught, caught like a rat in a trap and with just about as much hope of getting out—until someone far below opened up that mushroom-top again.

Meanwhile, he was in danger of suffocating.

There was no movement of air now, except for the natur-ally-rising exhalations, the used, filthy air from below, air which brought to his nostrils the stink of damp and musti-ness, of decayed animal bodies, of sweat and all other known human smells, an overpowering aroma like rotted death. He was now in what could be his tomb, a sealed and lead-lined concrete tomb.

He felt faint and dizzy, his legs and arms aching from the strain of holding on. Soon he must slip, slide down into the unknown darkness. His thoughts grew fantastic, dreamlike; the darkness began to people itself with strange shapes and faces, the blood pounded again in his ears, in his head, as he tried to suck in what air there was. His lungs felt con-gested, useless as they heaved away in great dragging sighs.

He was on the point of slipping down the rod when he felt the movement, the turning movement which told him they were opening up again, and then a moment later he felt the first draught of air sweeping up, sweeping over his body and drying out the sweat which drenched him. He hung where he was until the rod stopped its turning and the top was fully open; and then, using his last reserves of strength, he hauled himself upward, hand over hand, until he was able to reach out and drag the top half of his body limply over the edge of the shaft onto the concrete. For a few moments he stayed there, taking in gulps of fresh air, feeling life come back. Then he heaved himself right out of the shaft, crawled across the top of the pill-box and dropped thankfully to the earth.

He slid down by the side of the wall, feeling the shake in his limbs as the nightmare, claustrophobic experience drained out of him. Then, when he was rested, he walked back to the road, found the bicycle, mounted it, and pedalled away as fast as he could for Moltsk.

Back in the port Shaw left the bicycle on the outskirts and caught a late bus to the Nikolai Hotel, feeling an overwhelming gladness at being once again in the world of light and human sounds. When he reached the hotel he went straight up to his bedroom. He took off his jacket, nicked out a thread in one of the seams with his fingernail, and pulled. The seam ripped a little way and he got his fingers in and brought out some sheets of very fine crackle-proof tissue covered with a mass of tiny figures and letters. He was busy for twenty minutes, covering a sheet of paper with pencilled words and numbers, and then he re-stowed his code-book, brought out his battery shaver, and slid the back open. From inside he lifted a tiny morse key, set it up for transmission, and hitched the end of a flex to a wall where it held fast on a rubber sucker-cap. Then, reading off the three-figure groups from his pencilled jottings, he tapped out his message to the British Embassy in Moscow for immediate retransmission to White-hall. He repeated it through once more and when it was passed he dismantled the transceiver and slid the back of the shaver shut. Then he burned his notes in the flame of his lighter and went to bed.

Next day he kept on the move around the town, eyes and ears on the alert, unobtrusively watching down by the dock-yard and out by the northern road. There was a considerable movement of troops, and indeed the town seemed to be filling up with them now as more and more drafts came in by train and went in trucks to barracks on the northern outskirts. There were other vehicles on the move as well, heavy lorries like those of the night before, streaming out towards the military area with their cargoes of packing-cases guarded by armed men of the Red Army.

That evening, after an infuriating day of getting precisely nowhere, Shaw waited inconspicuously near the medical research center and waylaid Triska Somalin as she ran down the steps and towards a small red car parked near the building. She looked extremely attractive, he thought, neatly and tastefully dressed with a small fur cap set rather cheekily on her thick black hair.

Smiling he said, "Good evening, Dr Somalin. Going anywhere special?"

She seemed nervous, but pleased to see him. She said, "Oh, no. Just home."

"Change your mind, then?"

"No——"

"It's a woman's privilege, at least in England it is. Isn't there somewhere we can eat, and have a drink?" He lowered his voice. "I want to talk to you."

She met his eyes and said, "All right. But why not the flat?" She smiled, a little shyly he thought. "I am a good cook, Mr Alison."

"I don't doubt that, but have a change away from it. Save the washing-up and try someone else's cooking." He added, "It wouldn't be risky for you, would it—to be seen with an Englishman, I mean?"

She shook her head. "Oh no, not now." She was looking pleased, he could see; lights danced in her eyes, as though no one had asked her out for months. She said, "Thank you so much. I shall be delighted."

"Well, that's fine. Come along then, let's go right away."

"It's early to eat yet. . . ."

"Well, then, we needn't hurry en route."

They got into the car at once and she drove off. There was a nice little place, she told him, where they could get a good meal and where it was quiet, and they would be able to talk, a little way out of Moltsk to the south, in a small fishing-village. She said it was simple and down-to-earth but she would prefer that to the glitter of the more sophisticated places where the officers and important civilians ate so noisily and so drunkenly. Shaw agreed. As she drove, they talked; and Shaw told her about the pill-box and about his own experience in the shaft. She had not, she said, heard anything from Igor Bronsky about a tunnel.

He asked, "What do you make of it, Triska?"

She seemed to start a little at his use, his unexpected use, of her first name; it had slipped out almost unconsciously. He felt her arm brush against his, then a sudden pressure as she took a bend a little too fast and leaned against him. She said, "I don't know. I can't help you very much, though I should like to, with theories on those matters. But if you want just to talk things out, to clarify your thoughts perhaps, then I shall listen. Will that help?"

He said wearily, "I hope so, Triska. I've talked to myself all day . . . not aloud, I hope! . . . and I've got nowhere at all. I can't see the woods for the trees at the moment. Let's assume someone is going to blow up all that lot, all those nuclear devices in this storehouse. Where does that get them—except probably to blow Moltsk and district off the map!"

"It is an insoluble mystery, Peter."

He laughed brittlely. "That's all very well. I've got to solve it." He paused. "Look, Triska. I dare say you've picked up odd scraps of information from your cousin. Can you think of any way by which I can get into that tower? Could I tag myself on to some kind of working-party, for instance, perhaps arrange for some genuine worker to disappear and then take his place . . . that is, assuming there are civilian workers employed on the project, digging out the tunnel and so on? I did see some civilians in those lorries."

She said, "Yes, there are, both men and women, Igor has told me——"

"Well, d'you happen to know where they assemble—I suppose they're taken to the military area from Moltsk?"

"No." She shook her head. "They do not come into the town at all. They live in the barracks, some of them, the ones you saw would have come from there, and others live inside the military zone. They do not leave their quarters at all, ever—except to work!"

He groaned. "I suppose I might have worked that out for myself, really. The security's bound to be very stringent, of course. I suppose the troops are confined to the camp and the barracks, too?"

"Yes, except for the officers."

"That's no go, then. I can hardly pose as anything so exalted as a Red Army officer and expect to get away with it." He stared savagely out of the window. A little later Triska stopped the car on some high ground behind the town and they looked down on the cluster of lights below them. Away to the north Shaw could make out the loom of the floodlights around the tower.

He felt Triska moving against his shoulder and then she said in a low voice, "It is terrible, Peter. I would like to see your Air Force come and blow this place up. How can people have such schemes?"

He reached out his hand to her. "I know . . . but don't worry. I don't give up easily. I'll find a way out."

"I don't think you are going to, Peter. I think there is so little time left now."

He heard the break in her voice and a moment later the tears came, racking sobs which shook her body in her helpless fear and anger. His arm went round her, went round her shoulders comfortingly and held her close to him. For a

102

moment she seemed to yield, then she withdrew with a smothered exclamation and gave a small, shaky laugh. She said, "No, Peter, no."

After a couple of drinks they had dinner and a bottle of wine, sitting in a dimly lit room hung with fishing-nets and looking out over the cold waters of a small harbour. There was only one other couple in the place; lovers, by the look of them. Shaw wondered what future there could be for them or anyone else when, soon enough now if something didn't fall into place in his mind, more and more of the world would be a police state and more and more forced labour would be demanded of the Russian people who would be sent abroad to colonize anew the war-shattered British Isles. Under the extremists' expansionist policy the end-result would be more slavery for those at the bottom. It had always been that way, even in the British Empire. Ironically, the Englishman's working conditions had worsened, he had become himself a near-slave labourer, with the early days of the industrial revolution and the empire-building, had improved again only when the Empire had begun to fade away. Now, short of a miracle, it was to be the Russian's turn. . . .

Shaw and Triska didn't talk much during dinner but afterwards when they drove back into Moltsk they seemed to be very close and he had a feeling of being suddenly very much alone when she left him, discreetly, some distance short of her flat and he walked on down to the Nikolai Hotel.

He went to bed and he had been asleep for some five hours when there was a knock at the door. As he woke the light flicked on and the door crashed inward and three men in M.V.D. uniforms walked in with guns in their hands.

FOURTEEN

Shaw hadn't time to go for his own gun and it wouldn't have helped much if he had. A Webley .38 against three Kalashnikovas just wasn't on. The leader of the M.V.D. party, a long-faced, grey man with a slit of a mouth and gleaming dentures which were so large that they gave him the appearance of a dangerous horse, snapped, "You are the man Alison?"

Shaw said calmly, "Yes. What of it?"

103

"You will come with us, please."

"Like hell I will." Shaw stared back at him. "What's all this about?"

The N.C.O.'s teeth came to with a snap. "I am sorry. It is orders that all aliens report immediately to headquarters."

Shaw smiled without humour and relaxed a little. His first natural thought had been that they had caught up with him, that the abandoned van had been found in Petroslav or that Gorsak or Gelda had after all been taken alive and forced to talk. But now it didn't seem that way; he didn't suppose the M.V.D. often said they were sorry about this sort of visitation, for one thing, and no doubt he ought to be feeling grateful they hadn't simply dragged him out of bed. However, he knew he had to put on an act, so he said, "I'm not getting out of bed at this time of night unless you give me a better reason than that."

"You will get your reason at headquarters, Mr Alison."

"That's all very well——"

The N.C.O.'s gun jerked. "Come quickly. Dress yourself, or we will do it for you. There are other aliens in Moltsk and we have no time to waste on you."

Shaw studied the man's granite face. He didn't know what he would be letting himself in for, but he obviously had no choice. Those blank, dead faces were the faces of men who kill at a moment's notice if you put a foot wrong . . . kill, without altering their expressions by so much as a flicker.

He shrugged and got out of bed.

Slowly, deliberately slowly, he got dressed, pulling on a coat and trousers over his pyjamas. While he was lacing his shoes the N.C.O., rocking impatiently on his heels, said, "Your passport. It also is wanted. You will give it to me, please."

"All right, all right." Shaw stared at him with raised eyebrows and put his hand in the breast-pocket of his jacket. "Here it is."

"Good." The man took it. "Now you are ready."

"Well, if you say so, laddie, I suppose I must be." The men formed up round him and he was urged towards the door. As he was taken downstairs and across the foyer to the steps, he saw small groups of Red Army officers chattering excitedly together and looking as if they too had just got out of bed; but a silence fell as the procession shouldered its way through, and they saw the uniforms of the M.V.D. After that they just moved aside and stared at Shaw as he was led away.

The policeman put him into a closed car which quickly

pulled away and drove through the night-lit streets, streets which were deserted except for occasional groups of soldiers posted at points along the roads as though standing by in case of trouble. As they pulled up outside M.V.D. head-quarters, he saw an armed body of soldiers marching down a side-street, behind a rumbling tank.

Something was up, all right.

He was ordered out of the car and the escort fell in again and marched him up a long flight of steps and through an imposing doorway into a gloomy corridor, a bare, concrete-walled passage which somehow had the very smell of death and agony about it. Then he was turned towards a door with a card on it saying COLONEL ROGOVIN, and he entered a large office, an office as austere as the passage with several hard chairs ranged along a wall. A pale-faced man in plain clothes, evidently Colonel Rogovin, sat at a desk dealing with some papers. He took no notice when the escort clanked to a halt in front of him. He went on with his work, puffing at a cigarette, and then, after two full minutes, during which time Shaw attempted to speak but was peremptorily silenced by the N.C.O., he looked up, thrust his chair backwards, stubbed out his cigarette and lit another. He had a long neck which weaved from side to side as he stared at Shaw—rather like a snake, Shaw decided.

Rogovin stared coolly for some seconds and blew smoke towards Shaw in a long, contemptuous stream. Then he said, "His passport."

The uniformed N.C.O. put the passport down on the desk. Shaw, who didn't like this third-person treatment, hung on to his temper but it took a big effort. "Just what," he demanded icily, "does all this mean, Colonel Rogovin?"

"Patience." Rogovin was looking at the passport, flicking the pages right through to the end, examining the various visas and rubber stamps which signposted "Peter Alison's" journeys on behalf of W.I.O.C.A. But he seemed to be giving the document only a cursory examination; the check seemed to be more a matter of form than a really close scrutiny. Then slowly he turned back to the Uzhgorod entry and Shaw found his legs trembling a little. He trusted Carberry to do a first-class job, but Latymer had specifically warned him—and the warning hadn't been necessary—about the M.V.D. He broke out into a light sweat, and Rogovin glanced up at him, asked, "You are hot?"

"Not particularly. Just tired. Your chaps got me up rather early, you know. It's stuffy in here, too."

Rogovin—Shaw had mentally christened him Snake's-head—said indifferently, "Get the Englishman a glass of water."

There was a rattle of metal equipment behind him and one of the troopers went away, came back with a glass of water which Shaw drank, though he didn't want it in the least. The plain-clothes man murmured, "You are, of course, a guest in our country, Mr Alison—and a distinguished one, since you represent W.I.O.C.A. We do not wish to treat you with impoliteness." He finished going through the passport for the second time, and slammed it hard on the desk. "Neither do we wish to inconvenience you, and I regret the necessity of bringing you here at this hour. Now—your W.I.O.C.A. connexions, Mr Alison. I understand you are attached to the Moscow office?"

"Who told you that, Colonel Rogovin?"

Snake's-head snapped. "I ask the questions. We have our avenues of information."

Yes, Shaw thought, remembering the forms he had filled in—the Nikolai Hotel most likely. He said, "Yes, I'm from Moscow. I'd like——"

"One moment. There are questions which I am forced to ask you. This you must understand and forgive. Now. For what purpose have you come to Moltsk from Moscow?"

"To investigate the possibility of establishing an office in the town, and also incidentally to pay a courtesy call on a certain Professor Godov, who was for many years connected with W.I.O.C.A." They would probably know he'd been out there anyway, he thought; the hired driver would quite likely have reported it. He added, "You can check all that with Moscow if you want to."

Rogovin nodded and made a note on a sheet of paper. "I understand." He made no other comment but went on, "With what section of W.I.O.C.A. are you connected?"

"Literature." Rogovin went on staring at him and he couldn't resist adding, "That's to say—books."

The colonel glared at him coldly. "It is kind of you to explain. The point had not escaped my notice that books were literature." He went on moving his neck and staring, and Shaw came to the conclusion that it was a mannerism, a nervous tic which he couldn't help. "In the broad sense, that is. You have read *Dr Zhivago* by our own writer, Pasternak?"

"In parts."

"Which parts?"

106

Shaw grinned. "Well now—I read it when I knew I was being sent here, you see, so I read only the parts approved by the Soviet."

"You trifle with me. Do not do that." Rogovin's eyes glittered angrily and then he scrawled on his sheet of paper, which appeard to be a report form. "What else?"

"What else what?"

"What else have you read?"

Shaw lifted an eyebrow. "Very much else, too numerous to mention. We've got a writer or two, back in England." Anticipating the next question he added, "Dickens, H. G. Wells, Bennett, Bernard Shaw, Maugham, Priestley." He sweated again now; he didn't like this. He was going to get caught solid before long . . . and then he realized that he wasn't, after all. Snake's-head was losing interest already and in fact none of the questions had had much bite behind them. The man had simply been going through the official routines.

Shaw knew he was dead right when Rogovin snapped suddenly, "Very well. Now then, please listen with great care and attention. You have been brought here because I am instructed to inform all aliens personally that until further notice they are confined to the town and district of Moltsk— that is, in your case you will not be allowed to return to Moscow or, of course, to leave the U.S.S.R. for any reason whatsoever. Your passport will be returned to you in due course. For now—it remains here." He held the document up tantalizingly, then dropped it into a drawer which he pushed shut. "You need have no fear for your safety, I assure you. We are not arresting you, Mr Alison, but merely making provisions for your own good."

"What do you mean?"

Snake's-head stared at him for a few moments in silence, then leaned across his desk and said softly, "During the next few days you will hear and see—certain things. Disregard them. Much of what you hear will be rumour, and none of it, or the seeing, concerns you. You will see, for instance, armed parties of troops and armoured vehicles in the streets. Do not worry, do not fear. I say again, it will not concern you and it will not threaten your safety. Unless, that is, you should be so unwise as to show undue curiosity, in which case, and I warn you of this officially, the soldiers may shoot you. You will make no attempt to communicate with anyone outside the town and general district of Moltsk or, for instance, to get any word through to your relatives in England." He shrugged. "You will not be able to do so, of course—but I want to make sure you understand that if you are discovered in any attempt to do so, you will be arrested and, if found guilty, will be sentenced to die. Beyond this, there will be no undue restriction on your movements, and I trust your stay with us will be a pleasant one. I regret that it has been necessary to interfere with an official of your excellent organization. . . ."

Shaw cut in, "What about Professor Godov? Shall I be able to go out and see him?"

Rogovin said, "Godov lives within the district of Moltsk, which extends just to the north of Emets. But I do not advise you to go to see him again, Mr Alison, for such might be construed as an act unfriendly to the Soviet Union."

"Why's that? He's——"

"Yes, you are going to say he is harmless and old, and so he is, but his views are suspect, Mr Alison. I have no more to say about that. Meanwhile, the Soviet extends its welcome to its guests, Mr Alison, and will return to its normal policy of complete and joyous freedom within a few days. I have nothing more to say." He reached out for a form on his desk. "I shall issue you with temporary papers, and then you will be free to go."

They evidently had no suspicions whatever about him—yet. His room hadn't been touched in his absence and even his Webley was still where he had left it, as large as life under his pillow. He looked at his chest-of-drawers, saw the innocent-looking battery shaver still there in its case. He opened it up; that too seemed to be untouched. These people were no doubt absolutely confident of themselves, confident that no one could stop their plans. It was obvious that the extremists were winning out now, were most probably mounting their full-scale take-over this very night. In four days the London Conference was due to break up and the Soviet Foreign Minister would be on his way home. Something had to happen before then. There was also another worry. So far that faked passport had held up but to date it had never been under really close examination—not even tonight. Now the M.V.D. would have all the time in the world to amuse themselves with it if they chose to do so. It was perfectly likely that they would give all aliens' papers a fresh and thorough going over—and if that happened his life wouldn't be worth twopence.

After breakfast he risked a phone-call to the medical research centre and asked for Dr Somalin. When Triska came, rather breathlessly, to the phone, he asked, "Can you meet me in the Lenin Gardens at lunchtime? I'd . . . very much like to see you, Triska." He put all the meaning he could into that short conversation and she said yes, she would fix it and she would be there, by the gate into Nikolai Street.

He was impatient now for the darkness, the comparatively long darkness of early autumn in those high northern latitudes, for there was something he had to do now and he couldn't do it except under cover of the night; and first he needed Triska's help. He remained in the hotel for a time, studying any newspapers he could find, looking for any clues to the current situation. There were none of that day's papers, however, and the hotel seemed unusually empty, even the vodka-swillers having deserted it. It left a curious feeling behind it, a feeling of mounting doom, of foreboding. The few hotel servants spoke in low tones, and shut up like clams whenever they saw him looking, just as the Army officers had done when they'd seen the M.V.D. men during the night. It wouldn't be safe to ask the servants any questions at this stage, even if they were likely to know the answers. . . .

Shaw, chain-smoking away, liked things less and less.

He met Triska at one o'clock, by a big evergreen just inside the Nikolai Gate, and she looked haggard and tired but pleased to see him. She had some food with her, and she drew him farther into the gardens where they sat on the grass under a warming sun. Once they'd sat down he said, "You look a bit under the weather, Triska. Not well, I mean."

"Oh, it is nothing. Just that I am—worried."

He nodded. "Try and leave the worrying to me, my dear. After all," he added with a touch of bitterness, "it's not your country that's going to blow up!"

She turned to him and gave him a cold, reproachful look. "That was not called for, Peter. It was not a nice thing to say, either."

"I'm sorry," he said penitently. "I didn't mean it quite like that. Look, Triska. Things are hotting up." He told her about the night's events, then asked, "Have you noticed anything strange today?"

"Strange!" She gave a strained laugh and then glanced over her shoulder as if to make sure there was no one about, and then she went on quietly, "It's come, Peter. What we were talking about."

He felt very cold suddenly. "You don't mean—for God's sake, Triska——"

"Not that the threat has materialized, Peter, no. Not quite yet." She moved closer to him then, and smiled at him in a curiously starry-eyed way, as if he was beginning to mean something to her personally. "I mean the extremists have come into the open, Peter."

"That's what I suspected. How sure are you of this?"

She said, "I am quite sure. They told us this morning, at work. Our director himself told us."

"I see. What's the full score, Triska?"

"The score?" She turned her face up to him, puzzled. "What's happened, I mean?"

"Oh . . . yes. The Minister of Defence has taken over the Government—behind the scenes only, at the moment. But he is now in effective control. It seems that the Minister of Defence is to be our new leader. The old faces are still there to be looked at, but they will not stay there afterwards—when this thing is done, they will be liquidated."

"Your director didn't tell you all *that*, surely?"

"No, only that there is to be a new regime. The rest I was well able to work out for myself, Peter. Your Embassy will not now be allowed to communicate with London, except on routine matters—this you must expect, because for now the West must not suspect anything. All dispatches will be very heavily censored, I imagine. Our Director said that Moltsk is itself now largely out of communication with Moscow for the time being and will remain so until things 'settle themselves'—that was his expression. All except official telephone lines have been disconnected, the post offices are closed, no newspapers have come through pending a special edition of *Pravda*. Meanwhile we must all be prepared to declare for the new people in power. Soldiers are ready in case of trouble and they will impose martial law if necessary." She closed her eyes and leaned against him and he felt the shaking of her body as she whispered, "Oh, Peter, it is all so terrible."

"I know, Triska." He squeezed her arm. "Look, why d'you think your Director told the staff at the centre when it seems that the people as a whole aren't to know yet? I don't get it."

She said quietly, "If you knew Russia you would understand better. The people in Russia are simply that—the people—whatever the claims of equality we make for all of them. Do you see? We, the doctors of the research centre and others, are superior-grade citizens, in effect. *We* are told these things, because if we were not told we might find out for ourselves. Perhaps I do not explain very well, but——"

"That's good enough, I get the point. God . . . this was all beautifully planned, wasn't it! They must have got the right commanders posted to this area all ready to take over. Men who could be relied on to sway their troops, I suppose. Easy enough with the Defence Minister behind it, of course." He stared into the distance for a long time and then he said quietly, "Well, it's no good moaning, Triska. I got you here to help me. Will you?"

"Yes," she said at once. "I told you I would, in any way you want if it helps our two countries. Tell me?"

"Right. Now, remember I told you about that air-shaft?"

"Yes, Peter."

"Well, I've been thinking since. . . . I missed a cue the other night. . . ."

"What do you mean?"

He said slowly, "I should have gone on down when I had the chance. You see, I believe that's one way I can get into the tunnel, in fact the only way, and I've got to try it."

"But, Peter, you——"

He laid a hand on her arm. "Don't worry about me. I'll be all right. I know already that it's big enough to take me, and it's only a question of sliding down. Getting out isn't going to be easy, I know, but I'll back myself to do it somehow. There's nothing else for it anyway, Triska. You see, I've got to know what's in the tunnel—that's vital, it's the hub of the whole thing. Now, there are some things I'll want, and it'd be safer if you made the purchases for me, even though what I want are men's articles—clothing and so on." He added, "You can say you want 'em for your cousin if anyone does ask. . . ."

That evening, Shaw and Triska rendezvous-ed in one of the main streets. Moltsk was quiet so far, in spite of—or perhaps because of—the heavy concentration of troops. Shaw got into Triska's little car and they drove out along the northern road towards Emets, passing a convoy of heavy lorries on the way. As they drove Shaw handed Triska his transceiver for safe keeping and so that it would be handy when he got back; he struggled out of his clothes in the back of the car, pulling on a thick leather windcheater over his shoulder-holster. Then he got into rough worker's trousers and heavy boots. He pushed a pair of rubbersoled shoes up into the windcheater. He removed his wrist-watch and handed it to Triska.

Then he was ready.

When they reached the pill-box, which he was relieved to

see was open, Triska stopped the car and Shaw said, "Well—you know what to do now. Remember to brief Godov that if he's questioned at any time, you've been with him all the evening—went there straight from work. Come back along this road at three A.M. Give me an hour. If I haven't got back from my swim before then—buzz off. And in any case don't hang around if you see any troops or transport. That's an order. You've got to do exactly as I say from now on. Promise?"

"All right, Peter," she said in a low voice. "I promise. Take care of yourself."

"Don't worry about me, I'll get back somehow. I've got to." Impulsively he leaned across and kissed her, and then quickly he scrambled out of the car and slammed the door. He said, "Off you go, now."

She drove off and he watched the tail-light of the little red car speeding along the road for Emets and then he went quickly across the marshy ground towards the pill-box, heaved himself up into one of its slots. His flesh creeping with the overriding fear that the mushroom-top would be wound down once again, he slithered on his stomach towards the central shaft. He stowed his torch safely in his pocket and then felt for a tin of petroleum jelly and a pair of tough leather gloves also bought for him by Triska. He opened the tin, put the gloves on, and rubbed the petroleum jelly into the palms.

Then he put the tin back in his pocket, took a deep breath, grasped the central rod firmly, and slid his legs over the edge of the concrete into the lead-lined tube. He eased his body down until he felt the lead enclose him and then he let himself go down, for the second time, into the claustrophobic blackness.

FIFTEEN

The distant whir of the fan came up to him, funnelled by the narrow space—the fan which could put a possible finish to what he meant to do; for if he couldn't stop the blades, smash off one or two, and then crawl on down through the gap, he would be caught as he had been the other night, only much more so. Like a butterfly in a bottle, he wouldn't have a hope—he had no idea how deep this shaft

112

ran, but it must be fairly deep and he didn't fancy his chances if he had to climb back up again.

Once he was below the screw-thread he let himself go, dropping down the central rod as it ran through the greased palms of his gloves. The upflowing air seemed stuffier and filthier than ever and the temperature rose steadily so that soon he was wet through with sweat. In the total darkness and the nauseating smell he continued that alarmingly fast descent, dropping free, on and on and on into the very bowels of the earth. He could feel the friction-heat on his hands now, even through the thick leather, and after a while he began to feel the burning pain and he realized that an unevenness, a slight roughness in the rod, was wearing through the gloves. He had to grip harder and thrust out with his boots and body to slow his fall, and after that he went on down hand over hand, feet pushed out sideways against the lead lining of the tube.

After some minutes of this he found that he was tiring badly, as much from lack of good air and the consequent body-draining heat as from actual physical effort.

His arms felt like lumps of lead and soon his legs had gone the same way. Still he slid downward, on and on into the stifling blackness, filthy and sweat-drenched, the noise of the fan louder and louder, beating into his brain. Every now and again he stopped, held himself suspended by his hands and by the pressure of rump and knee and shoulder against the tube's walls, until his very inertness and weight, and the effort of pressing outward, began to tire him as much as the descent itself. Then on again, on and on endlessly, down into claustrophobia, fearful that his limbs would give out and he would drop like a stone.

He had never for one moment imagined that the tube could possibly go so deep as this.

His breath came in sobbing gasps and his body was just one big ache and he felt that he couldn't go on, that he must give in and drop. And then something happened below him. The noise of the fan died away and a few seconds later he felt his whole body twist round.

They were screwing down the mushroom-top again, operating the controls below him.

The air grew thicker, fouler, unbreathable—just like the other night, only far worse at this depth. It was as if he were sealed in a closed container from which the oxygen had been drawn off. The heat was much more intense now and he could feel his body wasting away in sweat, sweat which filled his eyes as if he were under water, sweat that rolled from his brows, his hair, from every part of his body.

Then, looking downward between his knees as the rotary motion stopped, he could just make out the very faint glow of distant light through the now motionless blades of the fan.

He couldn't have so very much farther to go—but it was useless to try to descend while men were working there, right below him. Now that they had shut the lid and switched off the fan it was reasonable to assume that they were packing up, at any rate for the time being. He stopped and waited for a little over three minutes and then he saw the light go off.

He went on then with fresh hope, painfully sliding down the rod again. A few moments later he felt his feet hit something and he braked with his body. Then his knees were forced up to meet his chin and his body stuck fast. He felt warm metal beneath him.

The fan.

It was blocking the tube completely, as he had expected it would, pivoted round that central rod.

He waited for some minutes and then, when no sound came up to him, he reached out for a blade of the big fan, testing it for strength. As he had expected, the metal was light, thin and pliable and the blade twisted upwards quite easily. Feeling in the darkness Shaw dealt with each blade in turn until the fan, if he could have seen it, must have looked like a flower with its petals closed up for the night. He reached down with a leg, gauging the clearance. It would be a tight fit; the circular fan-motor, positioned around the rod, was a bulky affair. Slowly, carefully, Shaw let his body downward, felt both legs go through the gap. For a moment he stuck fast. He almost gave way to panic, but then a kick of his legs and a big exhalation of breath allied to a final convulsive heave did the trick. The fan-motor gave a cracking sound, tilted a little on the rod, and he was through with no more damage than a ripped windcheater and a grazed chin and shoulder.

After that it was easy.

It was still pitch dark below and he simply slid down the rod with the remnants of his gloves and his boots helping him, and then suddenly his feet flew out sideways as they came clear of the shaft's constriction and a moment after that he hit the bottom with a thump and went flying over backwards.

He stayed where he had fallen, reaching for his gun and then keeping dead still and quiet. There were distant noises of men at work along the tunnel—and he'd been right, it was a tunnel—where he could see a faint glow of light; but in his sector there was absolute stillness. He listened for five minutes, ears attuned to catch any near-by sound and react instantly. Then he reached into his pocket for his torch and, shielding the end with his hand so that it gave only a dim red glow, he shone it around. Faintly he could see sheer rock, jagged rock, all round him—above, below, and on both sides. Moving his fingers to let through more light, he directed the beam upward, saw how uneven the clearance was. In parts the roof was barely visible, in other parts there was little more than three to four feet between roof and floor, and the lateral measurements also seemed to vary quite considerably. In the roof near the air-shaft he saw a heavy block of concrete mounted on rails which ran across the opening—possibly another sealing device—and on the ground was an electric motor, presumably for moving that heavy slab.

Somehow the whole aspect of the place gave Shaw the impression of being natural rather than man-made, neither blasted nor excavated but formed, perhaps, by some freak internal movement of the earth's crust, maybe millions of years back in pre-history. He flashed the torch along the tunnel away from where the sounds of men working were coming. Nothing there, just blankness and the heat—enervating, frightening heat. He sweltered. He judged the temperature to be in the region of 140 degrees Fahrenheit, possibly more, and that must mean that he was a devil of a long way down into the earth. He got up and walked along the tunnel for a little way, sweat pouring off him at every step. The place seemed to go on and on into the blank emptiness and after fifty yards or so he turned back, faint now with the loss of body-moisture. He wondered how the men kept at work down here; his clothing felt just as though he'd had a steaming hot bath in it.

He struggled on back and went beyond the air-shaft, making in the opposite direction now, cautiously and slowly, towards the human sounds and the faint light in the distance. Just beyond the air-shaft the tunnel seemed to narrow again and take a very slight left turn, and beyond this the gangway was down to no more than two or three feet. And in a moment, as his shaded torch swung round, he saw why. The whole place, higher here, was stacked from top to bottom with row upon row of shining metal objects, cone-shaped, sinister.

Shaw examined them.

He had never seen anything like them, couldn't identify them. They bore no markings whatsoever. Going on, he found that this stack continued, tightly stowed, into the far distances of the tunnel . . . there must be hundreds of thousands of them if the stowage continued right the way along to the sea-tower at the end; these must be what those lorries had brought. As he went along slowly, he found that the canisters varied in size and shape. Some were cone-shaped as he had already seen, some were oblong, others square; there were some enormous finned objects which looked more like conventional guided missiles and must have needed mechanical handling to get them in place. Whatever else this place might be in addition, it was most certainly a store all right. That part of it was perfectly genuine, and all this stuff would be quite safe down here so far under the earth, safe against any imaginable attack. It was so damned logical, he thought . . . and it was logical, too, to keep the place as secret as possible.

Getting nearer now to the work going on ahead, he removed his heavy boots and slung them around his neck, put on the rubbersoled shoes from under his windcheater, and then went on again in dead silence towards the pool of bright light. The tunnel stretched away ahead, endlessly. Thinking back to the surface he estimated that it must be a good five miles all the way to the tower itself . . . five miles of those weird contraptions. What in God's name could they be? Were they some diabolic new weapon, could the tower in fact be some brand-new missile-launching platform, would it perhaps spray these containers out over Europe, in close but spreading formation on the principle of a sporting gun, or the old "Hedgehog" anti-submarine weapon that had been used by the Allied navies back in World War II?

On the other side of the coin, of course, it could simply be the site for some big new underground test explosions, with no immediately hostile intent whatever.

Had Rudintsev imagined things, had rumour bred rumour and the wild stories mounted until this place had become a mystery and, as such, a potential threat in the mind only? No . . . too many sane people had sensed something in the

116

air. Godov wouldn't be misled by baseless rumour, for one, and then there were all the outward and visible signs of a *coup d'état* in progress. If this tunnel was innocent that needn't necessarily be connected, of course, but. . . .

Again no. There had been too many pointers. There was a threat all right, and this had to be the hub of it.

Shaw walked on slowly, his gun in his hand. Soon he could see men working, most of them stark naked, some with trousers only, in that narrow gangway, could hear orders being shouted in hectoring voices. There were women too, working alongside the men, their naked bodies glistening in the light. It was a quite fantastic scene of slave labour. Only the whips were missing. Shaw sensed a feverishness in the air, as though the men were working desperately against time, stacking more and more of those shining metal cases, sweat running off their naked bodies so that they gave the effect of working in a glass fishbowl. Some way ahead, Shaw fancied, the big stack came to an end—so perhaps they had only quite recently started stowing these things and were now working round the clock to get the job finished.

Suddenly some of the lights went out ahead and one more whole section was in darkness. Beyond that, far beyond now, the work was as intense as ever. Shaw pushed on quietly, not hurrying. It seemed as though, when each section was filled, the lights went out and the workers moved on. After a time Shaw came to the second of the air-shafts, the first of those inside the military area, and this too had its fan switched off and all was silent as the grave, silent and hot, stifling. No doubt this shaft was screwed down as well, lead-sealed from the fresh air above. . . .

Shaw's thoughts were nipped off then. He had seen the light moving towards him.

SIXTEEN

He was only just in time.

Someone was coming back along that tunnel with a light on a wandering lead. Shaw looked round quickly for somewhere to hide; there wasn't anywhere. Doing the only thing he could he dodged back beneath the air-shaft and crouched down in the lee of the stacked canisters where the stowage

117

had been discontinued to leave the space below the shaft free of encumbrances.

Still as death, he waited.

Two men and a woman came past, naked like so many of the others and following their leader, who wore the peaked cap of a Red Army officer. Without looking into the recess the officer said in Russian, "We will close the western shaft first, then come back to this one."

"Yes, Comrade Major."

They went straight on and in the back-glow from the electric bulb Shaw's eyes followed the woman who was in the rear of the line, saw her swelling, pointed breasts, her long flanks ridged with muscle and the perspiration glistening on a bottom as small as a boy's. Hard work in this filthy atmosphere would keep anyone slim enough . . . as the procession went past Shaw caught the acrid tang of body-sweat, sharp yet heavy on the air. They passed on into the darkness, back along the tunnel where he had been himself earlier. Again there was silence; Shaw wondered what his next move should be. If he went on, he would be caught in a sandwich between the working mob ahead and those three when they came back. Yet he couldn't stay here, obviously. "Closing the shaft" no doubt meant swinging across that heavy concrete slab on the rails in the roof so as to complete the final seal from the upper air, and in doing that they couldn't possibly miss him.

Once again he shone his torch through his fingers. Up on top of the pile of containers, where the natural irregularities of the roof made close stowage impossible, he found after a time a gap that might be big enough to take him until those men and the woman had gone on back to the workings. Switching off the torch and putting it in his pocket, he reached upward, heaved his body on to the pile, steadied a loose container which seemed on the point of dropping, and then lay there dead still under the lee of the roof. Again there was absolute quiet and stillness, broken only by the thumping of his own heart. The wait on top of the pile seemed endless, but at last he heard the men and the woman coming back, the light on its lead swinging in front of them, and soon they had stopped below the shaft. Looking down and keeping dead still, Shaw watched as the workman went to the electric motor and switched it on. The woman was standing by the officer, her naked breasts rising and falling as she struggled for breath in the filthy air, sweat showing damply on her thighs and stomach. There

118

was a high whine as the big concrete slab—which Shaw now noticed was also backed with a layer of lead—began to slide across the opening on its greased rails, inch by inch. There was a lot of load on that motor. The officer, a good-looking, well-built man in his early thirties, was showing signs of impatience and after a moment he snapped, "Is it running at full speed?"

"Yes, Comrade Major."

A sigh whistled through the major's teeth and he looked down at the woman. Meeting his eyes, her lips parted and the tip of her tongue protruded momentarily; then she looked away—scared, perhaps, at having let the officer see her thoughts. But he grinned back at her, and then said something, which Shaw couldn't catch, to the motorman. Then he reached out a hand to the woman, placing it on her breasts and letting it slide down her body. Her hips moved a little and Shaw heard the hard breathing of the major, and then together they turned away and went along the gangway below Shaw, towards the distant working-lights. As they passed along he heard a low gurgle of laughter. Then they were gone into the darkness, silhouetted against the distant glow, leaving the light on its wandering lead with the motorman.

The shaft was very nearly sealed now.

The man at the controls was watching closely and Shaw could hear stertorous breathing. All the man's attention was on that sliding concrete slab when Shaw, slowly, carefully, silently, brought up the Webley and aimed. The Russian had reached forward and had just cut the motor when Shaw squeezed the trigger of the silenced gun. The man spun round, his head messily shattered, and dropped without a sound. The soft plop of the silencer echoed eerily in the tunnel, but it was the kind of noise that would be lost in the working racket ahead and Shaw wasn't worried about that. He scrambled down from his perch, picked up the wandering lead and pushed the bulb behind the stack of containers so that it gave only a dim glow into the gangway, then he dragged the body close up to the containers and started pulling down some of the pile and re-stowing it so the body was covered against any casual glance if anyone should chance to walk back up this way again.

After that he took off his own clothing except for his trousers and stuffed the garments away out of sight on the top of the stowage. He fixed his holster so that it swung uncomfortably but securely between his legs and then he picked up the light and moved out into the gangway, going forward now quickly and without hesitation, just one of the civilian labour force.

Soon he emerged into the full light of the next section along, where the tunnel widened out considerably.

There must have been six or seven hundred men and women working here, working as a huge human chain and manhandling the metal containers into place, continuing that great stack right along from floor to roof. Lifting and straining, singing snatches of songs from time to time. Never letting up—working away like horses. Shaw was close to the third air-shaft here; this one, which was still open, seemed to be drawing air downward, for, though foul enough, the atmosphere was a little fresher. No-one looked twice at Shaw as he made his way along, assuming, probably, that he had been detailed for some job or other away from the gangs.

He slid past the greasy naked bodies until farther along he heard a shout: "You there!"

He half turned and a big, hairy-bodied N.C.O. carrying a sub-machine-gun grabbed him by the arm and swung him round close to a thin-lipped, sadistic face. "Where d'you think you're off to, comrade?"

"I——"

"Get on with it—no excuses! If this job isn't finished by the day after tomorrow, we shall all be in the Siberian labour camps. You know that as well as I do. And however much you grumble, all of you, about the heat . . . you'll not find the cold of the Siberian plains to your liking!"

Shaw was pushed violently backwards and almost fell. He staggered into one of the women, felt the contact of naked flesh, heard her laughter and a coarse joke. Holding on to his temper he joined in with a team of men and women stowing the pile near where he was standing. He worked for perhaps half an hour and then a siren sounded out loudly and the N.C.O. roared at them to pack up.

They stopped work thankfully, all along the tunnel, but there wasn't much chatter; many of the workers were too tired, too spent, even to talk. This was evidently the end of the shift—they wouldn't be able to keep going for long at a stretch down here anyway. Shaw simply followed the motions of the others and made for a kind of assembly square a little way along where a mass of clothing was hung on hooks or piled on the floor. The men went to one side, the women to the other, and they seemed to be grabbing the first articles of clothing that they came to, clothing that was

120

all much of a pattern: rough trousers like enough to his own and short pyjama-like coats of heavy material, and coarse shirts. It was like a prison rig. Shaw grabbed with the others, taking one of the shirts and a coat but retaining his own trousers; each man, as he got dressed, went ahead, marshalled by the N.C.O.'s, towards a turnstile gate where the tunnel narrowed again. As each man came up to the turnstile he was checked on an automatic counter and handed two salt tablets and a mouthful of water from a metal jug. Once through the number-check, the workers piled into a line of small, open trucks drawn up on one lane of a double-track miniature railway running into the brilliantly lit distance. As soon as everyone was in, Shaw among them, there was a jolt and the little train started up. It ran on the flat for some way and then started up an incline. Farther along they passed another line of trucks coming up from the other direction—the relief shift reporting. Then they came below the fourth and last of the air-shafts, the one that rose above the sea. This one, like the third, was still unsealed.

Farther on the tunnel, its walls, roof, and floor lead-covered for some twelve feet back from the entrance, opened out into a large round compartment; that compartment must have been a couple of hundred feet in diameter and it was regular, with none of the natural characteristics of the tunnel proper. This, Shaw realized, must be the actual base of the tower itself. There were many doors leading off to stores, workshops and the like; looking back at the entrance to the tunnel Shaw's attention was caught by a vast lead-and-concrete door to one side of it, a door that was ready for sliding across on huge greased rails like outsize girders. Shaw had never seen anything to equal it for size; that door must have been all of twenty feet thick and, once run across, would be driven back into the lead-covered entrance of the tunnel until it slotted neatly to form a complete seal, blocking the tunnel off like a well-driven cork. Down into the main compartment which he was in, a series of twelve big open-platform lifts descended in groups of three, all of them ready now to take the workmen up, presumably to the top of the tower for the run along the pier to the camp on shore. These lifts were quickly filled as the crowd surged forward, twenty at a time riding on each.

Shaw was in the second batch to go up.

The lifts rose swiftly, breathtakingly fast—alarmingly so as the walls of the tower flashed by; but even at their high speed it took them nearly five minutes to reach the top of the tower, the air growing cooler all the time so that sweat dried quickly on their bodies. That tunnel must be deep indeed in the western end where Shaw had descended, for the railway along its latter stretch had risen for nearly the whole of its distance and yet they were still so far from the surface.

At the top of the tower, doors slid open and the workers spilled out of the lift-house onto the wide, flat roof—and into the cold bite of the wind.

Shaw looked round swiftly, taking it all in, the layout and the chances.

This was where he had to make his getaway—if he could.

The top of the tower was surrounded by a guardrail, and beyond that was the sea thirty feet below, and then, farther out, the circle of small constructions carrying the defensive boom. If he could get into the water without being spotted he would back himself to swim under the boom all right—the cold wouldn't be too bad this far off winter conditions—and then make his way to the shore beyond the limits of the military area long before anyone found out what had been going on. *If he could get into the water. . . .*

That looked utterly impossible now and he had to face it.

The whole of the tower was brilliantly lit from the floods on tall standards at intervals along the guardrails, and there were four observation-posts mounted on the perimeter. These posts were each manned by two guards armed with automatic weapons, and their fire would cover the whole area very adequately indeed. It didn't look as though he had a hope in hell. Perhaps it would be easier to get away from the shore end after all . . . but no, that wouldn't do. Once he was forced to enter some mess-hut or other in that military encampment, someone would realize very quickly that there was a stranger around. He could get away with it—had done so—down on the workings, where all the men were mixed up and wouldn't know all their mates, but that wouldn't be possible in the camp. Nor, for that matter, would he be able to cross the wire out of the military area. So it had to be done now—and quickly, before the men were hustled into the line of trucks waiting on the pierhead to drive them shorewards.

He looked round again, almost desperately now, pushing his way nearer the tower's side through the ranks of workers, the ranks which were thickening as more and more came up from below from the other groups of lifts. It seemed that for some reason—security, no doubt—all the men were being kept together in the floods and under the guns and

122

not allowed into the trucks until the whole lot was up from below. Then Shaw caught sight of something on the wall of the nearer lift-house, just above his head now—a big, square metal projection which looked as if it might be a junction-box.

If it was—then it could conceivably control those floods! But that didn't help much; the box was well out of reach.

He was wondering how he could reach it when a bell began clanging, like an action-alarm; for one terrible night-mare second Shaw fancied the whole thing was about to go into action right here and now, that he had been too late. Then the bell stopped and he saw that a Red Army captain had lifted a telephone off a hook. The Russian spoke for fifteen seconds, his face hardening in the glare of the floods, and then he slammed the phone back on the hook and swung round. Voices were stilled as he called for silence, raising a hand, and then he shouted: "The relieved shift will remain here for questioning. One of your number has been murdered."

SEVENTEEN

At once Shaw, taking advantage of the frightened confusion of the workers, pushed his hand down the front of his trousers, grabbed for the already silenced Webley, flattened himself against the wall of the lift-house, raised the gun and at once fired upward.

He hit the junction-box with his first shot, loosened it, and fired twice more in as many seconds. On the third shot the box disintegrated and there was a sheet of blue lightning which fizzed and crackled over the heads of the frightened mob of workers. All the floods went out together, leaving a total and vibrant blackness behind.

That did it.

Instantly there was complete chaos on the roof, with officers shouting, and men yelling and getting in the way of the officers who hit out at them savagely and indiscriminately with fists and boots and gun-butts. Shaw smashed his way through the mob and reached the guardrail. As he climbed over in the darkness and dived in, losing his gun as he did so, there was a rattle of automatic fire, a long burst followed by screams of agony as the Kalashnikovas' 7.62 mm. cartridges sprayed into the mass of bodies.

Shaw hit the water cleanly, went into the cold sea with hardly a ripple; keeping well under the surface he swam quickly for the perimeter and the boom. Through the water now he could see a searchlight sweeping the area, probing, like a vengeful finger, a directing beam of death trying to seek out anyone who might have gone over under cover of the panic—he was sure he hadn't been personally spotted and as things had happened he fancied his chances were more than good. Whoever had been fool enough to give the order to fire was going to regret it soon; because of that mad burst of bullets they could never be sure, now, of what had happened while the lights were out. With luck some bodies would have gone over the side and their numbers would be all to hell.

Inside a minute Shaw was moving below the boom; and then he was fighting for his life as his legs and arms entangled in the heavy steel mesh of an anti-submarine net, which closed over head and body grippingly, like some wicked metal octopus.

Every struggle seemed to make matters worse. He felt that he was being dragged down deeper and deeper into the icy water by steel chains round his feet. His lungs were bursting now; curving himself into a tight ball he freed his head and arms and then he reached down towards his feet, managed at last to get one leg free. Time stood still. Above him the searchlight played on the water, sweeping in an arc, then pencilled back to the tower's roof. Shaw felt as if he was really done for this time . . . and then all at once the net moved on some underwater current and he was clear again. Blood drummed in his ears as he kicked himself away from the net and forced himself to go deeper yet, down and down until his ear-drums cracked and he felt sick and giddy, down and down towards the foot of the mesh.

The net seemed to reach to the very bottom of the sea. He couldn't go on like this for much longer. He made one final effort and went deeper . . . and then his reaching fingers found the heavy weights at the bottom of the mesh. Pulling himself down, he glided beneath the net, kicked clear again, then let himself go upward as slowly and gently as his bursting lungs would allow.

He wondered how he could ever have done it.

He didn't know how long he had been underwater when at last he surfaced for a few quick gulps of air—but it must have been quite a time. It was no short stretch from the tower to the boom alone, although his dive had carried him well clear of the tower and he was a strong, fast swimmer. And now he was some distance from the boom itself, making seaward for a while and not hurrying, idling along for the time being to get his wind back.

Treading water, he looked towards the tower.

The floods had come on again now and once again the whole area of water between tower and boom was brilliantly lit. A small boat had left the tower and was making for one of the boom-carrying constructions. Shaw watched it being pulled round the net, its armed crew peering into the water all around. Then he felt a series of alarming shocks through the water, followed by a number of dull thuds, and water churned up inside the boom. They were putting down small charges to drive men to the surface, but Shaw was well outside their effective range. He heard a loud yell then, and the men in the boat started to grapple something inboard. They must have found a body. Shaw hoped it would satisfy them.

He started swimming again.

It was very cold, worse than he had thought it would be; had it been a few weeks later this swim would have been impossible, he could not have lived in the water for more than a few minutes once winter's rapid drop in sea-temperature had set in. Farther out he met the tide which, flooding strongly, carried him on towards the port. When he judged it safe he turned over on his back and floated and then when the current had carried him far enough, clear of the military area, he struck out again, turning across the current and making for the shore. He could tell from the beams of torches moving out from the direction of the camp that no chances were being taken, but they hadn't got far along the foreshore yet and, choosing his time carefully and keeping submerged again and invisible until the very last moment, he was able to leave the water, unseen in the darkness, and then crawl slowly on his stomach up the beach, away ahead of the flashing torches and under the shelter of a big groyne. After that it wasn't long before he was across the coast road and running along behind the beach, a bitter wind slicing into his wet clothes and his body and his teeth chattering madly, running fast into the barren, bush-dotted countryside that lay between the coast road and the road from Godov's house where Triska would pick him up.

Behind him, the search was already tailing off and once again Shaw was grateful for that stupid burst of gunfire. In any case they would never think for one moment that an outsider could ever have got into the tunnel.

Meanwhile he was ahead of schedule. He had expected that he would have had to spend much longer inside the workings that had turned out to be the case. That meant a long, cold wait and he flattened himself into the beginnings of the marshy ground below the western verge of the road—and waited. Once during that wait a squadron of heavy tanks rumbled past but none of them stopped and nobody saw him.

Ninety minutes later, as he was trying to rub some warmth into his limbs, he saw the lights of a car coming along the road from Emets. The car was going slowly, as though the driver was keeping a look-out, and soon he was able to recognize Triska's little car. Stepping into the road he waved her down and he heard her gasp of relief as she stopped and pushed the door open. He got in gratefully, out of the wind.

She said, "Oh, Peter, I didn't say so, but I was sure I should never see you again!"

He grinned and said lightly, "As a matter of fact you nearly didn't, but it takes more than a swim and a bit of trouble to kill me."

"Yes, but. . . ." She broke off. "Those clothes! Get into the back and change quickly. There is a towel there."

"No sooner said than done, I assure you." He was shivering violently now, barely able to keep still. He heaved himself over the seat-back and pulled off his wet clothing. Finding the towel he rubbed himself down until he began to feel a comfortable glow all over. The he pulled on dry underwear and his grey suit. Smiling but anxious still, Triska turned round and handed him a flask of raw spirit, which he took two or three big gulps from and immediately felt a whole lot better.

He asked, "Godov gave you this?"

"Yes. And there is something else for you. When I told Godov you meant to swim for it, he said you might have to jettison your gun——"

"And he was dead right! It's on the bottom somewhere off the tower. Don't say you've got a replacement?"

"Yes, I have." She brought out a beautifully kept Luger automatic and handed it to him with some spare ammunition. He examined it appreciatively.

126

"It's a beauty, Triska," he said. "Somehow I don't associate Godov with guns though."

"Oh, it wasn't his, he would never use a gun except a sporting gun, Peter. It is old Josef's, Godov's man, you know? He took it from a dead German outside Stalingrad—Volgagrad—and now he gives it to you with his blessing."

"He's the one who deserves the blessing," Shaw said gruffly. "It's going to be worth its weight in gold, believe me. We've a long, long way to go yet."

"Have you found out much?"

"Little enough for certain," he said. He told her what he had seen and added, "One of the N.C.O.'s said something about it all having to be completed by the day after tomorrow—that's to say *tomorrow* now, which incidentally is when the British ships come in. . . ."

"Do you see any connexion, Peter?"

"Well no, frankly I don't. But the very fact of a time limit being talked about means that tunnel's no mere store—right? It's what we're after, I'm certain of that, though I still don't know what they mean to do." He looked at his watch. "Let's go, Triska. I want to get a message off to the Embassy for London, and I'm not risking a transmission so near the military area. If anyone picked it up locally they'd smell a rat right away."

"Where do you want to go, Peter? To the Professor's house?"

He shook his head. "No, I think we'll head back into Moltsk. I told you that M.V.D. character warned me against seeing Godov again, and I don't want to get too many questions asked about me. For similar reasons I'm not keen to roll up at the Nikolai at some freak hour. I'm going to ask you to put me up at your flat for what's left of the night, Triska. I'm sorry, but . . . well, I've got to have an alibi in case I'm questioned." He looked at her hard. "Do you see what I mean?"

She nodded, "Yes, I do."

"And you . . . don't mind?"

There was a funny look in her eyes as she said quietly, "Why, of course not. I shall be very pleased, Peter." As she started up she said, "You are sure your Embassy will be able to pass on your message? Remember there will be heavy censorship, Peter."

"I'm remembering. The answer is—no, I'm not sure at all. But they're pretty good, you know. They don't like it, but they rally round! They'll find a way of slipping it through in

127

some innocent-looking routine transmission under any circumstances short of a complete shut-down."

"And then you'll get more orders?"

He shrugged. "Depends. If I do, they'll come direct from London at eleven P.M. Moscow time tonight." He explained about the routine broadcast from London and added, "They've only contacted me once so far, though I've listened whenever possible. Once we're in the field, you see, we're forgotten men! All they want is our reports to them, and they do the rest . . . but what they'll do this time is anybody's guess. I'm glad I'm not in their shoes."

She looked at him oddly as the car rushed along for Moltsk. She asked, "It does not worry you, that you are in your own shoes?"

He laughed. "Wouldn't do much good if it did! Anyway, I'm used to it by now."

As they neared the flat Shaw asked, "What about cousin Igor?"

"Oh, that's all right. He's on duty. I wonder you didn't see him in the tower! He won't be back till lunchtime."

When they were in the flat she switched the electric fire on and Shaw sat by it, coding up a message for Latymer telling of all he had seen and indicating the N.C.O.'s words about completion. He transmitted this at once and then warmed himself right though by the fire while Triska made him a hot drink. After that—bed; and Shaw slept like a log, flat out and dreamless, until the broad daylight coming through into the bedroom brought him wide awake and he found himself warm and comfortable in Triska's arms. She was stroking his forehead and there was a strange expression in her face, a look of loneliness and longing.

Shaw took her wrist in his hand and asked quizzically, "Well? Why are you looking at me like that?"

She coloured. "Oh . . . no special reason, Peter. Except perhaps that I am fearful of what may happen to you."

"Don't start thinking like that," he told her. "I'm used to this sort of thing, remember? I'll get by."

"I do not think you take enough care. You have never thought of giving it up, this life of yours?"

"Often!" He laughed. "I've got a chief who doesn't think I should, though." He sat up. "It's getting late, Triska. I must go."

"No. It is early still, you did not sleep for long." The odd look was still there, tender and sad, and her colour was high, her lips slightly parted. "You need not go yet."

He said uncomfortably, "I've got some thinking to do, and I want to show myself at the Nikolai——"

"Back on the road, Peter, you said you could do nothing more until eleven o'clock tonight. A few more minutes will make no difference to your thoughts, Peter, or to the hotel. Then I shall get breakfast while you bath and dress and after that the day is yours, yes?"

He looked down at her as she lay beside him and then suddenly his hands were on her body, pulling urgently at her nightdress, and she helped him, lifting her arms so that he could pull it over her head. He felt her small cup-like breasts straining against him and he took her in his arms and crushed her to him. His lips came down on hers, hungrily, and he felt the surging warmth of her body against his own. Then she gave a small cry and he felt a shiver run through her, a shiver of eager surrender, and her thighs moved a little beneath him.

They were just finishing breakfast and it was still barely nine o'clock when the doorbell pealed and went on pealing. Triska started and went very white, then left the room and answered the door. Shaw jumped up in consternation when he heard her say, "Igor! Why, you are——"

The reply was thick with drink in spite of the early hour. "There has been trouble. I am sent into Moltsk to talk to some of the families of the civilian workers."

Then the door of the sitting-room, which had been ajar, was jerked violently back by the resounding kick of a heavy boot. Major Igor Bronsky lurched into the room, his eyes bloodshot and, as they took in Shaw, angry.

Bronsky walked up to him slowly. He demanded, his voice harsh and his heavy white face twitching, "Who is this?" He slewed round on Triska as she came in behind him, nearly losing his balance as he did so. "Who is this man?"

She shut the door and said quietly, "Mr Peter Alison of the Workers' International Organization for Cultural Advancement. From Moscow. Peter, this is my cousin——"

"When, from Moscow?"

Shaw said, "Some days ago."

"What do you do?"

Shaw told him and he made a crudely anatomical remark. "A genius, yes? Ah, me! Why is your hair not long, genius?" He belched, and walked round and round Shaw, looking at him in wonderment and speaking in an irritatingly high-pitched voice which he seemed to find amusing. Shaw put him down as a buffoon, though a sinister one. "Poets, painters, pimps. I spit on them." For one moment Shaw thought the man was really about to spit, but he refrained. "The poet has spent the night in your bed—are you going to tell me that, Triska?"

She faced him, eyes flashing. "And what if I did tell you that, Igor?"

He shrugged heavy shoulders and lowered himself into a chair. "I would say this: that I do not admire your choice, that if I were you I would prefer to bed with a man rather than a poet, but that your morals are not my concern, Triska. You are my cousin, not my wife or my mistress, and your particular style of beauty makes no appeal to me or I would have put you to bed myself before now." He looked her up and down. "There is not enough flesh . . . me, I like something to get hold of."

She said disdainfully, "You are drunk."

Bronsky gave a cynical laugh. "Drunk! Dear Triska, I have not yet had time to get drunk. When I am drunk, I can no longer move. Until that happens, I am sober. But enough of this. You now, poet," he said truculently. "What do you know of death?"

"Death?" Shaw raised an eyebrow and smiled. "Not very much, I'm afraid, Major. And you?"

Bronsky pulled a flask from his hip-pocket and drank, wiping the cuff of his uniform across his lips afterwards. "Plenty. Death is my trade. I kill, I am trained to kill, because I am a soldier, poet, a soldier, of the Red Army." His words were slurring badly and his head had begun to weave from side to side. "Last night a man was killed in . . . my place of duty, you understand, and now I have to question the relatives of his comrades to see who the murderer may have been. I investigate the enmities among these people. I shall investigate very thoroughly. Perhaps I investigate some of the women first." His glance was on Triska's breasts, suggestively, roving down her body; then his red-flecked eyes swung back towards Shaw, glittering, and he veered off on to another subject. "You English. I feel sick to the stomach to look at you. So smug. Oh, so damn smug!" Unsteadily he leaned forward and waved a finger in Shaw's face. "You believe, I am told, that the sun shines from your collective fundamental orifice. You . . . are going to get the damn biggest shock of your life, poet."

Shaw smiled acidly. This man was well worth encouraging a little further. He asked, "Really?"

"Really!" Bronsky mimicked him. "Triska, how you can bear to sleep with a poet . . . it revolts me, it is almost an unnatural practice. Poet, it will not be long now."

"Oh? What won't, Major?"

"Aha, you would so much like to know!" The mouth sagged stupidly but the eyes were hard and glittering still, like black diamonds in the pasty face. "You would like to know . . . and damn me, poet, if I do not tell you! It cannot matter now . . . you cannot leave Russia now that strong men are in the Kremlin. What does it matter now, poet, tell me that?"

"I don't suppose it does, if you say so."

Bronsky made a contemptuous gesture. "Of course it does not. Now I will tell you. One of our ministers arrives today, here in Moltsk. The Minister of Defence. And do you know who he will have with him poet? Do you?"

"I've no idea."

"*Lawrence Carew*. Now do you see?" Bronsky sat back complacently, triumphantly, watching the effect of his words.

The effect was there, right enough.

Shaw's hands had clenched behind his back and his lips had gone very dry. Carew—of all people! Shaw knew that name only too well, as indeed the whole of England knew it. Carew had been a nuclear physicist, a brilliant man, and thirteen years ago he had flitted to the East. There was said to be nothing Lawrence Carew didn't know about nuclear matters, and his loss had sent Whitehall and Washington as well into the biggest panic for years—and, in due course when it all came out, Moscow had been openly exultant about his defection, as exultant as the West had been dazed. Carew had for some years now been a full citizen of the Soviet Union. And, ironically enough, as Shaw now remembered reading in the papers, it had been W.I.O.C.A. that had given Lawrence Carew his start in life, put him on the road to his studies and laid the foundations of his reputation.

Shaw stifled his racing thoughts. Bronsky was looking at him narrowly, grinning in vindictive triumph still. Shaw said indifferently, "I don't see anything very special in that. All I can say is, I hope I don't come across him."

Bronsky gave a gust of coarse laughter. "I very much doubt if you will, poet! He will not be here long. Tonight a reception is being held in honour of the Minister at the Baku Hotel. Certainly Carew will be there, but I need hardly say that *you* will not be among the distinguished guests, poet. And now I have a good joke to tell you." Bronsky gave another great laugh and slapped his thigh. "You would like to hear it?"

"Go on."

"Very well, then. Do you know why Carew is coming—officially, that is? He comes to welcome your British admiral, who arrives tomorrow with his poor little fleet of impotent warships. Your admiral will have to receive Carew with full honours, as the welcoming representative of a host country. Is not that a fine joke, poet? That we should arrange for an Englishman to meet the British admiral?"

He roared with laughter again.

"Very funny indeed," Shaw said dryly. "A nicely calculated insult. Clever. But I think you've forgotten one thing, haven't you?"

"I do not think so, poet."

"Then I beg to differ, Major Bronsky. You see, the moment Lawrence Carew steps aboard a British ship, he's on British soil. He'll be arrested at once, taken back to England, and charged with treason."

Bronsky stared at him for a moment and then put his head back and laughed until tears ran down his cheeks. Shaw didn't like the implications of that helpless laughter at all, but Bronsky clammed up after that and he couldn't get any more out of him.

Ten minutes later, having discovered after threats and bad temper and cajolery that there was no alcohol in the flat, Bronsky lurched away angrily, presumably to carry out his duties in the town, and when the outer door had slammed behind him Triska came up to Shaw and said anxiously, "You must be very careful now, Peter. Igor is a dangerous man——"

"Yes, I know, so Godov told me, and he looks it too. But I don't think he'll bother me much, Triska."

She insisted, "You must not be too sure. When he is sober, which he will be sooner or later, he will realize what he has said to you, and remember—he is a good communist and a Party member. I am frightened, Peter."

"But why? He——"

"I told you! He will realize that you know too much."

"He hasn't told me all that much. And people often forget what they've said when they've been drinking."

She shook her head. "Not Igor. You must believe me. He

has a devil's memory for all he says, even when he is much more drunk than now."

"Well, maybe. But he won't shop me, if that's what's worrying you. He won't want to let out that he's opened his big mouth!"

"No, I agree entirely, he will not. Don't you see? What he will do is to kill you himself, Peter." She grasped the lapels of his jacket and looked into his face pleadingly. "I know Igor so well."

He said, "All right, Triska, I take your point. You may be right, but if you are he won't be the first person who's tried to kill me, and you can take it from me, he won't be the last either. I'm much more worried about Carew. You know who he is, of course?"

"Yes."

Shaw walked up and down the small room, like a frustrated tiger, then swung round sharply. "If Carew's on his way in, then we can't have long to go. That stands out a mile. The link's too obvious to be ignored—and they don't keep the brass hanging about. Besides, the Defence Minister's coming himself, and you told me he's the big shot. The Foreign Ministers' Conference doesn't break up for another three days, but whatever's going to happen . . . well, I'd say it's likely to happen any time after Carew gets to Moltsk, and pretty soon after at that." He paused, frowning. "Wait, though! We *may* be able to rely on having until our ships get in . . . they won't forgo their little joke, as Bronsky called it. They'll be looking forward to that like bloody kids. Also that might tie in with what the N.C.O. said down in the tunnel about completion by to-morrow. D'you know, I wouldn't be surprised if the thing's tied in some way with the arrival of our fleet—that the whole damn show's timed for the arrival itself!" He clenched his fists impotently. "God, Triska, if only I knew what it is they're going to do. . . ."

"I understand." She looked at him in a scared way, her face white and drawn. "Peter, what do we do now?"

"Just a moment." He ran a hand through his hair. "This is where you go to ground, I think—at least from to-night onwards . . . we don't want to start arousing suspicions too soon. I take it you'll be safe enough in your medical centre —I mean, Bronsky couldn't get at you there? I ask because he may try to get at me through you." He gave a tight smile. "You see, I am taking him seriously!"

She nodded. "I am glad, Peter. And I shall be perfectly all right at the centre, I assure you. I need not leave the building all day, and I will not have him admitted if he calls."

"Right, fine. Now listen. You leave at six, don't you? I'll meet you outside then——"

"What about you? What are you going to do?"

He said grimly, "Lie as low as I can—consistent with finding out as much as possible about Carew's movements after he gets to Moltsk. I'm going to get hold of Lawrence Carew and get this thing settled once and for all. Once I know what's really going on in the tunnel, there's just a chance I may be able to do something about it and anyway if Carew disappears, my guess is there'll be such a God Almighty flap they'll have to postpone their plans if not cancel them. And I may need your help, Triska."

They left the flat soon after and he saw Triska off to work in her car; then he walked quickly through to the Nikolai Hotel and went straight up to his room.

He locked the door and took out the Luger. He checked the slide. Full. Things were hotting right up now and he would be needing that gun very soon. And if it did so happen that Bronsky came for him, then the Russian would stop a bullet. Triska's cousin or not, it was far too late in the day to let a sneering drunk like Bronsky ball-up his plans.

EIGHTEEEN

Shaw left the Nikolai at ten-thirty and strolled out into bright sunshine, sunshine which glittered on soldier's weapons and on the metalwork of tanks and armoured vehicles and personnel-carriers. There were some big guns on the move also and he saw some missile-carriers going out of the town towards the north. He began to have fears for the safety of the fleet when it approached Moltsk, dropping south through the Barents Sea . . . until he remembered again the little joke over Carew. If they had anything in store for the British ships, they would hold it until afterwards.

He went on along Nikolai Street, turned to the left at the end past an ominous-looking tank waiting with its gun pointing down to cover the whole thoroughfare, and fifteen minutes later he walked into M.V.D. headquarters, as bold as brass. He was far from easy underneath, though he knew he had a first-class hand to play.

He demanded to see the officer-in-charge, and when, after considerable and nerve-racking delay, he was taken into an office, he found that he was confronting the same plain-clothes man as had impounded his passport—the man he called Snake's-head.

Rogovin recognized him and seemed surprised to see him. He said, "Well, Mr Alison. To ask for your passport yet is quite useless."

Shaw shook his head. "I don't want my passport, Colonel. I'm quite happy in Russia. My trouble's a different one."

"So?"

Shaw had assumed an expression of puzzlement. He said, "Well, it's most extraordinary, but I've lost my invitation card. I really can't think what can have happened to it . . . unless those troopers of yours pinched it—took it by mistake, I mean—when they came for me the other night."

Snake's-head looked at him with cold hostility. "My men are most careful, Mr Alison. What kind of invitation was this?"

"Why, to the reception at the Baku Hotel to-night, of course——"

Snake's-head pounced, looking triumphant. "How do you know about that?"

Shaw said, "Why, because I was invited! I wouldn't have heard about it otherwise, I dare say. You see, my Moscow office was given advance notice that Dr Carew was visiting the port and they were given the invitation, which they passed on to me and asked me particularly to make use of it." Shaw drew now on his memories of Carew as reported in the Press at the time of his disappearance. "I expect you know that Dr Carew's university training was paid for by my organization—he was a steelworker's son, elementary education, no money—only brains. So naturally we take a very great personal interest in him. It's most annoying to have lost the invitation, Colonel. I was hoping to meet Carew myself, you see."

"*You* hoped to meet him—you, an Englishman?"

"Yes. I've told you why." Shaw shrugged. "Oh, I know what you're thinking, Comrade, but then you don't quite understand." Shaw brought out a W.I.O.C.A. handout that Chaffinch had given him in Moscow and flourished it at Snake's-head, who looked bored and irritable. "My organization doesn't let things like that upset it. Culture is international, after all. It transcends all barriers of class, race, and colour. We of W.I.O.C.A. are dedicated, you understand—

I'll leave you this pamphlet—to the wonderful cause of pro-
moting peace and goodwill and understanding throughout
all the nations of the world—spreading culture everywhere,
whatever men's political beliefs and so on may be. We of
W.I.O.C.A. . . ."

Shaw kept it up for some time, improvising with confidence, watching the glazed look in the policeman's eyes.
At last Rogovin could take no more of it and he broke in
angrily, "Yes, yes, yes—I understand perfectly. I am a very
busy man but I will see if by some mischance your invitation was taken the other night."

Irritably he slammed his fist on his bell-push.

The policemen concerned were sent for and hectored long
and loud but with no result. They had seen, they swore it, no
card; they had touched nothing, in obedience to the specific
order of the Soviet as to personal freedom and the in-
violability of private property. Shaw's passport was brought
out in case the card should have been slipped into it. It was
flicked through page by page, and then flicked over again.
Even Shaw himself was allowed to give it a third going over.

But there was no card.

Snake's-head, tired of the whole business by now and
weaving his neck angrily, snapped, "I am sorry. But—there
is no card!" He threw up his hands.

"Well, yes, so I see." Shaw sighed. "It's most unfortunate.
My Council believes in——"

"Yes, yes, *yes*——"

"Er . . . I was wondering, Colonel, if perhaps you could
issue me with a pass of some kind?"

"No."

"Oh, dear." Shaw clicked his tongue. "My Council isn't
going to like this. I'll be in trouble." He gnawed at his lip.
"Are you certain there isn't some way of giving me a pass?
I mean, you know who I am, don't you? You've got my
passport."

Snake's-head rapped his fingers on his desk. "Mr Alison,
you are a nuisance. You are taking up too much of my time
with this frivolity. Certainly I, Colonel Rogovin, have the
power to issue you with a pass if I am satisfied, perfectly
satisfied, as to your bona fides and that you had an invitation in the first place, but I refuse absolutely to do this without authority from your own office in Moscow. And," he
added triumphantly, "since all communication with Moscow
is temporarily suspended, even the telephone, I do not see

how you can obtain such assurances for me! Please, will you go away?"

"Just a moment. Your telephone—the official police-line? Is that cut too?"

"No, it is not!" Rogovin glowered at him. "No telephones are *cut*, the service outside the area of Moltsk is merely suspended until further notice. This naturally does not apply to any official lines, but——"

"Well then," Shaw said happily. "I'll give you the number. I'd really be awfully obliged."

Rogovin clenched his fists in despair. "You will leave me alone thereafter, Mr Alison, if I agree to this as a special concession?"

"Yes, of course I will. I'm sorry to be such a bother."

Rogovin reached out for his telephone and asked for the line to Moscow. Shaw didn't know how he got through the next half-hour; he was sent outside while the connexion was being made and Rogovin turned his attention to other matters meanwhile. Chaffinch had looked an intelligent kind of man, but this thing was certainly being sprung on him without notice. He hoped, too, that Chaffinch, if he was going to back him, would be able to square his own yard-arm through the Embassy afterwards.

Shaw was brought in again when the call came through and he realized that bluff had paid off. From Snake's-head's nods and grunts he could see that Chaffinch was backing him to the hilt. At the end of that conversation the M.V.D. man banged down the receiver and reached into a drawer. He pulled out a pad of official forms and scrawled on the top one. In dead silence he signed it and rubber-stamped it. Still in silence he detached it and held it out to Shaw.

"Thank you so much," Shaw said.

After Shaw left his office, Colonel Rogovin pressed his bell again and a uniformed man came in.

Rogovin said wearily, "There is more work for you and me, Bulyin, in connexion with the Minister's reception. There is a fool of an Englishman who has lost his invitation. Because he is a high official of W.I.O.C.A. and has some contact with Comrade Doctor Carew, I have issued him with a pass signed by myself—but now, my poor Bulyin, you must redouble your precautions. Who knows who may have found that lunatic's original invitation? Why, the only person we can now be sure of is the Englishman himself. . . ."

NINETEEN

"You have not seen Bronsky?" Triska, fresh and desirable in a neat suit, looked up anxiously into his face when he met her as arranged outside the medical research centre.

He said, "Not a sign of him all day. Now look, Triska. I'm going to hook Carew at the reception. I don't expect a great deal of trouble for one reason and another. I want you to wait in the car, clear of the Baku Hotel—park somewhere quiet along the northern end of the street, ready to get away as soon as we're in. Give me until . . . let's say nine o'clock. If I haven't turned up then, drive out to Godov's house and lie up there till I get word through to you or come myself. All right?"

"Yes, Peter."

"And you'd better have this again." He handed her the pocket transceiver. "I'll want to use it later on but I'd rather not risk having it found if they decide to frisk the guests."

An hour later he took a car to the Baku Hotel, a tall, ultra-modern, hideous building near the outskirts of the town.

He got out on a broad concrete sweep in front of the hotel, one of scores of guests arriving for the reception. He walked up the steps to the doorway into the foyer, where half a dozen uniformed M.V.D. men were checking the invitations and every now and again frisking someone; having anticipated this Shaw had the Luger strapped to the inside of his right leg. As it happened, however, Snake's-head himself was there when Shaw came in and he gave Shaw one look and said something to one of the troopers. They didn't bother with him after that.

It was a brilliant scene, reminiscent of the one in that London Embassy so short a time ago. At the head of a great staircase the Minister himself stood, fat and squat and ugly, to welcome the guests. He was flanked by bowing, smiling local V.I.P.'s and a strong-arm squad of guards with their right hands in their coat pockets. Behind him, and also greeting the guests but looking as though he wanted more than anything else to keep out of the limelight, was a pale, short man with thick glasses, blinking nervously. He was a good deal older than his Press photographs, but of course that had been thirteen years ago; however, even though he was nearly bald now and was sallow and wasted-looking, Shaw recognized Lawrence Carew right away.

Shaw filed past in the queue and shook the Minister's hand. The Russian smiled affably and nodded, and then Shaw was welcomed by Carew. When Shaw was announced as an official of W.I.O.C.A. Carew's bulbous eyes looked at him keenly, as though gauging, and gauging with cynical amusement, the reaction of a fellow-countryman to a traitor. Then Shaw was swept on by the pressure of the men and women behind him and Carew was busy with a portly, fawning Russian and his wife. Turning into a large room at the top of the stairs, Shaw spotted Colonel Rogovin again and made a point of pushing through the crowd to have a word with him.

He said, "Good evening, Colonel. I'm awfully grateful to you for that pass, you know. Most obliging of you."

"It is nothing, Mr Alison. I hope you will enjoy yourself."

"Oh, I will. I must have a word with Carew . . . thank you again."

Rogovin escaped with obvious relief and Shaw drifted on, found a waiter with a tray of drinks. Circulating as best he could in the crush, he found himself near a group of Englishmen, business executives and salesmen from their conversation, talking together in a corner. He heard the name Carew mentioned after a while, contemptuously, and a few references came up as to the way their passports had been impounded so arbitrarily. Then they began discussing the implications of what appeared to be going on in Moscow and what effect it was going to have on the Five Powers' talks and the prospect of a summit conference. Idly Shaw listened for a while in the hope of picking up something that he might have missed, but there wasn't anything and he moved on. It was at least a comfort to know that he wasn't the only Englishman present; if he had been, then the M.V.D. might well have taken more interest in him.

He drank sparingly, keeping a half-full glass in his hand and refusing all the blandishments of waiters and the Russians to whom, for the sake of appearances, he talked now and again.

He was waiting his time now. He felt keyed-up, tense in his stomach. He knew he had to wait until the reception was nearly over. After forty-five minutes he went off to the cloakroom, where he shifted the Luger to his pocket.

The chance came when the Minister himself was on the point of leaving and Carew had lingered for a word with a couple of the guests. Carew, Shaw had noticed, hadn't been much of an attraction in spite of his reputation as a backroom boy. It could be that few people knew about him simply because he was a backroom boy, or again it could be something in his own personality, which seemed to Shaw to be meagre and unattractive.

Shaw went over to him slowly, casually, drifted up behind him as the other two went off. He said, "Dr Carew."

Carew jumped and swung round, his eyes large and protruding behind the heavy spectacles. He said, "Oh. You surprised me." He gave a nervous titter. "Why—it's the W.I.O.C.A. man. Do I know you?"

"I doubt it." Shaw kept his voice low as he became aware of a thickset man watching from a corner, a man who could be Carew's bodyguard. "I'm not all that anxious to make your acquaintance anyhow, Carew, but it so happens I want a word in your ear." He put his right hand in his coat pocket. "Don't start looking for your pals, Carew, if you've got any. I've got a gun in my pocket and it's lined up on your stomach and if you take so much as a deep breath I'll spill your lunch on the floor. Right?"

Carew licked his lips, his face grey. He said, "I—I don't understand. I don't know you. What do you want?"

"I'll tell you that later. Listen, I don't want to start anything unless you force me to, but just bear in mind that my life isn't all that important—and I've got just a hunch, Carew, that if I kill you somebody's plans are going to get mighty bitched up for a while. I'm willing to give my own life for that. So don't make the mistake of thinking I'm bluffing. I'm not. Now—just relax." His eyes hardened. "Go on, Carew, or I'll really get dangerous."

"I—I can't relax just——"

"Try. Or I'll kill you. If anybody gets suspicious, you've had it, Carew. Just look as if you're enjoying an interesting conversation . . . ah, that's better!" he said encouragingly. "Hold it that way. Now pull out your handkerchief and get rid of those beads of sweat on your forehead. It's not all that hot in here."

Carew did as he was told, his hand shaking badly.

Shaw asked, "When are you leaving here?"

"In—in two or three minutes——"

"What are your plans for this evening?"

"Nothing. I—I'm staying in the hotel, you know. I . . . they're going to send my dinner up to my room."

"Well, I'm sorry, but your plans have changed, Carew. You're coming with me. Now, I happen to know that you got your start in life on a W.I.O.C.A. scholarship. I won't go into details, but I've already established that link with you so far as the M.V.D. is concerned and there won't be any trouble whatever unless you make it yourself. If you do— you know what will happen. So now you'll just tell that tame bodyguard of yours that you're coming with me and on your way out you'll chat to me about how grateful you are to my people for putting you on the road to the stars. If anyone else talks to you, keep up the same line but get rid of 'em as quickly as you can. Get it? I'll be right behind you all the time—and I speak fluent Russian, by the way."

Carew's eyes stared, glassily.

"And take that scared look off your face! When you've done that, start walking to the staircase and speak to your guard on the way. If you don't want to be ripped up the backbone, don't take chances. You'll be dead long before anyone can grab me."

Carew went across the room towards the tame gunman, with Shaw close behind. The scientist spoke to the bodyguard, who nodded obsequiously and then accompanied Shaw and Carew down the stairs. As they reached the bottom and headed for the exit, Shaw glanced at the M.V.D. who were still on the doorway, saw that they were not taking much notice of the departing guests. But he nudged Carew's back with the muzzle of the Luger and Carew, taking the hint, began talking in a high-pitched voice, mouthing platitudes for all he was worth and doing his level best to avoid the sudden rip of metal in his back that would end his life. They went on down the steps and at the bottom Shaw came up alongside Carew and propelled him along to the end of the line of official cars and beyond them out into the road, still accompanied by the bodyguard.

Looking ahead he saw Triska's car parked in the shadows.

Something had made the Russian gunman suspicious just as they came up to the little car.

Shaw heard the man's warning shout to Carew and saw him bring out a gun. Quickly he lifted his hand and reversed the Luger, brought it down with a cutting movement, hard across the curve of the Russian's neck, and then he caught him as he fell. Triska had already pushed open the front

141

near-side door and Shaw heaved the body in, motioning Carew to follow into the back. No one had seen a thing.

After that it went off perfectly.

Within half a minute of reaching the car Triska was driving along the northern road for Godov's house, while Shaw sat in the back with Lawrence Carew. The unconscious bodyguard was slumped in the front seat alongside Triska; and Shaw, who had removed the man's gun, was on the alert for trouble as soon as he came round. The Luger was held right into Carew's side, and the scientist was looking deathly white and frightened.

As they cleared the town's outskirts Shaw asked, "What about Bronsky, Triska? Still no trouble?"

"No, I have not seen him, Peter."

"I dare say he's genuinely forgotten about the whole thing after all."

Triska didn't answer and Shaw turned his attention to Carew. He said harshly, "Now, Carew. You're going to talk and you're going to talk fast and fully. You're going to talk about that tower in the sea, and the tunnel leading off it. I've been down there myself, so there's no point in holding anything back now. In fact, Carew, you're going to tell me the whole story behind what's building up in Moltsk and what your people intend to do. If you don't talk, you're a dead man. I can soon lose a body in the marsh out there." He nodded out at the bleak swamp to the left of the road. "On the other hand, if you help me, I'll promise to do my best to get you out of the country so that your current bosses won't liquidate you when I've done with you."

"You couldn't get me out and you know it." Carew's voice was still high but somehow he gave Shaw the impression of being less scared now, of having command of himself again. "Besides, I don't want to go back to England, if that's what you mean."

"It's what I mean all right, but would you just like to tell me *why* you don't want to go back, Carew?" When Carew didn't reply, he asked, "Is it because you're scared to face your own countrymen—or because you don't want to walk into a nuclear attack of some kind? Because you can set your mind at rest about that. I'm here to stop it taking place—and as soon as you've told me all I want to know, that's what I'll be doing. Now. . . ." He jabbed the Luger savagely into the man's body and Carew gave a grunt of pain. "Come on. I haven't got all night. I might shoot in . . . let's say the next thirty seconds."

Carew turned his head and looked into Shaw's eyes. He flinched at what he saw there; and then he muttered, "It won't make the slightest difference now, anyway. You're too late. Much too late."

"I'll risk it, thanks. Just start and I'll form my own conclusions. If it won't make any difference, you won't lose anything by talking, will you. . . ."

Carew gave a sudden cynical laugh and said, "How right you are." He began talking soon after that and once he'd started he showed all the confidence, the convinced confidence of the Party fanatic. He clearly had no fears that anything could possibly go wrong now. He said, "I expect you've heard of Kazenadze."

"No."

Carew said, "He's a geologist. A big man—the biggest, as a matter of fact, world famous. He's got all the Western experts licked into a cocked hat and his papers are studied in universities all over the world——"

"Cut the blurb," Shaw snapped, "and give me a summary."

"Oh—very well." The car rushed on, touching sixty-five and expertly handled by Triska. "Kazenadze was concerned with the drillings for oil off the Peninsula. There'd been a report, you see, that there was an oil-bearing stratum below the sea-bed, but it turned out to be a false hope. Kazenadze hadn't been called in at the start, he was rather too big a man for that, but when they found they hadn't any oil to speak of, they got him along to carry out a fresh and much fuller geological survey. Well—as a result of that, he found a natural tunnel, a kind of fissure, a flaw if you like, in one of the strata of the earth's crust, fairly deep down or comparatively so——"

"That's the tunnel I mentioned just now, the one I was in?"

Carew nodded. "Yes. Well, there wasn't any more oil anyway, so it was decided to abandon the project. The workings remained unused for quite a while and then the authorities thought they should make some use of Kazenadze's fissure, since it was there waiting. Seeing how deep it is, they approved a scheme to use it as one of a series of deep stores for nuclear devices, ballistic missiles, and so on——"

"Yes, I know about that. Do I take it that as far as the legitimate government in Moscow is concerned, it's still in use as a store—and that all that part of it was quite genuine?"

Carew nodded again. "Yes, that's entirely so. Well now—the first thing they did after that was to build that tower over the spot where, according to Kazenadze, the fissure starts, which as it happens was near where they did the first oil-drillings. That end of the fissure was blocked off solid by rock—the tower itself is bedded in rock. For various technical reasons it was more practical to have the store entrance there, rather than bore down to the fissure on land—for one thing, a cylinder had already been sunk and it was largely a question of extending it. The air-shafts were sunk later on. Well, the fissure was used secretly as a store for quite a time and then not so long ago Kazenadze, who apparently had been carrying out large-scale geological researches on the fissure in the meantime, came up with a brand-new theory, a startling theory altogether—and he got in touch with certain people in Moscow who asked him to keep his ideas to himself until a more propitious time."

Carew paused and Shaw said, "Well—go on. What was this theory?"

"I'm coming to that." Carew smiled faintly; he showed no trace of embarrassment for what must have been his own part in the plan. "Kazenadze had a theory that the fissure went quite a long way through the earth, and he plotted its course right across the Kola Peninsula and then across Finland, and found that it continued roughly in a south-westerly direction. From there on, of course, he couldn't get any more readings himself, and he had to accept a long delay. But eventually, with the help of teams of agents working in the West, who were themselves helped by fellow-travellers and so on—I was able to put him in touch with some of them myself, as a matter of fact—he plotted the course of the fissure as closely as possible from on-the-spot checks and readings . . . right along Scandinavia and the North Sea to England, where it runs from north to south fairly close to the surface until it blocks off somewhere below Winchester." Carew paused, his spectacles gleaming at Shaw. "So there's your fissure: Moltsk in North Russia to Winchester in Hampshire and running, as it happens, pretty well down the length of Britain. Much of the ground below which it runs has been excavated by coal mining, which means an even thinner ceiling in places. Now, as to Kazenadze's actual plan, which is based on this theory . . . I've told you he went to certain people in Moscow, including the Minister of Defence and my own Minister, rather than to the Council of Ministers as a body—he did this because he knew the State as such would never back him, and in this he was quite right——"

"So he had to get his pals to arrange a *coup d'état*?"

"In a sense, yes. I prefer to call it pressure, rather than a *coup d'état*. You see——"

"Don't bother." Shaw kept all emotion out of his voice. "Let's have the plan itself, Carew."

Carew smiled. "Oh, but surely you've guessed, haven't you?"

"Perhaps." Shaw felt nausea, disgust. Carew's very matter-of-factness had pointed up the horror of what he now had to suspect. "I'm getting there, but let's have it in full, then I'll be sure, won't I?"

"Very well." Carew shrugged. "That fissure has been well and truly crammed in the last few days. Crammed to capacity with nuclear devices of various types. As a matter of fact, Alison, by the time the stowing operations are completed tomorrow afternoon it will have been packed with nuclear material to the extent of well over two thousand million tons T.N.T. equivalent. *Two thousand million tons*. All the sections will have been fully prepared for nuclear detonation and the whole lot will be fired by an electrical impulse from a control-room in the tower. By this time, of course, the Moltsk end will have been very heavily sealed off, so you see the explosion will take place behind locked doors as it were, in a very confined space—confined, I should say, until it spreads along the fissure, which in fact it will do very quickly. This area will not be damaged at all. Data from the recent series of tests, underground tests on Novaya Zemlya, with bigger and bigger bombs being exploded, helped to determine the load the fissure would carry without erupting this end. The released forces will simply seek the line of least resistance and travel along that natural cavity in the earth's crust until they reach that point in Hampshire——"

"By which time they'll be well and truly spent! Look at the length of the fissure!"

Carew smiled. "Wishful thinking, Alison! There are other forces . . . I'll come back to that in a moment. Now, the explosion is expected to deviate a little en route, through various side-fissures, and cause some nuclear upheavals in the Scandinavian countries. But the main effect will still be felt in Britain." There was no shame in Carew even though he was speaking to a fellow-countryman. Shaw realized that in his heart the man must always have been a convinced communist, must have been indoctrinated years ago, even probably in his student days. "There, at Winchester, the various forces will hit against the end of the fissure and

145

recoil back along that thin-ceilinged north-south line—and split England like a sausage in a frying-pan!"

Shaw scoffed. "Sheer exaggeration. As I said, the forces'll be spent. The blast from a hydrogen explosion isn't all that terrific . . . nothing like what people imagine, anyway. It's more a question of fallout—and that'll be trapped underground."

"I dare say you like to think so." Carew shrugged, full of confidence. "You're underestimating H-bomb blast. I agree that an H-bomb dropped on the surface is more dangerous, in the wider sense, from the point of view of fallout than an explosion erupting from beneath the earth's surface, but an underground explosion of the kind and size we've planned is a different thing from anything that's ever happened before—and it'll be very devastating when it's channelled towards a thin earth-ceiling. And remember this as well: two thousand million tons of T.N.T. equivalent is approximately equal to one thousand times the explosive force of all the bombs dropped on Germany and the occupied countries during the whole of the last war. Put it another way: all the conventional bombs that could be dropped in a war lasting *six thousand years* will go off in that fissure tomorrow afternoon. That lot has to come out somewhere, and, as I said, most of it will hit England. Now, take the places along that north-south fissure . . . Winchester itself, Oxford, Birmingham, Manchester, Glasgow, and many more. They'll simply vanish in a nuclear earthquake, an earthquake which according to Kazenadze will spread to east and west of the line of fracture——"

"Did you say . . . an earthquake?"

Carew nodded. "I did. That's something England hasn't had before, isn't it? There's another thing, too. According to Kazenadze—and this was what I meant when I mentioned 'other forces' just a while back—according to him the fissure dips sharply en route before it rises again towards the British Isles. Taking the curvature of the earth into account as well, it dips far enough to bring it fairly close to certain thin-skinned strata not so far from the earth's centre . . . do you see what I'm getting at?"

Shaw's face was grey. "Volcanic forces. . . ."

"Yes, that's right," Carew said. "It's perfectly possible, and indeed probable, that the explosion will mix with so-far-dormant natural forces, volcanic forces as you say, also gases and other turbulences. These forces, once released, will in effect push the fallout before them so that it is funnelled up

146

over the British Isles. You can imagine the result. A nuclear-volcanic eruption, a nuclear earthquake of phenomenal proportions, won't be easily dealt with, Alison. Your nuclear stockpiles, your missile-sites, your airfields and power-stations —they'll almost all be destroyed along with a good deal else . . . factories, ports, water-reservoirs, roads, and communications . . . need I go on? The Continent is sure to get some of the fallout——"

"So will Russia, ultimately."

Carew shrugged. "We accept the risk. It will be heavily diluted by the time it reaches here, and we've made great strides in protecting our people from the effects of fallout. There are deep shelters, with stored food—pre-cooked and packed and deep-frozen. It's all on an enormous scale. There's even underground reservoirs for drinking water. We've also made some really big advances on the medical side, the treatment of people affected by fallout——"

Shaw called, "Is that right, Triska?"

She nodded as she stared out ahead at the road leaping up into the headlights. "Yes, Peter, we have made progress."

"I see. Go on, Carew."

Carew said, "I think I've given you the whole picture. This explosion'll be touched off while I myself am welcoming the Admiral aboard those ships of yours. It's all quite foolproof —they don't even need me to carry out the firing. All the work has been done and the actual firing procedure is . . . well, lengthy for reasons of safety checks, but really *very* easy. I'm nothing but window-dressing at this stage, though of course the whole thing has been carried out under my personal direction. So, you see, no one's going to get in that panic you talked of, when they find I'm missing. At least, not enough to make them postpone any plans." He smiled. "You've miscalculated, Alison. If it were possible, they would even advance the plans now!"

Shaw said savagely, "I rather think not! You're forgetting it's all supposed to look like an accident. I'm shortly going to call up our Embassy and get a message through to London. Once that goes out the whole world's going to know about this. I doubt if even your extremist friends are mad enough to go ahead after that happens!"

Carew laughed. "My dear Alison . . . aren't you being a little naïve? You'll never get word through to London now —the Embassy will have been forced off the air already. I don't know, but I expect our people have put guards on all their transmitters, or at least put them out of action for the

147

time being, until the new Government is firmly established. No, no—it'll still look like an accident. An accident of fate, something which we couldn't possibly have controlled or foreseen, an upsurge of natural forces suddenly released, in which our own delegation to the London Conference will suffer with the rest. The only possible accusation that can be brought against us is that we triggered something off unintentionally by underground tests on Novaya Zemlya, and even that's stretching it a bit. Why, even the control-room in the tower will be dismantled within an hour after it's gone into action! It's absolutely self-contained inside the tower, and it was rather hastily rushed together anyway, because we had to bear in mind that the Kremlin wasn't to know what was going on, and we didn't want to give them any ideas. It'll be easy to take apart, and when that goes, so does all the evidence." Suddenly Carew laughed. "Why, even your admiral—old Carleton—will see for himself that we weren't up to anything nasty!"

Shaw had very nearly squeezed the trigger of the Luger; the only reason he hadn't done so was because he thought it too easy a way out for Lawrence Carew. Better, perhaps, to leave him to his Russian masters. They would cut him down to size one day, as they did all their leading lights sooner or later, and that way Carew would taste more bitterness, more gall when he came to think, in the years ahead, about what he had done for Russia. Even a man like Carew might one day discover a conscience. As to England, Shaw could frankly find no hope whatever now. Even if Whitehall should decide, on the strength of his own earlier reports, to blow up the tower with either a bomber force or missiles they might achieve nothing except to save the Russians the trouble of firing the fissure.

England could be in danger of eruption just the same.

Suddenly Carew asked, "What are you going to do with me, Alison?"

"That remains to be seen. Can you think of any reason why I shouldn't kill you here and now, Carew?" His feelings were getting the better of him. He lifted the Luger, feeling again the urgent desire to kill this man. "Can you?"

Carew huddled himself back in the corner of the car and gave a faint hiss of breath, but he said evenly, "Frankly, I suppose not. But you won't shoot me, Alison—not now, not for no real reason. You're . . . too damn British for that. You'll have to let me go—after tomorrow. There'll be the biggest manhunt you ever saw. But if you treat me decently until then, I'll put in a word. After all, you've only been doing your duty, haven't you? They're bound to see that, and if you haven't harmed me, well . . . you see what I mean?"

Shaw was about to give some short answer when he saw the sudden movement of the bodyguard in the front seat. The man had probably regained consciousness some time earlier and had been listening . . . his shoulder was moving, the arm coming up stealthily, and then, as Shaw was about to dive forward and yell a warning to Triska, the man's hand grabbed for the wheel. In the same split second Shaw fired. The car gave a leap as Triska's hands jerked on the wheel, and then resumed its course. The bodyguard slumped without a cry, blood gushing from his neck.

Shaw asked, "Dead?"

Without slackening speed, Triska glanced sideways, looked at the body in the light from the dash. She said, "I don't think there's any doubt, Peter."

Shaw swivelled savagely round on Carew. "Too damn British, am I?" he said. "If I were you, I wouldn't try my luck too far!"

After that they drove on in silence, each busy with his own private thoughts. They flashed by the little village of Emets and turned up for Godov's house, saw lights in the distance. Then as they approached the metalled driveway through the swamp, Triska gasped and said, "Peter, every light in the house is on!"

"So I see. I don't like the look of that."

She accelerated up the drive and then pulled up with a scrape of tyres and jumped out. Shaw yelled at the girl to be careful but she took no notice and ran ahead for the front door. With Carew ahead of him and the Luger ready for action, Shaw followed Triska into the house and he was half-way down the passage to the old man's study when Triska came out, white and shaken.

She said, her eyes wide and frightened, "Peter, he's dead! He's been shot through the heart."

"Godov?"

She was crying now. "Yes."

He went up to her quickly and put a hand under her arm. He said, "Easy, Triska dear. You're sure he's dead?"

"Quite sure. . . ."

He went forward with her, pushing Carew ahead of him. In the study he found the old man lying face downward on the floor, half across a smashed chair. Bending, he felt for the heart, looked at the white head dappled with blood from the pool in which he was lying. He got to his feet again and said, "Bronsky. I'd bet my last cent it was Bronsky."

She said, "Yes, I think it could have been. But, Peter— the house . . . it is so silent. Where are the others—Anna and Josef?"

"I don't know, Triska, but I'm going to find out." He took the Russian bodyguard's gun from his pocket and handed it to her. He said, "It's loaded. Keep an eye on Carew and use this if you have to. I'm going for a look around."

TWENTY

"Bronsky . . . are you there, Bronsky?"

There was no reply and Shaw ran along the passage, stopping for a moment at the end to look carefully round the angle of the wall. It was all quiet; he turned to his left through the hall and went down another passage which seemed to lead to the kitchen. He jerked the kitchen door open and stood back with his gun ready, but nothing happened. Gingerly he edged forward. The cupboards, big deep cupboards where a man could have hidden very easily, had their doors hanging open and their contents scattered wholesale by someone in a hurry to find something or somebody. Then he saw the bodies, in the horrible attitudes of sudden and shocking death. Anna, the old housekeeper, slumped across a big basketwork chair; Josef—he assumed it was Josef anyway—face down on the floor in a pool of blood with one arm outstretched as though he had been mown down while trying to reach towards the door-handle. A bloody line of blackened holes ran right round the old fellow's back, and this, together with the fact that the big window behind him was shattered, seemed to indicate that the killer had fired a raking burst from outside and then, most likely, come in through the window to find Godov once the servants were out of the way.

This bore all the marks of a man of Bronsky's type.

Sick at heart Shaw turned away. If only old Josef had had his Luger . . . but even with it, he would never have stopped Major Igor Bronsky. Bronsky had probably been to the flat in Moltsk and found it empty, and had come here looking for Triska. Shaw left the kitchen and made for the hall and the staircase, intending to take a look round the bedrooms. Then, just as he put a foot on the bottom stair, he heard the faint sound behind him, turned in a flash and saw the Russian uniform. Bronsky had an air-cooled automatic in his arms and his eyes were slits in the white face. There was a roar and a spurt of flame and Shaw flung himself sideways, came down heavily on his right side, firing as he did so. Bullets zipped into the woodwork of the staircase, there was a stink of gunsmoke, and Shaw fired a second burst from the Luger. There was a scream and then Major Igor Bronsky was tearing at his throat and blood was gushing. A moment later the Russian crashed heavily, choking in his own blood and gurgling, and then he lay with legs and arms twitching slightly as his life drained out of him.

Shaw got to his feet and crossed the hall.

As he did so he felt a sharp pain in his side and a warm, sticky patch. Cursing, he put his hand in his pocket and it came away patched with blood; but he wasn't much worried about that. What was really serious was the fact that his heavy fall had smashed up his transceiver—he'd taken it back from Triska earlier—and now there was absolutely no way of sending any warning through to the Embassy. Possibly they couldn't have got his message passed to London, possibly they could; what was certain was that now he couldn't receive any signals at all.

He swore savagely.

As he looked up he saw Triska's white, scared face at the end of the passage. He gestured her back and then walked along and followed her through to Godov's study. He saw that her eyes were red with crying, but she seemed to be in control of the situation and she had Carew, who was sitting hunched in the chair in which Shaw had sat when he had first seen the old professor, covered with the gun which he had given her. Godov's body was still on the ground but Triska had now covered it with a rug.

She asked, "That was Igor, Peter?"

He nodded and said briefly, "Yes. I'm sorry, Triska. It was him or me."

"It doesn't matter. He was nothing to me, that Igor. And he had killed . . ." She stopped suddenly and looked at him hard, then she went on steadily, "Peter, there is something I must tell you now. I think perhaps it no longer matters. It is this. Professor Godov was my grandfather."

He stared at her. "Your grandfather?"

She nodded. "My paternal grandfather, Peter. Somalin was

my mother's name. My parents were . . . not married, you understand? My father let my mother down badly—he disappeared across the frontier before I was born, but . . . grandfather made amends for him, for his son. Grandfather did not want the relationship to be known, not because of what his son had done, but because he was afraid the blood relationship to a man with his record in the Party would be bad for me if it was known to everybody. Yet we were very close, Peter . . . so very close."

Shaw nodded. He felt that this explained quite a lot—for instance, why the two of them shared so many views despite the great difference in their ages, why Godov had been so keen for Shaw to contact the girl—he might even have wanted her to be taken out of the country? He said, "Triska, I'm terribly sorry. I feel it's so much my fault—all this."

She shook her head firmly. "Do not think like that. He is better off now, and he wanted so much to help, I know that. He was an old man, to be living in a world of which he so much disapproved, and now, if he has gone where he always believed he would go, he will know how much he has helped. We will not talk about it any more now, Peter."

"Just as you like, my dear." He put a hand on her shoulder. "In any case, we've got to move now, and fast."

"Where to?"

He said grimly, "North! Up the Kola Peninsula. I'm assuming you'll come with us—out of Russia, I mean? Because that's where we're heading, Triska."

"Yes," she said at once. "Of course I will come. There is nothing to keep me here now, but how do you——"

"Good girl!" He glanced across at Carew. "Now, this is what I'm going to do—I got the idea when Carew here mentioned the British ships." He saw the sudden flicker, the wariness in the scientist's eyes. "Those ships are due to go alongside the outer mole in Moltsk dockyard at 2 P.M. tomorrow. Let's give them a maximum speed of, say, twenty knots . . . it certainly won't be more, because they've got an old heavy cruiser with them, a pre-war job used as a training-ship, and she's heavy on oil fuel at high speeds. Right. . . ." He frowned in concentration, calculating quickly in his head. "They'll be . . . somewhere off Vadsö now, I'd say. And that ought to give us plenty of time."

"Time for what, Peter?"

He said, "Time to go to sea and board one of them!"

"But how?" She wrinkled her brows, astonished.

"Listen, Triska," he said. "It shouldn't be too difficult.

152

We'll head up north from here and take the coast road till we're well beyond the military area—a long way beyond. Somewhere up the coast we're bound to hit a fishing-village, or some kind of community anyway, on one of the fiords. It'll be pretty primitive to say the least of it and it shouldn't be too difficult to grab a boat——"

"But there will be a chase now, surely—they will know Carew has disappeared?"

He said grimly, "I expect so, Triska, and that's all the more reason to get on the move—fast! We can't do any good here now, that's certain, and they may have rumbled me by now. So—we pinch a boat and go to sea—I'll head out across the route our ships'll be taking, and we'll make contact with them at sea and go aboard. The farther north we can get, the sooner we'll reach them."

"Suppose you miss them? There's a chance of that?"

"My dear, there certainly is a chance of that—but it's not going to happen to us. I know that route—I was at sea myself, and I did an Archangel run during the war. You'll be in good hands." He remembered Latymer had advised him against trying to board the ships, but that had been when the fleet was going to Leningrad. It was more in the world down there. He added, "It's the only thing to do, Triska. My radio's had it and I've got to get word through to London and tell them what's going to happen. I can do that direct from any of the ships——"

"What for?" Carew broke in. "What's the point of that?"

Shaw said harshly, "Plenty of point, Carew! It's no good looking scared. You're going to face that trip and like it."

"But really . . . all London can do is to send in a force to destroy the tower, and you must realize that if a bomb goes down there, there's at least a chance it'll set off an explosion at once, never mind the correct procedure for detonating nuclear material——"

"Oh, yes? That's exactly what I had in mind myself earlier, I admit—but like you, I was forgetting that lead-and-concrete door, the one that seals off the fissure. I've been down there, remember? I've seen it, Carew! Bombs won't penetrate that, but they'll do away with the firing circuits from the control-room——"

"Yes, but the door won't be shut till the last moment!" Carew was clearly terrified of that sea trip. "Nothing will be sealed off until we're ready to fire."

"Why's that?"

"Several reasons. For one thing, the stowing will be going

on throughout the night and tomorrow morning, and it follows that the final procedures and the completing of the circuit can't be done till the job's finished. That doesn't in fact give us very long before your ships are due alongside. Because of the need for secrecy, it's had to be a very tight schedule. Also——"

"Save it! " Shaw snapped. "'Don't you see that if you're right and the tower goes up *with the door open* it'll be Moltsk and not England that'll get the benefit of it?"

"Moscow. Comrade General Berida. And hurry." Colonel Rogovin, grey-faced with worry and with his hand shaking badly, put the receiver back and sat in silence, his fearful thoughts nagging at him. It was all too clear—now—that the man Alison had fooled him, that he should never have given him that pass. But how to convince Major-General Berida that he had acted in good faith? To suppress information would be worse than foolish; it would mean death. . . .

Rogovin broke out into a sweat as the telephone shrilled at him. He reached out slowly, reluctantly now, and took up the receiver again. He said, "Comrade General Berida? Rogovin, Comrade General, from Moltsk."

The instrument snapped at him in a small explosion of irritation. "Well, Rogovin?"

"Comrade General, I—I have to report a disappearance."

"Go on. Who has disappeared, Rogovin?"

He could scarcely get the words out; they stuck in his throat and choked him. His voice hoarse, he said them at last. "Comrade Doctor Carew." His face grew greyer, sicker, as he listened to the furious, amazed noises at the other end of the line. It was a tirade—and naturally he had expected no less. He said obsequiously, "Yes, Comrade General . . . yes . . . yes. It has all been done, everything, I assure you. Yes. Patrols, Comrade General, on all the roads leading out of Moltsk. Even the foreshore is being watched. The ferry terminal is under heavy security guard . . . yes . . . yes, Comrade General. We are doing everything in our power. . . ."

The telephone barked at him. "Everything is not enough, you must do more. Now give me all the details of his disappearance. Leave nothing out that has any possible bearing, Rogovin."

"Yes, Comrade General." Rogovin made a full statement and included the information that Dr Carew had last been seen in company with one Peter Martin Alison, whose passport Rogovin had at this moment in his office. He explained the circumstances fully; he had no option. He insisted, shaking in his shoes as he did so, that he had no reason whatever to doubt Alison and that he still did not doubt him. Berida, however, went on making extremely threatening noises at him and finally told him that he, Rogovin, was being held personally responsible for the safe interception of Dr Carew. And then there was a crash in Rogovin's ear and the line went dead. Rogovin put the instrument down and sat back, wiping his forehead. Then he jammed a finger on to his bell-push and kept it there.

Triska made a flask of hot coffee and collected as many blankets as she could find in the bedrooms to help keep out the bitter cold of the Barents Sea. Shaw made Carew help him remove the dead body of the latter's personal gunman from Triska's car, and they stowed it in an outhouse, covering it with a deep pile of logs.

They left soon after that, but in a car that had belonged to Godov, for though it was old-fashioned and heavy it was bigger than Triska's and it had more speed. They had plenty of petrol aboard, for the old man had had many cans of it in his garage. Shaw was driving and Triska, in the back seat, had the bodyguard's gun still covering Lawrence Carew.

As they sped down the drive to the Emets road she asked, "Do you think they will come here, to the house?"

"I'm pretty sure of it, but it won't help them much." He remembered that Snake's-head was well aware of his contact with Godov. "I'm surprised the M.V.D. hasn't turned up already, as a matter of fact, Triska. I only hope we get north of Emets before they do come along." Once on the road he slammed his foot down hard and the big car rocketed forward; in no time they had flashed past Emets where, though they didn't know it, the line from Moltsk was humming furiously and radio orders were being beamed to a patrol ahead. And it was only fifteen minutes later as they were roaring north that they saw the winking lights, lights which were waving them down.

Shaw snapped, "See that?"

"Yes, Peter. It may be an ordinary road check——"

"And it may not! In any case I'm not chancing it. The flap'll be on now." He narrowed his eyes, gripped the wheel hard. He snapped, "Hold tight, Triska, and watch Carew. I'm going right for them now."

The probing headlights played on two motor-cyclists, their machines nose to nose across the road, and the levelled

155

guns. Chromiun barrels—Kalashnikovas! They weren't going to come through this, not without one hell of a lot of luck. Shaw could almost fancy he was staring right along the barrels of those guns when his foot rammed hard down on the accelerator and the car seemed to jump forward through the air, roaring down on the motor-cycles like an express train. There was a ripple of light from ahead, red tongues of flame, and then the windscreen went blank as neat round holes appeared. Shaw leaned forward swiftly, holding the wheel dead centre and smashing away with the butt of the Luger until he had cleared his view. Reversing the automatic quickly he fired through the empty space, but couldn't tell whether or not he had hit anyone. A bullet snicked the jacket material on his left shoulder, more flew singing past his head, and then he heard a high scream from behind. No time to look round now . . . his face hard and his lips tight and bloodless he sent the car forward and a second later it hit. The men hadn't been able to get completely clear and the car took both their front wheels together. It reared up for an instant and the wheel seemed to come alive in Shaw's grip, then the heavy vehicle had bounced back on to the road and they were clear and away and belting north. Shaw had had a momentary glimpse of machines and men whirling into the air and then, just before his tyres screamed round a bend in the road, he caught the first flicker of fire reflected redly in his driving-mirror.

He called anxiously, dreading to hear no answer after that one scream, "All right, Triska?"

"Yes, Peter." He felt an overwhelming relief. "I ducked in time, but Carew has been hit. The car is like a pepper-pot."

"Is Carew bad?"

"I think so, Peter. One of the bullets has smashed the side of the skull. He was hit also in the fleshy parts of his arms and in the shoulder, but the skull . . . he is unconscious now."

"Uh-huh. Do what you can for him, Triska——"

"But of course! I am a doctor, Peter."

"Sorry!" He grinned briefly into the streaming wind coming at him through the smashed screen. "I'd like him kept alive just for the pleasure of handing him over in England, but don't worry all that much if he pegs out. He's not worth an ounce of your effort or pity really."

A little later she said, "Peter, you speak of handing him over in England. Do you really think. . . ." She broke off.

"That England's going up?" he asked, a confident, exultant note in his voice now. "Not if I can help it! It's early to speak yet, but I think I may have got just the right answer—something that'll mean we needn't have a war on our hands after all."

"What is it, Peter?"

"Sorry, but I'm not saying. Not yet. We aren't clear yet, Triska, and the less you know the better—just in case."

"Yes," she said. "I understand that. You are right."

They rushed on through the night, grim and unspeaking now. There were low sounds from the back now and then; otherwise the only noise was that of the blipping tyres and the engine and the wind blowing a bitter hurricane into the speeding car. Outside, the desolate country was quiet, peaceful, deserted. They were running a little inland now of the rock-bound coastline and there were no more road-blocks this far north. There didn't seem to be a telephone-line, and Shaw felt safe in assuming that they wouldn't have been reported ahead; there would be scarcely anybody up here to be reported to anyway. They should have a clear road from now on and all they had to do was to find a boat.

It was all clear astern as well—until Shaw noticed the headlights a long way behind on the twisting track. He cursed into the night then. That could be the pursuit from Moltsk itself—the M.V.D., who would have found the bodies in Godov's house and had very likely decided to check the roads to the north. The car was rocketing along at speed, and faintly Shaw caught the whine of a police siren.

TWENTY-ONE

"They're right behind us and I reckon they've got the legs of us." Shaw spoke bitterly. "Looks as if I've been rumbled after all . . . it won't have been all that hard for them to work out after what's happened and they may have bowled out my passport into the bargain. Triska, we've got to polish off those bastards or we've had it."

She said, "Yes, I think so too. But will we have any chance in a running fight, Peter?"

"It's not going to be a running fight," he said. "I'll wait till I'm in a good position and then we'll sacrifice the car. You'll see."

He drove on flat out, the accelerator almost through the boards. The pursuing car hadn't much of an edge on him after all, he found, though they closed the distance enough to make Shaw use the first likely section of road that he came to. This was at the bottom of a steepish gradient running through a rocky outcrop that hid them from the car behind. At the bottom the road took a left-hand turn—not a very sharp one, but it would have to do. Shaw jammed on his brakes and the big car screamed to a stop farther along. Quickly he slammed the gears into reverse and backed up until he was some six feet short of the bend. Then he positioned the car broadside across the track and snapped at Triska to get out. He went round to the back himself to help her with Carew and together they got the scientist—and the blankets and coffee—behind some rock boulders clear of the road and took cover themselves.

Shaw slipped off the "safe" of the Luger and then they waited.

A little later they heard the M.V.D. car speeding up in the distance, its siren blaring, a high whine in the night air. Then it reached the top of the gradient and they heard the rushing sound and the flying grit as it came down.

Shaw reached out a hand. "Hold tight, Triska. Any minute now. Leave it all to me."

Blinding headlights swung round the bend, travelling fast. Travelling too fast. The M.V.D. hadn't a chance. Shaw heard the screech of tyres as the brakes were rammed on but it was far too late to save them. The vehicle tore into Godov's car at very nearly full speed, ploughed through it, reared up with its smashed bonnet in the air and all its windows shattered, and then plunged over on its side. The bonnet appeared to have been driven right back into the bodywork and as the first flicker of flame licked up Shaw caught the gruesome sight of a staring face protruding through the jags of the windscreen, its tongue lolling out and blood spurting from the severed arteries of the neck. By some miracle one of the men inside was alive, apparently even unhurt. An arm came through a side window, then a uniformed body. The man, dazed, clambered out on to the track, a revolver in his hand.

Shaw was out from cover now intending to make the man talk and tell him what the score was back in Moltsk; but the policeman had seen him and had brought up his gun. There was a stab of flame, a bullet whistled harmlessly by, and then Shaw had emptied the slide of the Luger into him.

The man fell back against the car as the flames roared up and enveloped both vehicles in the sheeted flame of a funeral pyre.

The road thenceforward deteriorated into a mere cart-track and Shaw realized that they couldn't have driven much farther in the car anyhow. They stumbled on by torchlight, making the best speed they could with Carew carried between them. They saw no one, no sign of life whatever in this rocky, harsh land. Godov's car had taken them well north before they had abandoned it, but even so they had walked for nearly two hours before they saw the lights ahead, a glimmer from scattered dwellings at the foot of what seemed to be the sheer rock sides of a fiord.

"It must be a village . . . just what we wanted!" Shaw was grinning with relief. "Right on the shore, too. Come on, Triska. We've just got to get to the fleet before those bastards get to us."

They pressed on faster, with fresh life now that they had the last lap in sight. Carew was in a bad way now; before they had left the car Triska had put makeshift bandages on his wounds and done everything possible for him, but the man was clearly very sick and Shaw felt that he wouldn't get through the night, could never hope to survive the trip to sea in a small boat; though if they could keep him alive until they boarded one of the ships, then the naval doctors might, he supposed, be able to save him.

They flitted like shadows in the moonlight between the few dwellings that formed the village. It was nothing more than a cluster of little huts fringing the shores of the fiord, one of many craggy inlets on that rough, inhospitable coast, and there was no sign of life out of doors.

As they went down to a shelving beach Triska pointed ahead. "There—there are some boats."

"So I see. Come on. We'll have to take the first likely looking one."

They crept on, coming now right down to the water's edge. Several fishing-boats of varying sizes were riding at anchor or secured to small mooring-buoys out in the fiord, which was being whipped up into wavelets by the wind coming in from the sea. None of the boats carried any lights and they all appeared as deserted as the village behind. The nearest one, which was some twenty yards from the shore, was a biggish open boat with a single mast and an engine.

Shaw pointed it out to Triska and said, "She'll have to do. I'll take Carew out first. You stay here. All right?" He added, "Cover me with your gun if you have to."

"All right, Peter."

Shaw waded out through the shallow water with Carew, his

159

breath leaving him momentarily as the icy water soaked into his legs. Putting the scientist carefully onto the bottom-boards of the boat, he turned away and went back for Triska. Taking the girl and the bundle of blankets in his arms, he carried her out and lifted her into the stern-sheets. He said, "I'll have to leave you to steer once we're out of the fiord. Meanwhile you just sit there—and get those blankets round you. I'll unshackle from the buoy." He waded to the bows and quickly cast off one end of the buoy-rope and pulled it, hand over hand, through the ring of the buoy, then chucked the end back inboard. Then he went aft to Triska.

"I'm going to push her out as far as I can," he said. "I'll get wet to my neck, but there isn't a hope of remaining dry anyway, once we put our noses out there." He gestured towards the sea. "That way we shan't make any noise, and if anyone does happen to wake up and look out of his window, we'll be moving so slowly they won't realize we're going out. Now—shove the tiller over to starboard—no, the other way—that's it!" He added encouragingly, "You'll soon get the hang of it."

He put his weight behind the boat's counter and shoved.

Quietly, slowly the boat eased to sea, scarcely seeming to disturb the chop of a sea already getting rougher as the wind increased in gusts outside. It was going to be a foul trip, Shaw knew; he was frozen through already—but he would warm up soon when he started hoisting the sail—he wouldn't risk the noise of the engine yet—and he wasn't going to let anything stop him now.

When the water was up to his chest he heaved himself over the gunwale, bringing in a slop of water with him as the boat heeled to his weight. He rooted about in the bottom until he found a tatty sail; he began sorting out the tangle of canvas and rigging and after a time he was lucky enough to find a canvas dodger evidently cut to fit across the fore end of the boat. He said, "This'll help to keep Carew dry. I'll give you a hand—we'll make him comfortable up this end and then I'll rig the dodger."

Within five minutes this was done and he had the sail hoisted as well. He felt the boat heel over and take a grip on the water as the wind filled out the canvas. Then he moved aft to take over the tiller for the remainder of the trip out of the fiord. Tacking into the wind, they moved out, travelling faster now, dipping into short, breaking seas. Half an hour later they had passed a headland to the north and were clear of the fiord, sailing on a nor'-nor'-westerly course to intercept the British fleet.

As they left the lee of the rocky fiord the full force of a freshening wind hit them and the boat lay well over. Rising and falling to the lift and scend of the seas they flew onward, with the icy spray flying in their faces, Triska's clothing already nearly as soaked as Shaw's and heavy with the bitter seas.

TWENTY-TWO

"God damn and blast!" Latymer raised his fists in the air helplessly and added, for the tenth time since he had arrived with the Chief of the Naval Staff in the Admiralty's Operations Room, "I wish to heaven the P.M. would get cracking, Sir John. There may not be much time left now."

"I know that, Latymer." The First Sea Lord's voice was quiet; he was apparently untroubled—until one looked into his eyes. "We can't hurry them, though. Two speeds . . . dead slow and stop—they must take their time." He put a hand on Latymer's shoulder. "Remember that in spite of Shaw's signals we still don't know just what the threat is. The Cabinet's still hoping for more news from Shaw."

"God knows how they expect to get it, with the Embassy off the air!" Latymer snapped. "I've told 'em myself, we've got enough to go on already! The P.M. ought to order the Vulcans into the air and have 'em standing by with their missiles to blast that tower off the face of the earth—before it's too late!"

"My dear Latymer—that's a big decision to expect from any man before we know all the facts. The newspapers have been full of the success of the Conference to date . . . we've *got* to be one hundred per cent certain before we commit an act of war, otherwise there'd be no support whatever from the country, let alone the rest of the world! Don't you see?"

Latymer swung away angrily and started once again to pace the floor of the Operations Room. Shaw had given them all he could. Shaw had said that in his opinion the tower and tunnel were the trouble centres and he'd even passed a date when he thought things would happen—tomorrow afternoon . . . Latymer looked up at the clock. *This* afternoon—it was after midnight now.

And this afternoon the fleet was due to enter Moltsk. . . .

The atmosphere in the Operations Room was tense, vibrant with uncertainty as the naval staff waited for word from Downing Street. W.R.N.S. ratings, their eyes watchful and anxious, stood round a large table where the movements of the British ships were being plotted hour by hour on the charts, showing the whole route out from England. Latymer stopped his restless pacing and looked down at those charts. A red circle marked the position of the tower as estimated by Shaw; the varying positions of the ships were shown by a series of crosses stretching from a point to the west of the Needles and extending round the North Cape to the current position in 31° 15′ East longitude, 71° 00′ North latitude —or in plain language, passing well to the eastward of Norway's Varanger Fiord and nearly into Russian territorial waters. Six ships in all. The aircraft-carrier *Invincible*, the old heavy cruiser *Lord Cochrane*, and the frigates *Turbulent*, *Harrier*, *Foxhound*, and *Petunia*. This group of ships was commanded by Vice-Admiral Eric Carleton wearing his flag in the *Invincible*. He was a man of whom Latymer knew little though he had made a point of having a very private and unofficial word in his ear before the ships had sailed from Portsmouth, warning him, as he had promised Shaw he would, that a man from his department might make contact with him. Latymer could not foresee what the Admiral's reactions might be if anything should happen in Moltsk that afternoon. Men were not made into supermen merely by the fact of being promoted to Flag rank, and all admirals were not *ipso facto* good ones; and Carleton had never before enjoyed an important seagoing command. He had done well in a shore job but that didn't count. There was nothing against Carleton at all, of course, but Latymer had gathered that he was a prim and proper fellow who went entirely by the book; so much that he was known to his subordinates as Careful Carleton. Moltsk, or rather what was likely to happen in Moltsk, had not been itemized in Queen's Regulations and so nothing specific had been laid down as to how to deal with it; a state of affairs that could catch a bookish admiral on the hop. Carleton had, of course, been kept informed by radio of the situation as it was known to Whitehall, but only in broad terms, and he had been given no precise instructions or guidance whatever. In these circumstances Careful Carleton might dither. Had Latymer been in

Carleton's shoes and back at sea again, he would have read between the lines of the signals; and, rather than wait for orders that might never come, he would have used something of the Nelson touch and would have entered the arrival channel for Moltsk with his guns cleared away for action so that he could if necessary blast hell out of that tower on the way in, taking it for granted that someone in chairbound authority was unwilling, scared, to give the sensible order until the whole situation had been revealed down to the last hair's breadth of Intelligence.

Latymer almost jumped when a telephone-bell jangled into his thoughts. He hoped it might be Carberry with more news from Shaw, positive news, but, as he had known in his heart, it was not; a junior officer hurried to answer it and then spoke to the First Sea Lord, who went heavily across the room and listened for some moments. As he put the phone down Latymer looked at him inquiringly and asked, "Well, sir?"

"Prime Minister himself." The Chief of Staff spoke abruptly. "You've got your wish, Latymer—and I can only hope to God it's the right thing to do. Four squadrons of Vulcans, supported by jet fighters, will take off one hour before dawn. Meanwhile," he added, "I'm ordered to recall the fleet."

Water, icy water, slopped continually into the boat as Shaw strained his eyes ahead through the thick darkness. There was still that bitter wind and it was blowing more strongly now, straight off the Arctic snows; and a lash of rain was in it too. The waves, short and breaking, were bitten off in spray which blew into their faces stingingly, so that it was an effort, an agony, to keep their eyes open and watch the seas ahead. Slivers of ice in the rain had raised open weals and cuts on Shaw's face and in spite of the hot coffee from the flask he was chilled through and through again, his fingers numbed as they gripped the bucking mast to windward. He had insisted that Triska and Carew have all the blankets, and Triska was huddled in the stern nursing the tiller and keeping an eye on Carew, forward under the canvas dodger. The scientist was moaning all the time now in delirium and when Shaw had looked in at him his face had been just a white, contorted blur. Shaw didn't believe he could possibly last much longer now.

Stinking weather, he thought, as the cold wind went right

to the marrow of his bones; but it had its compensations. The seas were empty, had been empty ever since, when they had been not far out from the fiord, he'd seen the loom of an unlighted power-boat outlined distantly against the northern sky and he'd hauled down the sail and stayed motionless, invisible with the high rock mass behind him, and then got clear away to sea once the coastal patrol had roared off southward.

The cold was the enemy now; nothing else.

Shaw looked down at Triska, feeling a rush of pity for the girl. She'd already been terribly seasick but she was bearing up wonderfully under the filthy, dangerous conditions. He called out, "Keep it up. Not far off the track now. We'll pick 'em up soon."

"Suppose they have already passed, Peter?" Her voice came to him thinly against the wind, though he knew she was shouting. He called back to her reassuringly, though he was far from happy himself. He had to keep that cheerful front whatever happened, had to see to it that she kept her spirits up. This cold was deadly, enough to make anyone give up hope, and once you gave up hope you gave up trying to keep alive, and then the cold really got you and you'd had it.

He stared ahead again, straining to keep his eyes into the lashing rain. The boat ran on into the restless, hostile seas. Minutes dragged by like decades; half an hour later there was still nothing, nothing but sea and black sky and the wind and the biting rain, and Shaw began to wonder. . . .

He scarcely dared to believe it at first when he saw the lights through the murk. Then there were the bulky shadows, darker than the night, and he felt wild, flooding exultation.

He narrowed his eyes into the weather and then, as if in confirmation of his hopes, he saw the white masthead lights coming clearly into view one by one; and then a little later the green sidelights of the British fleet as it approached and bore down from the north, standing well to the eastward of the little, plunging boat. Then he made out the big black bulk of an aircraft-carrier and behind her the fighting-top of the old cruiser; ahead and on the bow, extended as an escort screen around the heavy ships, he saw the smaller shapes and the lights of the Home Fleet frigates.

He shouted, "It's all right, Triska. It's them!" He was shaking with excitement and relief now, but he still had to wait until they were within range of his torch; powerful as it was, it wasn't a signalling projector and it would be dim by comparison and extremely difficult to read, so low in the water, in that filthy night with the breaking seas obscuring it. He doubted if any of the look-outs of the fleet would see his unlighted little boat itself. Soon, when he had tacked across to close the distance and the range seemed right, he began sending.

The dots and dashes flicked out, spotting the water ahead of the open boat, directed at the frigate on the fleet's starboard bow. Well clear of the others, she was his nearest ship.

There was no reply.

Majestically the ships steamed ahead, bearing down to pass him. Shaw cursed aloud, oaths ripping back along the wind. Those bloody signalmen on the flag decks of the fleet—asleep, the whole goddam lot of them. . . .

Fury didn't help. Shaw tightened his lips, went on flashing. The ships remained silent, not speaking to anyone in the night, proud and haughty and self-contained.

That torch just wasn't getting there.

Still no reply. But then, a moment later, the ships began a private conversation between themselves, a conversation conducted with flashing lights from the Flag to all ships in company. Shaw watched in alarm, reading the signals as well as he could.

And then—very slowly, very majestically—the black shapes moved. The green light of the leading ship seemed to swing round to starboard and then vanish, to be replaced soon by a red one.

The escorts were turning.

Detaching from the fleet to pick him up? The signals hadn't looked like that, though Shaw was admittedly rusty on fleet procedure these days. They were turning too far . . . soon Shaw, watching in growing consternation, could see the port sidelight of the *Invincible* as the carrier slowly turned towards him—turned to approach, but went on turning. They wouldn't turn the whole fleet to investigate a flashing light!

Triska shouted at him, "Peter . . . what is happening? Have they seen us?"

"I—don't—know!" His voice was high, savage, and bitter. "They're turning in succession . . . towards us, yes, but. . . ."

He broke off as his heart was forced at last to accept what his brain had told him already. The fleet was turning. Turning right round through 180 degrees, swinging back for home. Shaw's lips flattened back against his teeth almost in a snarl and he went on flashing, flashing uselessly, flashing like a senseless maniac who couldn't help his actions.

Above the high whine of the wind he heard Triska crying.

TWENTY-THREE

The leviathans of the fleet, standing high above the escorts, the bitter, restless seas rising up their grey-painted plates and then streaming back again to join the whitened foam of the wakes, were busy with their own affairs as their bridge personnel prepared to execute the turn for home.

The chief communications yeoman on the Admiral's staff crossed the bridge of the flagship and reported to Carleton.

"All ships acknowledged, sir."

The Admiral, a tall, lugubrious and heavy-faced man of deliberate movements, nodded. Dressed in a thick sweater, monkey-jacket and greatcoat, Careful Carleton had come up to the bridge to watch the turn after he had been called with the changed orders from the Admiralty, and had insisted on lamp signalling rather than R/T. It was a fad of his that the communications staff should be exercised on lamps whenever possible . . . he shivered suddenly in that bitter wind. He wasn't sorry to be going home, not at all sorry, even though he would be going back to a country, if already at war, then certainly on the brink of it now that the Vulcans were going in. Soon he would have to break the news to his ships' companies. He rehearsed religiously in his mind the orders he would have to give so as to shift his command from a peace footing to a war footing . . . he ran a hand across his eyes and then became aware that the chief yeoman was still waiting expectantly and he nodded again, shrugged his big-boned body deeper into his great-coat as the rain swirled into the collar, and said, "Very well, chief yeoman. Executive."

"Aye, aye, sir." The chief yeoman saluted the Admiral's back and turned away. The lights winked out again as the short executive order to start the turn was passed to the fleet. The flagship's officer-of-the-watch, after a nod from the Flag Captain, bent to the wheelhouse voice-pipe and ordered twenty degrees of starboard wheel. The flagship began her slow, bulky swing, heeling over a little to port as the rudder took effect and centrifugal force acted upon her; and it was right in the middle of that turn that something was seen out in the heaving waste of water.

"Captain, sir!" This was the flagship's own yeoman, sharp and breathless. "Green one-oh . . . looks like a light flashing. Can't read it yet, sir. It's very faint——"

"What's that?" The Admiral lifted the night-glasses which were hanging from his neck on a length of codline and steadied them on the bearing, which narrowed to come dead ahead and then moved across to port as the aircraft-carrier went on swinging. "It's an open boat, by God . . . Flag Captain, negative the last order! Fleet to resume previous course. Quickly—those damn frigates'll turn onto 'em!"

As the orders went out Carleton held tight to the bridge screen, staring out ahead. As the ships turned away to port he let out a long breath and said, "That's as near as I hope I ever get to running someone down! Silly beggars . . . some confound Kola fisherman, I suppose, not burning his lights." he moved his sholders irritably. "Flag Captain, make to the starboard escort: Report names of officer-of-the-watch and look-outs. And you'd better shake up your own people. Someone's going to answer for this!"

When the ships had resumed their course Carleton asked loudly, "Well? Anyone read that light yet?"

"Yes, sir, just got it." The chief yeoman came across towards him. "He's using a pocket torch, I reckon, sir, and it was tricky to read." The man sounded puzzled, unbelieving. "He says he's a Commander Shaw."

Carleton stiffened, then barked urgently, "Well—go on, man! What does he say?"

"It's vital he speaks to you personally, sir, and if you were altering course for home he suggests you negative the order." The chief yeoman glanced up, expecting fireworks, but they didn't come.

Carleton said, "Oh. He says that, does he?"

"Yessir."

"Blunt, isn't he?" Carleton smiled briefly and turned to the Flag Captain, who was also showing signs of astonishment. "Commander Shaw has spoken. We obey. We hold our course, for the time being at least. Be so good as to tell the fleet so. And meanwhile, call up *Petunia*. Give her the bearing in case she still hasn't got it and tell her to detach and pick up Commander Shaw. She's to bring him alongside and send him aboard by breeches buoy."

167

A net was lowered from just below the break of the frigate's fo'c'sle as she swept up alongside. A Neil Robinson stretcher was sent down for Lawrence Carew and then Shaw and Triska scrambled up the net. They were taken at once to the wardroom without being bothered for explanations and they were given tots of neat Navy rum. Warm, dry clothes were hastily rustled up and they changed into them there and then; and within a few minutes they were alongside the carrier, under the lee of her vast, towering side, and waiting to be put into the breeches buoy for the short transfer across the windswept sea lashing up between the ships. The frigate's doctor had said that in his opinion Carew hadn't long to go, but that he would be better off in the big ship with her steadier motion and superior resources. So Carew was also sent across and he and Triska were taken to the sick-bay as soon as they were aboard the carrier. Then the frigate swung away and raced ahead of the flagship to resume her station on the bow.

Shaw was taken straight up to the Admiral's sea-cabin where he remained closeted alone with Carleton for some considerable time during which, after satisfying the Admiral as to his identity, he gave him the whole story as quickly and briefly as he could, right from the start.

Carleton listened intently and in growing astonishment. When Shaw had finished he said, "I can't believe it. It's fantastic, Shaw."

"I know, sir, but—may I ask how much of all this you knew before? Did you know about that tower, for instance?"

"Yes, I did indeed." Carleton nodded heavily. "I was told by signal not long ago——"

"Well, sir," Shaw broke in urgently, "may I ask you to take the rest on trust? Carew could confirm it all if he were fit, but he's in no condition to talk now."

"Yes, yes, I see." Carleton got up and took a turn or two up and down the small cabin, two steps one way, two the other, hands clasped tight behind a long back, frowning anxiously so that the blue-chinned, lantern-shaped face hung in heavy, fleshy folds. Then he stopped and looked down at Shaw. "Very well," he said abruptly. "I'll take your word for it, Commander. I had a word with your chief before we sailed, so I feel I am safe . . . yes, yes. Now, I'd better tell you my end of this. It's very brief. I've been ordered home, as you obviously guessed when you saw us start the turn, and meanwhile it's been decided to send in a force of Vulcans to smash that tower of yours."

Shaw's head jerked up. "Has it indeed! Are they in the air yet, sir?"

"No, they're taking off an hour before dawn. Why?"

"I think they should be negatived, sir. Immediately. Top priority." Shaw's voice was sharp with anxiety.

"What the devil d'you mean?"

"Just that, sir. Cancel them." Shaw sat forward, his fists clenching. "It's vital. Sending in the Vulcans will only lead to all-out war——"

"I'm only too well aware of that, my dear fellow! It's a filthy prospect—a filthy prospect—but what else d'you expect Whitehall to do, Shaw? Just sit down and take what's obviously coming?" He stared frigidly, lips tight, neck stuck out.

Shaw said tautly, "No, sir. Not that at all. I've got a better idea—that's all. And it's going to work. May I put it to you, sir?"

"Certainly, but let me have it quickly." Carleton peered at a clock on the bulkhead. "Remember, I've got an order I'm supposed to obey. I'm supposed to be steaming for the North Cape and home and I'm going to have the Admiralty on my tail directly, asking why I've not reported my new course and speed. So I do hope you've something convincing to tell me, Shaw." He added, "Frankly, I don't see what else anyone can do, other than try to smash up that tower."

"Quite, sir. That's what I'm aiming to do, but in a different way, a safer and in the long run a much more effective way." He paused. "Now, sir. That tower's big and wide and deep, it goes way below the sea-bed. Carew tells me that for one reason and another the sealing door down below won't be shut until almost the last minute. Now—if we can smash that tower and fill it up with sea-water, thousands and millions of tons of it, that's all we need to do—they've had it! Don't you see, sir? The fissure will flood right up and they'll never be able to use it again, ever, not if they pump for a thousand years—and even if they do get the door shut, we may still be able to flood the control-room inside the tower itself——"

"Yes, yes—but how do we achieve all this, Shaw? By gunfire? Torpedoes? Bombs from my aircraft? No—just a moment, Shaw, kindly allow me to speak. Surely that'll have precisely the same warlike look about it as the Vulcans, with only a fraction of the chances of success?"

"No, sir!" Shaw shook his head, sweat beading his forehead now. "I don't mean gunfire, sir, nothing like that at all——"

"Then what——"

"I mean—ram!"

Carleton started. "Ram? *Ram the tower?*"

"Yes, sir! Split it into fragments and let the weight of water do the rest. Let the Barents Sea itself pour down and finish the whole thing off for good and all!"

Carleton went on staring at him, hands behind his back, eyes narrowed. Shaw went on desperately, "I'd suggest using the *Lord Cochrane,* sir. She's obsolete, expendable, and heavy. She's still got a good turn of speed at full power, and she could smash that tower in seconds once she's worked up to maximum revolutions—just as effectively as the Vulcans! Well, sir?"

Carleton licked his lips, looked down at his shoes and eased his knees up and down. He said, "Dear me. You've put me in a quandary, Shaw. There's a *chance* of success, I admit. But the timing . . . it'll be such a close thing, won't it? You say they won't flash the fissure until we're alongside in Moltsk, but now Carew's disappeared they may advance the firing. If we let the Vulcans go ahead, they can smash that tower within minutes of being airborne, long before we're due to enter——"

"*And start a war, sir!* Those Vulcans'll start a war with an apparently unprovoked attack. You can see what effect that's going to have——"

Carleton rocked angrily on his heels. "But good God, man! War is at this moment the lesser of two alternatives. You can't offer me any guarantee that we'll reach the tower before they fire it off, can you?"

"No, sir, I can't. It's a risk. But I think it's worth taking, because Carew told me quite categorically that they wouldn't go into action before tomorrow afternoon, that they'll be loading up and wiring-up right throughout the morning and until almost the last minute. It's a very tight schedule, he said. They'll know Carew's missing, I agree, but they won't know he's talked, and in fact I think I've got an idea as to how we can convince them that he *hasn't* talked."

"How?"

"Well, sir . . . I suggest you make an *almost* clean breast of things and signal the naval authorities in Moltsk that you've picked up a dead man in a drifting boat. Carew's going to die anyway before morning, so we'll be covered. The radar tracking-stations along the north Russian coast will have noted *Petunia*'s altering to pick us up anyway, so no secrecy will be lost in admitting it—in fact, it'd be suspicious perhaps if you *didn't* account for it. Tell 'em straight out that the dead man carried papers saying he was Lawrence Carew, and that he was alone. They'll probably come to the conclusion that Carew had another change of heart, realized at the last moment just what he was going to do to his own country, and then died trying to reach the British fleet. It'll all be perfectly logical."

"But surely they'll have their suspicions?"

"Yes, sir, but they won't be certain, and the fact that you've admitted picking up Carew at all will give it a genuine look." He added, "Can we leave that side of it for the moment and just go into the physical practicalities of ramming? What's your opinion as to whether the *Lord Cochrane* could smash into thick concrete and split it?"

Carleton said, "It depends on the actual thickness, naturally, but from what you tell me I believe she could do it all right. Yes, as a physical proposition I believe it stands up, Shaw." He frowned in thought. "Ten thousand tons at thirty-two knots . . . if they can raise enough steam on all four engine-rooms in time. Currently she's got two shut down." He pursed his lips and went over to a table below one of the ports. He switched on a bright light over a chart that was spread out on the table, the chart for the Kola Peninsula and Moltsk approaches. He said, "Come over here, Shaw."

Shaw got up and looked over the Admiral's shoulder. Carleton said, "The entry channel runs close in for some way north of Moltsk, certainly. That means we could make a straight approach rather than a sudden tight turn. It's just there—d'you see?" He traced a line with a pencil. "Where exactly is the tower?"

"There, sir." Shaw put his finger on the spot. "Just clear of the channel."

"H'm . . . soundings look all right, plenty of water there. It starts to shoal only farther in. Yes, yes . . . the approach to the tower is certainly clear enough. It *could* be done, certainly it could, from a purely seamanship point of view. It would be the end of the *Cochrane,* of course, and there would be casualties. . . ."

"I think we'll have to accept that, sir, when you think of what's in the balance now. They needn't be very heavy, since the ship's company will have been warned and they can mostly be on the upper deck as she runs in."

"Yes, yes. . . ." Carleton pulled at his lower lip. "What about retaliation? It's defended, presumably?"

"Only by guards with automatic weapons, sir, just to control the civilian labour. They've got Kalashnikova sub-machine-guns with an effective range of abour four hundred yards. Also there's some rocket-batteries on the coast, but I don't believe they'd tick over in time." Shaw kept his consuming impatience out of his voice with an effort. He wanted nothing so much as to take Careful Carleton by the scruff of the neck and shake him into action, into an awareness of urgency. "As for the boom, the *Cochrane* would go through that like paper. And here's the nice bit, sir. We could work it so it looked just like a genuine accident, something going wrong at the last minute. Caught with our pants down. Then they can't use it as an excuse, can't say we struck the first blow—all that sort of thing. It's tit for tat, sir!"

"Ah-ha." Carleton looked at him intently, his heavy face folded into deep lines. "How would you go about that, Shaw?"

Shaw was trembling now, striving to keep his feelings out of his face, but he thought: Oh, dear God! He clenched his fists, said, "Steering can jam at awkward moments, sir, as you know. No reason why the *Cochrane*'s helm shouldn't jam once she's headed a little off the channel, and something go wrong in the engine-room too. An old ship . . ."

"Yes, I follow." Carleton tapped the chart with his pencil, gnawing at his bottom lip, tall and gloomy, concentrating hard.

"Well, sir?"

Carleton said, "It's a plan, certainly. Yes. Well worth thinking about. But a very big decision to have to make, Shaw."

"Yes, sir."

Suddenly Carleton swung round. He said energetically, "I tell you what I'll do. I'll put it to the Admiralty with my recommendation that it be adopted. Does that satisfy you?"

Shaw let out a long breath and said, "Thank you, sir. But may I suggest you lose no time now? So far the home authorities don't even know exactly what's going to happen in that fissure—and I really would like to get the Vulcans called off."

Shaw knew it was going to work. Assuming that the timings were right, he couldn't see anything to stop it. After they'd hit there would be nothing the Russians could do about it, even if they did smell a rat and disbelieve that explanation of an unavoidable accident, as in fact they most likely

172

would. There would be far too much dirty washing around if they made trouble; they couldn't possibly use a jammed helm and a fault in the engine-room as an excuse for going to war, however phoney they might believe it to be, for to do so would be to admit to the world what the tower was there for.

Within the hour the answer was flashed through from the Admiralty and Shaw read the cypher as soon as it was broken down. It read: *Plan approved. Vulcans cancelled but will be held at instant readiness pending success or otherwise of ramming. They will be airborne at your E.T.A. Moltsk and can have missiles on target within five minutes of any signal from you reporting plan impracticable in conditions as you find them. It is however urgently hoped at highest level that Vulcans will not repeat not be required.*

Once that signal had come and he had definite orders, Carleton was a changed man. He acted quickly. There were urgent consultations between ships and Carleton went into the plan very thoroughly with his navigator and the Flag Captain and with the captain and navigator of the *Lord Cochrane*. The right moment for the ramming turn was plotted as closely as possible. In the meantime Carleton had given orders for a helicopter lift of all excess personnel from the cruiser so as to minimize casualties; and both his helicopter squadrons were engaged on this, dropping aft over the carrier's round-down to hover above the cruiser, which had now closed the carrier to a cable's-length astern; keeping as low as possible so that the radar tracking-stations ashore, which would be following the fleet all the way in, would not be able to pick up any aerial activity. Orders were passed to ensure so far as humanly possible the safety of all hands remaining aboard the cruiser, which the Admiral expected would have her fo'c'sle ripped right back to the bridge under the tremendous impact. Aboard the cruiser mechanics and engineer officers were working flat out and would go on doing so throughout the night and the next forenoon, bringing life to the two silent engine-rooms which had not been needed in the old vessel's role of training-ship, bringing them to life so that her four shafts could, that afternoon to come, send her flinging arrow-like, thundering through the water with a foaming bow-wave and tumbling wake to demolish the tower and all its works.

Ashore the radar tracking-stations kept their unremitting vigil on the British ships, handing them on from one to another along the coast, making reports by landline to grim-faced men in Moscow, the men behind the threat, the men whose very lives now hung upon complete success. These men were edgy, in a nail-biting mood as the hours ticked slowly past. No chances were being taken now; a big reception—though now, unfortunately, without Comrade Doctor Carew—had been prepared for the British Admiral in a spirit of complete friendliness, a friendliness that would effectively mask the iron fist to be revealed when it was too late—only after the fissure had been fired into the heart of England.

In the meantime certain further precautions were being taken—just to be on the safe side. The British Admiral's signal about Carew had appeared to be perfectly genuine; it fitted with such facts as were known—with the two disasters on the road north from Emets. One of the motorcyclists had been found alive and he had reported filling the escaping car with bullets, one of which could easily have hit Carew. The man Alison might also have been wounded and then, succumbing to the weather, have been washed out of the boat. . . .

Yes, it fitted; but the British, of course, were never entirely to be believed.

TWENTY-FOUR

And now there was not long to go.

The dawn was cold and grey and the sun was a dull and ominous red blob on the eastern horizon. The fingers of the look-outs, the men who were the eyes of the fleet and who were now alert for any hostile signs in the air and along the Russian coast, were stiff with cold although the morning watchmen had not long since relieved the decks. Away to starboard those men could begin to see that barren coastline, the dreary tundra stretching away, characterless and open in the clefts between the high rock walls. Some men, those who had served during the war, knew this run—as far as Murmansk anyhow; and they cursed it still. It had never brought anything but grimness and death. The Murmansk run, the last run of all for so many ships, so many men, so many cargoes. A cruel place in which to be attacked, to be cast adrift in a hopeless sea, a cold sea whose icy fingers dug

174

'nto men's entrails and stopped their breath; a sea in which in those days there had been no rescue, for the escorts could not stop to pick up survivors under threat of the German bombs and the shells; and there had been no helicopters handy. This run brought its memories of the long, weaving gun-barrels of the German heavy cruisers and the pocket-battleships, of the black crosses on the wings of the dive-bombers aiming sudden death at sailors who had struggled round the dehumanizing North Cape to bring the means of war to the Russian armies.

As the crews of the fleet looked out at Russia now, something stirred in the hearts of many of them. They sensed that they were steaming into a page of history even if that history could not in fact ever reach the printed page. Some of them grinned to themselves in anticipation as they eased stiffened fingers in frost-coated woollen gloves and went on staring through their binoculars. Others, below decks, as they turned oil-fuel jets in the boiler-rooms, or greased machinery, or simply woke up to one more day, were having similar feelings —particularly aboard the *Lord Cochrane,* now steaming so unexpectedly on her last voyage. Orders were being obeyed smartly and there was joking in the places where men worked, the brittle jokes of men before action begins. They were keyed-up, tense—but not unduly worried. They would get away all right, even if they did get a few broken limbs and a dowsing in the cold waters of the port approaches; it wouldn't be long before the helicopters had them nice and safe and drying out with a tot of rum aboard the carrier. Old Carleton, he always looked after his men.

He wouldn't fail them now.

Ready for anything that might happen, the cold wind sighing through the steel-wire standing rigging of the ships and cutting across their decks, the fleet steamed on for Moltsk.

At noon, with ninety minutes to go now, Shaw was on the cruiser's navigating bridge with Captain Wilson, waiting for the last reports to come in from the Engineer Officer. Shaw had asked if he could be aboard the *Lord Cochrane* for the operation and he had been delighted when Carleton had arranged with Wilson to let him handle the ship himself. He was now wearing a blue battledress uniform with the stripes of his rank on the shoulders—a uniform lent him by the cruiser's own commander so that when he entered Moltsk he would be, to all intents and purposes, just another ordinary naval officer. Peter Alison had vanished, and Shaw hoped with a certain amount of unkind pleasure that the M.V.D. were still being kept busy looking for him.

Within the next half-hour the voice-pipe from Number Two engine-room whined and Wilson bent to answer it.

"Forebridge. Captain here."

The Engineer Officer reported, "Numbers One and Four engine-rooms ready, sir, with steam for full speed."

"Thank you, Chief." Wilson, a square, stubby man with a cholerically red face, nodded in satisfaction. "Think everything's going to hold together all right?"

"Yes, sir." The voice came thin and hollow up the pipe. "For long enough, anyway."

"Good. I'm going to put the telegraphs to half ahead now for all four engines, Chief, and I want revolutions for eighteen knots—in other words, we keep to the present speed of the fleet for the time being. We shall increase speed gradually, all ships together, so that by the time we're coming into position to alter on to the collision course, we'll be going ahead at twenty-five knots. That means our own subsequent increase to full won't be quite so immediately noticeable to the people on the tower, not until it's too late anyway—we hope! All right?"

"Yes, sir."

"Now, we'll be in position for the run-in in sixty minutes approximately. I can't be more precise than that, because of the variations in speed. But when I want your full power, I'll give you a five-minute warning first, then I'll ring down Emergency Full Ahead. That's your cue. I'll want the lot then, Chief—all four shafts flat out and a bit more."

"You'll get it, sir."

"Thank you. You've done wonders in the time available." Wilson slammed down the polished brass cover of the voice-pipe and turned to Shaw. He asked, "Like to take over now?"

"With pleasure, sir." Shaw looked all round as he stepped to the Captain's customary position in the starboard for'ard corner of the bridge, feeling a peculiar thrill in being back aboard a ship again and in full control, if only for so short a time. He said, "I'd just like to run through the drill once more, if I may."

Ashore in Moltsk the Minister of Defence had arrived in the dockyard to meet the ships and to be present when the button was pressed in the tower's control-room, when months of planning and seditious intrigue would come to their final

176

fruition. Already he saw himself as Chairman of the Council of Ministers of the Supreme Soviet, the lawful holder of which office was currently—though not so overtly that the Russian people knew about it yet—in house-arrest within the Kremlin walls, together with the President and other high officials of the State—men who were known violently to oppose the Minister of Defence and his colleagues.

Just now the Minister was waiting in the naval Commander-in-Chief's office, having decided to have a word with the Admiral before going with the other V.I.P.'s to the outer mole for the official reception of the British fleet.

He asked, "You have your precautions all ready, Admiral?"

"But certainly! I do not anticipate using them, but they have been made as ordered. A helicopter will be spotting above the ships as they come in, Minister, and will at once report any activity aboard them. There will also be the guardship standing by, of course. The British will not be able to close up their guns' crews unobserved, I promise you that——"

"Good." The Minister nodded, seemingly satisfied. "You will ensure that there are no mistakes and that everyone is alert. The fleet must be destroyed at once if they attempt to use their armament." He turned away and walked over to a big window, where he stared out into the yard. In spite of his outward confidence, doubt and anxiety was invading the Minister's mind now. *Was* Carew really dead after all . . . and what had happened to that apparently so unimportant Englishman, Alison? He had vanished without trace, despite the best efforts of the infallible M.V.D. Carew, again . . . he must be dead, of course. It fitted, as he had told himself earlier. Yes—it fitted. Possibly, then, all was well. And certainly failure at this stage was simply not to be thought of. When the earth tremors from the fissure shook Moltsk and then when the reports came through from the tower in confirmation that everything had gone off according to plan . . . then he would officially take over the Government. The proclamations already printed would go up in the government buildings and the public places all over the Soviet Union, and the people would find themselves willy-nilly under the new regime. It would be too late for them to protest, except at the peril of their lives. He, the Chairman of the Council, leader of a mighty world-powerful country, would turn to the British Admiral in consternation, say that something terrible must have happened, that something had gone wrong. When the full news broke he would express heartfelt contrition, offer his condolences on the virtual extinction of a country, would promise retribution on those responsible for such a terrible calamity. The Russian people, he would say, would be shocked and horrified, would demand that the Old Guard whose ineptitude had allowed such a dreadful thing to happen be hounded out of the Kremlin . . . and, later, the British ships would be allowed to sail away to what was left of their shattered country, the great pretence being kept up right to the end for the benefit of the watching world.

The Minister began to glow again. He glowed for some minutes—and then, unaccountably, he felt a shiver run right along his spine. He turned suddenly and snapped, "Admiral, ask the tower when they will be ready."

The Admiral looked surprised. "But you——"

"I said ask them, Admiral Boronoff."

"Yes, Minister." The Admiral went to his desk and picked up a telephone. After a brief conversation he put the receiver back and said, "As soon as the ships berth, Minister, as ordered."

The Minister nodded broodingly. He paced up and down the room for a while and then said, "Call them again, Boronoff. Tell them to advance the firing as much as possible and to fire when ready, without further orders." He swung heavily round on Boronoff. "I have a curious feeling that all is not well. . . ."

TWENTY-FIVE

"Five minutes, Chief, then I want the lot."

Wilson spoke down the engine-room voice-pipe, crisply; then stared out ahead again, head sunk in his arms which were folded before him on the bridge screen. They were into the arrival channel now, with Moltsk ahead, coming in at twenty-five knots and sending up big bow-waves, proud grey ships of war bent on an errand of peace, all their guns and missile-launchers trained innocuously to the fore-and-aft line, tompions rammed home in the muzzles of the *Lord Cochrane*'s conventional, turreted armament.

The time had almost come.

One of the frigates—*Petunia*—was leading the fleet in. Behind her came the Flag, the great carrier towering like a huge grey-painted box behind the little frigate. Astern of the Flag, the *Lord Cochrane,* old-fashioned and solid, long, broad in the beam, with a knifing stem which clove the water back in wide swathes to port and starboard; astern again, the remaining frigates, all in Line Ahead. Their ships' companies, caps on square, wearing their best Number One uniforms with gold badges and lanyards in place beneath their greatcoats, were already fallen in fore and aft for entering harbour. Divisional officers in kid gloves and wearing swords walked up and down the ranks, putting a cap straight here, jerking down the front of a greatcoat there, squaring-off their men before the Russian Minister and his entourage boarded for the formal inspection. On the carrier's quarterdeck a ceremonial guard was fallen in with rifles and bayonets, to welcome the Soviet officials. On her flight-deck a Royal Marine band in white helmets played lively tunes, and another played brazenly on the quarterdeck of the heavy cruiser itself. On her fo'c'sle was fallen in such of her reduced complement as could be spared, carrying on the vital play-acting as long as possible.

It was a perfectly normal and peaceful scene, such as had been enacted countless thousands of times over the long years as units of the Royal Navy entered the world's harbours on their peacetime official visits. The Russian naval helicopter, already buzzing about overhead, would be able to find nothing whatever wrong, nothing out of place, except possibly for the matter of speed; and that speed, that twenty-five knots, was so essential to success that a chance had to be taken. It was, however, a fair and reasonable chance, for the ships were still some sixteen miles from the dockyard itself with the whole length of the channel yet to go—and Carleton, with his tongue in his cheek, had already warned Moltsk that he was a little late on his E.T.A.

On the compass-platform of the *Lord Cochrane* Shaw stood rigid, cool as ice as the moment of action approached. He could see the tower now, sticking up out of the sea like a great gasometer. He remembered when he had been on top of that tower, such a little time ago. . . .

Ten minutes until the actual moment of impact.

Shaw watched the clock in the fore part of the bridge, watched the direction of the ship's head on the gyro-repeater in front of him, his hands gripping the sides of the gyro-standard. He glanced at the almost expressionless faces of the bridge personnel. The cruiser's Captain was standing squarely, with his legs apart, his cap tilted forward, and his hands deep in his bridge-coat pockets, looking all round before swinging back to watch out ahead. He was whistling some nameless tune, flatly, between his teeth. Captains didn't normally whistle on their bridges; a prerogative by custom of the Captain alone, it wasn't one that was often indulged in—but today was different. The navigator was clearing his throat noisily, nervously, and rubbing his jaw; the displaced officer-of-the-watch, from whom Shaw had taken over for the run in, was tapping his fingers on the bridge-rail aft of the compass-platform and chatting over-brightly with the chief yeoman, something about a run ashore a few weeks ago in the Clyde, and a barmaid in a Rothesay hotel . . . the lookouts were scanning all around, phlegmatically going on with their work until they were ordered to clear the bridge and jump for what safety they could find.

There was a flutter in Shaw's stomach now. . . .

He looked up at the helicopter, passing low above the flagship. Three men waved from it, grinning down, all clearly visible, all nice and friendly, and a hand waved back from the carrier's high bridge in reply. Then the machine was passing slowly aft along the flight-deck, over the carrier's company lined up along the sides, over her own helicopter squadrons waiting—if the Russians only knew it—for the take-off order from Flying Control. But the Russians wouldn't know it, because there were no pilots in sight and the walkways were empty. The moment the order came to clear the way for take-off and rescue of the *Lord Cochrane*'s remaining men, the sailors on parade would scatter in seconds, jumping down into the walkways, and the pilots would race up from the briefing-room just beneath the flight-deck.

Somewhere aboard the carrier was Triska Somalin, who would remain well hidden throughout the fleet's stay in Moltsk. Shaw smiled to himself as he recalled how dubious Careful Carleton had been about guaranteeing her a passage to England; Shaw had had to work hard for that, but the Admiral had given in gracefully enough in the end . . . and he wasn't too bad really. He'd rallied round all right, as soon as he was relieved of the overall decision-making. The thing was being done now as carefully as Careful Carleton could make it; painstaking in detail always, he had excelled himself today and he had made a first-class job of it.

Nine minutes to go.

Shaw took a deep breath and said, "Warn the Flag, sir, please."

"Very well, Shaw." Wilson turned and nodded at his chief

communications yeoman. Nonchalantly the man lifted a green anchor-flag to a little above chest level, held it for five seconds precisely, then lowered it out of sight. Shaw knew that glasses in the flagship would have been trained on the chief yeoman for the last five minutes or so and a moment later the flagship began to swing, almost imperceptibly, off course to port.

The tower was clearer now, seemed larger, tougher, so much more impregnable in these, the last few minutes. Would they do it after all, Shaw wondered, or would the concrete prove too much even for the steel stem of the heavy cruiser? There would be iron girders and beams, supports. . . . Shaw sweated, eased his collar from his neck with a shaking hand.

Now the flagship had given them a clear track.

Just a little starboard wheel when they were ready to increase speed, and they would pass her clear. Now was the time of doubt, now was the time to wonder if the Russians in that infernal helicopter might begin to get suspicious too soon.

Shaw's lips moved in a silent prayer.

So far, he didn't think anything had been noticed. If it had been, perhaps it was being put down to poor station-keeping on the cruiser's part, a failure to allow for the small alteration made by the Flag, an alteration that had just kinked her wake.

Seven minutes.

In seven minutes now the rest of the fleet would be abeam of the tower. Before that time the *Cochrane* had to start the run and before that time too she would have hit the tower. Captain Wilson, also watching the clock, looked round at Shaw and lifted his eyebrows. Shaw nodded in reply and at once Wilson bent to the voice-pipe beside him and said quietly, "All right, Chief. Emergency Full Ahead."

The same order was passed to the wheelhouse and the telegraphs went over. Far below the Engineer Officer heard that order and saw the telegraph indicators swing forward, back, forward again in confirmation. Automatically he completed an entry in the log and nodded to a junior officer who was with him on the starting-platform; at once levers were pulled over in each of the four engine-rooms. The ladders and platforms and dials and gauges began to shake and clatter as though they were coming free of their moorings, as though the engines would sheer the holding-down bolts. The shafts, spinning dizzily already, spun faster and faster, and a sound as of generating heat and energy filled the enclosed steel spaces as the screws bit into the water to send the cruiser leaping forward.

Shaw waited, his heart beating fast and almost choking him, his nails digging hard into his palms, as the engine pitch increased. A shudder ran right through the old ship and the water frothed up alarmingly below her counter, coming nearly to quarterdeck level as sheer speed pushed her stern down. There was a deep though subdued roar from below, coming to them from the ventilators, as all four screws thundered ahead.

The *Lord Cochrane* seemed to hurtle through the water, wind screaming along her decks. Surely that helicopter was going to notice something now . . . she simply couldn't miss it!

The old cruiser drew level with the flagship.

On the carrier's bridge the Admiral was letting loose all hell, putting on a convincing act for the benefit of the low-flying helicopter's crew. Signals, phoney signals, flew between cruiser and carrier, upbraiding, explaining, speaking of sudden chaos in the engine-room. No chances at this stage, Careful Carleton had warned—act naturally. They were doing so. All was apparent hair-tearing and confusion as the *Lord Cochrane* began to race ahead, coming up now to the leading frigate and steering inside of her to port; and a moment later the chief yeoman sang out, "Helicopter calling the Flag, sir . . . asks, *What is going on?*"

Wilson snapped, "Admiral's reply?"

"Just a minute, sir . . . Admiral says, *God knows I don't*"

Shaw grinned briefly.

Five minutes—and now they were well ahead of both the Flag and the leading frigate. Bending, Shaw took a quick bearing on the tower and then he gave the action-order to the wheelhouse: *"Starboard ten!"*

The repeat came quiet, phlegmatic, from the cruiser's chief quartermaster: "Starboard ten, sir." A moment later, "Ten of starboard wheel on, sir."

And now—dead on the tower. Shaw snapped as he watched the bearing closely, "Midships—steady!"

"Steady, sir. Course 183, sir."

"Steer 183." Shaw's voice was hoarse, cracked with excitement now. "Lovely, Chief Q.M.! Keep her right there. Keep the wake as dead straight as you possibly can, or they'll know the helm's not jammed."

"Aye, aye, sir."

182

Shaw glanced at Wilson. "Right, sir."

Wilson stepped aft to the tannoy and switched on. He said steadily and clearly, "This is the Captain speaking. Clear lower deck, clear the fo'c'sle—all hands muster aft. You all know what to do. Keep well aft of the bridge from now on. Hold tight and—good luck to you all." He let go the switch and went quickly to the engine-room voice-pipe. "All up, Chief. Clear all engine-rooms, leave everything just as it is. We'll hit it about four minutes maybe less."

Then he turned and looked aft at the chief yeoman. "Yeoman, hoist the N.U.C. balls and call up the Flag by light. Tell the Admiral that our steering's jammed. Make it convincing and try to ensure that the helicopter reads you. Tell the main transmitting-room to warn Moltsk on port wave to the same effect and apologize in advance for any damage we may do. . . ."

He broke off. The R/T loudspeaker had come alive, and an excited voice in Russian was yelling thirteen to the dozen. It was answered by another. Wilson said, "Shaw, you speak Russian—what's all that about?"

"Helicopter talking to Moltsk. They're assuming already that our steering's jammed." He listened attentively. "Moltsk is telling the guardship to intercept!" He looked up, pointed to the port bow. Some distance off, a lean grey destroyer was waiting. "There she is!"

They held on, tense and expectant, silent, as the *Lord Cochrane* rushed on to her destruction. The Marine Band had gone, all the men had left the fo'c'sle and scrambled aft. On the bridge only Shaw and Wilson and the chief yeoman were left. The wind tore across them, spray flew aft along that wind as the water was whipped up by the racing bow, whipped up and flung back through the hawse-pipes and over the bullring, up over the guard-rails.

Shaw said, "We'd better stand by for real fireworks when they hoist it in that we aren't putting our engines astern."

TWENTY-SIX

From the Defence Minister in Moltsk dockyard the word was radio-ed at once to the tower. They all knew, those sweating men in the well at the fissure entry so far below, what was going to happen. The Tower Commandant had told them over the internal broadcast-system.

His voice high and sharp with fear, he had said, "One of the British heavy ships is going to hit us within the next two or three minutes. We must fire immediately. It is vital, I repeat vital, that the sealing door be shut the moment the last connexions are made to the firing-circuit. You will obey your orders. Obedience alone can save you. You will be brought up at once when the door is sealed. Any man who tries to use the lifts before that will be shot. That is all."

Below, after that, men worked feverishly, fumbling in their haste, sweating in their consuming fear. They could all guess what would happen when the cruiser hit; the panic in the Commandant's voice had told them more than his words. They would die instantly down there as the hurtling tons of water dropped clear down the lift-shafts with smashing force and fell on them to squeeze their bodies flat, and then, if the door was not shut in time, hurl them forward on the racing avalanche into the fissure, to mingle with the nuclear death that would never fire, send their shattered fragments on into the very earth itself. Somehow those last few vital connexions were made and up in the makeshift, hastily adapted control-room just below the flat roof of the tower, a series of red lights came up, one by one. The controllers, sitting before those lights and before batteries of dials and levers, also faced certain death as the vital seconds ticked past so swiftly; each second meant that they had less chance of getting clear even if the firing could still be successfully carried out—and that in itself was becoming doubtful now.

Or was it?

The cruiser hadn't hit yet and the guardship, the loudspeakers now told them in metallic tones, was already rushing in to intercept. As the speakers clicked off again, a hand began to move slowly round a large clock-face before the Chief Controller.

The man said hoarsely, "She moves—she shuts!"

There was a curious sound from the others; like hounds on the scent and eager for the kill, they were giving tongue. They were all grinning now, the immediate fear of death flowing away to be replaced by tension of a subtly different kind, an exultant tension.

If only that great door could move faster. . . .

The hand, which would move right round the clock-face in precisely sixty seconds would, when it came again to twelve o'clock, indicate that its master the door had shut, that the

184

fissure was finally sealed, that the main firing-lever could be eased over, circuits made, button pressed. Then the whole lot would go up and the British cruiser could do its worst. There would be glory in dying for the Soviet then, but there would be none if they were unsuccessful.

Utter silence now in the control-room as the hand clicked slowly, slowly round the dial in response to the impulses from below. The men could see in their imaginations the progress of that twenty-foot-thick slab as it edged across the fissure's mouth, ready to be slotted back into the opening. The Chief Controller's hand was fidgety, damp and sticky with sweat. Slowly, as his eyes watched the clock-face, his hand went out towards a red-painted lever at the side of a metal box in front of him.

Fifty seconds to go now. Forty-nine. Forty-eight. Forty-seven. . .

"Red two-oh, guardship moving in."

Both Wilson and Shaw had had their full attention on the shore batteries at that moment, watching to see if they would go into action, and they had temporarily forgotten the guardship. Now they swung round on to the bearing and saw the destroyer coming in and aiming apparently right amidships, evidently meaning to slice into them before they could reach the tower . . . or was she heading a little farther up?

Wilson shouted, "She's going to come across our bows and take the impact herself!"

"Yes, I believe you're right." Shaw bent to the azimuth circle and watched the bearing of the racing destroyer as the *Lord Cochrane* thundered on. Trembling with impatience and anxiety now, he kept the sights on the Russian, saw that the bearing was remaining perfectly steady and was not going to alter. The intention was undoubtedly for a collision and they probably wouldn't open fire. Shaw estimated that the destroyer would either hit them on the port bow and deflect them inshore, or, as Wilson had said, she would go a fraction ahead so that they would hit her. That would mean the end of the destroyer, but it would also mean the end of Shaw's plan and, unless Carleton could get off his signal for the Vulcans to release their missiles mighty fast, it would mean the end of a good deal more besides. They were judging it very nicely aboard the guardship, very nicely indeed. Shaw sweated, saw Wilson staring at him. They were going to hit, sure as fate they were, if Shaw didn't alter course away. Unless he could hold until almost the last second, and risk the kink in his wake that would tell the Russian ship unmistakably that his helm hadn't jammed at all. . . .

He watched, eyes narrowed to slits, everything in him concentrating on trying to judge the exact second when he had to take action, the moment when a small alteration, the smallest he could make, would be of the most use. His lips were close to the voice-pipe when he roared suddenly, "Steer one debree to port!"

"Steer one degree to port, sir." Then, "Course 182, sir."

They surely wouldn't see that fractional alteration mirrored in his wake. Shaw came upright. There was nothing more he could do now; the game was lost or won already. If they hit that destroyer it would be up to the Admiral. Whatever happened after that none of them in any of the ships would get out of Moltsk. They would be caught like rats in a trap, with everything that floated or flew or marched or fired coming at them from all points of the compass.

Nearer and nearer. . . .

Shaw had a curious impression that he had moved into another dimension, that he was watching all this detachedly from above, just as if the two ships were models approaching one another in an instructional tank ashore—and with precisely the same degree of absolute certainty as to the outcome. But the *Lord Cochrane* was racing on beneath him, 10,000 tons of steel very much alive and on the move, with her men waiting tensely about her after decks, trusting in his judgment, braced against the shattering impact that would come at any moment now, whether it was another ship's steel or the tower's concrete that they hit. Tearing inward, faster and faster each second it seemed, the wind raised by her passing screaming wickedly aft along her decks. Faces white, expectant, apprehensive, exultant—a mixture of all the emotions. . . .

"Shaw, she's going to hit!" Wilson's voice, high, shrill.

"It's going to be close, but . . . *hold tight, sir!*"

Shaw gripped the gyro-standard in front of him. He fancied the Russian had altered very slightly to compensate for his own alteration, but he couldn't be sure of that. The ships were flying towards each other now, meeting at a combined speed of something over seventy miles an hour and . . . they were going to hit now. . . .

Shaw's eyes took in the destroyer's fo'c'sle tearing towards him, then her bridge superstructure rushing down upon the cruiser's bows, passing beneath them now. He waited for the

186

impact with his eyes shut, all feeling drained out of him.

And then he heard a roar from Wilson.

"She's passed clear . . . God in heaven . . . well done, Shaw!"

Shaw opened his eyes. Wilson was almost dancing in front of him. Then he saw the destroyer's counter sliding out to starboard, slicing across the *Lord Cochrane*'s heavy forefoot. It was the world's closest thing . . . the two ships couldn't have cleared by more than inches. The Russian, fooled by Shaw's late alteration, had been put off her stroke just enough to ball it up. She had simply torn through the narrowing gap between cruiser and boom and now she was hurtling on into the shallows that Shaw had seen earlier on Carleton's chart. Her engines were thrashing astern now but it was too late to check her headway; as Shaw watched the Russian flew on and then, very suddenly and with a scream of tearing steel, she stopped. She had hit bottom inshore of the tower and she was a shambles on deck and settling fast enough to indicate that her bottom-plating had been ripped away. And then, just a fraction of a second after, several things happened almost together and Shaw forgot about the destroyer. The shoreside rocket-batteries opened up and the close-range weapons, the Kalashnikovas, started up simultaneously from the tower's roof, the terrified troops firing down blindly on the *Lord Cochrane* over open sights, each of them pumping out a hundred rounds a minute. Bullets snicked into steel screens and bulkheads, sprayed over the bridge, but you might as well try, Shaw thought, to stop a charging rhinoceros with a pea-shooter . . . then there was a spine-chilling *whoosh* as the rockets flashed overhead. Shaw and Wilson ducked—and as they ducked the cruiser took the boom.

The old ship's stem crashed through, biting hard and biting deep; as Shaw had promised the Admiral, it was as if the heavy steel mesh and the supports were made of paper. Her starboard side crashed along one of the concrete support piers and it toppled, almost powdered by the glancing impact of the *Lord Cochrane*'s armour plate. There was just a slight bump and that was all; and the cruiser was tearing on unchecked, her engines still racing ahead for the thirty-foot projection of the tower. It seemed to hang over the bows for an instant and then they were in the middle of an apparent earthquake. At thirty-two knots and a little more, ten thousand tons of flinging steel took the tower full and square, right on the point of the bow, plunging right on and in until the tortured stem twisted and ripped back right to the foot of the bridge trunking itself, the decks gaping wide and ugly, A and B turrets slewed sideways with their useless, broken guns twisted up like hair-curlers. The bows had gone straight through into the control-room itself, smashing connexions, killing men, bringing the concrete roof down on what was left. Then in deeper, so that the concrete began to crumble and split lower down, the beams and girders twisting and fracturing and falling down onto the cruiser's gaping deck. The *Lord Cochrane* reared up like a stallion, riding high, riding up onto the crumbling framework, driving in, the angle sending her quarterdeck right under to vanish beneath a boiling sea as the screws thundered on; thundered on until the shafts, fracturing, buckling as the ship began to break her back, jangled and juddered to a stop. Men everywhere were flung about like dolls, into the sea, into bulkheads and guard-rails and stanchions and into the half-submerged after turrets. There were screams from aft as some of them went overboard to die horribly in the flailing screw-blades, before the shafts had stopped. Ahead of Shaw, Wilson unthinkingly standing braced with his arms pushed out ahead of him like steel rods against the for'ard screen of the bridge, had hit the structure violently. Both his arms had crumpled and his rib-cage had smashed against the screen. The bridge itself was a shambles, was leaning over drunkenly to port. The chief yeoman was in a pool of blood in the port wing, under a smashed signalling projector, a big thirty-inch which had come clean off its moorings. At the last moment Shaw had turned his back and hung on to the rail above the chart-table in rear of the compass-platform, and though his arms felt as if they had been almost torn from their sockets he had, so far as he knew, suffered nothing worse than a dislocated shoulder and a full quota of nasty bruises.

He ran now towards the chief yeoman, found that he was only knocked out and had a smashed jawbone. Then he saw that the foremast had cracked, was canted forward over the bridge itself. He ran back and grabbed Wilson with his good arm, dragged him into the port wing with the yeoman, and just got him clear before the foremast went. It came down on the bridge with a crash; a tangle of steel-wire rigging and wireless aerials and yards trailed forward on to the gaping fo'c'sle. And then something else happened: the remnants of the *Lord Cochrane*'s fo'c'sle seemed to drop, down and down and down . . . and suddenly Shaw realized why. The impact had cracked and split not only the top of the tower but it had also smashed the structure far below and now, under the strain, under the tremendous pressure of ship and water, the riven blocks were disintegrating, plunging down the hole itself behind the descending sea. As he had planned, millions upon millions of tons of the Barents Sea were rushing, cascading down into the fissure. It was a mad nightmare of debris and bodies as the Russian soldiers were hurled away into the plunging water, drawn by the movement of that water into the vortex of a whirlpool, down that terrible deep hole, legs and arms flailing, spinning like tops to vanish into the chaos of smashed lift-shafts and concrete and girders, to drop and drop until they hit the bottom and were swept into the fissure itself. Some of them were trapped, as their bodies swirled downward, between the twisted girders and the lift-shafts, and they remained there as the water and debris dropped past to skin and flay their bodies so that they were left as near-skeletons, skeletons which themselves began to break up. The water swirled and roared beneath the fragments of what had been the control-room where the indicator, still intact on an isolated steel beam, showed the great lower door as only half closed. That water would go on swirling and filling the fissure for a very long time, would go on and on until that enormous length was entirely filled with the sea and then, and only then, when the Barents Sea reached England, the mad whirlpool would stop.

Shaw felt dazed, light-headed; all that he was conscious of in that moment was that one hundred per cent. success had been achieved and the Vulcans would not be needed now. The rocket-batteries were silent, no doubt obeying an order to refrain from any further hostile acts until more was known . . . and there wouldn't be any more trouble, of course; the whole organization behind the *coup d'état* would already be crumbling just like that tower. . . .

Meanwhile the *Lord Cochrane* was breaking up; there was a roar of escaping steam from the engine-rooms and boiler-rooms, pipes and gauges blowing off all over the place; the decks were buckling and splitting still, all the superstructure slowly caving in. The Shaw heard a noise overhead and he looked up and saw the helicopters coming in from the flagship, and he realized he had to do something about helping the injured; and for a start he got hold of the Captain and the chief yeoman and dragged them painfully towards what was left of the bridge ladder.

Ten days later Shaw was in Room 12 at the Admiralty, having left the carrier in Portsmouth whence he travelled up in a fast official car with Triska Somalin. After he had made his full personal report to Latymer the Old Man said, "I suppose I need hardly tell you, Shaw, I was sweating drops of blood. As it is, though, the explanation of an accident appears to have been accepted with as good a grace as possible."

"Grace!" Shaw laughed. "There wasn't much grace about our reception at Moltsk, sir!"

"So I gather from Carleton's report. However, the official line is reasonably graceful. They haven't much choice, of course, unless they want to come out with the story in full." Latymer grinned. "What about that Defence Minister—how did he take it?"

"Badly, sir! He was in a hell of a froth. There was some little bloke with him who seemed to be putting the fear of God into him. Has there been much news out of Russia since, sir?"

"Precious little that's reliable. Quite a crop of rumours. All we know for certain is that the Kremlin's made a formal protest to our Government, asking for action to be taken against those responsible for letting such an accident happen. To keep the peace, Russia will be informed that such action is being taken, but that's just as far as it will go, I need hardly add."

"And the *coup d'état* boys?"

Latymer shrugged. "The official line is that there's been a reshuffle, which I take to be an euphemism for a purge or bloodbath. As a matter of fact I've just an idea your friend the Minister of Defence has already departed this life, together with a few other highly placed personages. I think we can assume that the Kremlin's back to normal and there's nothing more than usual to worry about—oh, and you'll be glad to hear that Chaffinch is in the clear. He managed to slide out from under. Also they never did link you with that business on the Hungarian border, and I assume—I don't know—that your man there got away with it. I'm pretty sure they'd have made him talk if he was arrested. . . . The only pity about all this is that Lawrence Carew died. A lot of people in this country would have liked a chat with him— but you couldn't help that, I know." He shuffled some papers on his desk. "Now, what about that young woman of yours, what's-her-name? You'd better wheel her in and I'll see her —alone, I think. I've got to make certain she doesn't talk

. . . we've got to keep faith, if that's the word, with the Kremlin. Hoodlums are hoodlums the world over, but the Kremlin is the Government, if you follow. Tact, that's what's needed now. No point in exacerbating anyone's feelings."

"I entirely agree, sir." Shaw got to his feet. "By the way, what about the Foreign Ministers' Conference?"

"*What* about it, Shaw?"

"Was it really successful?"

Latymer gave a short laugh. "Don't be so naïve. Of course it wasn't. But what does that matter? No conference has ever solved anything yet, my boy, and it never will! It's the people behind the scenes like you and me that keep this old world from falling apart, though damned if we ever get any thanks for it." As Shaw moved to the door Latymer added, his eyes twinkling suddenly, "It's a new experience for Careful Carleton to have a female aboard his flagship, I hear. We're all expecting a memo from him daily, suggesting an amendment to Queen's Regulations—so that next time he knows what he's done this time—if you see what I mean!"

Shaw said with mock primness, "I've nothing but praise and respect for Admiral Carleton, sir." He added, "For what my opinion's worth, I mean that."

Latymer grinned. "A very proper sentiment from a mere commander, Shaw. I would have expected nothing less. Seriously—I absolutely agree, of course. Now get that confounded girl in. . . . I shan't keep her long and then you can take her off and show her the sights of London or—um—anything else that takes your fancy. And take that keen and anticipatory look off your face, Shaw. An acquaintance of mine at Eastern Petroleum rang me this morning, and in the course of conversation it emerged that another of your lady-friends is coming home earlier than expected. She went aboard the *Oriana* at Fremantle two days ago—so you'd better watch your step!"

PHILIP McCUTCHAN'S
Commander Shaw Counterspy Novels

GIBRALTAR ROAD   (F1050—50¢)

Introducing Commander Shaw, of British Naval Intelligence, on the trail of a man who *must* be found, if Gibraltar isn't to blow up higher than Hiroshima.

REDCAP   (F1051—50¢)

"REDCAP," an apparatus vital to maintaining a hard-won, atomic-control agreement among the Western powers, is threatened, and Commander Shaw is given the job of protecting it.

BLUEBOLT I   (F1069—50¢)

To Commander Shaw goes the task of searching the African jungle for a man called "Edo," and of crushing Edo's plan for world domination.

WARMASTER   (F1127—50¢)

Determined to stop an organization plotting world conquest, Shaw, in a race against time, searches out the conspirators in New York, the Argentine, and the far corners of the world.